Cats of Katlyn
THE TALE OF TAILEY

L.R. SLACK

 FriesenPress

One Printers Way
Altona, MB R0G 0B0
Canada

www.friesenpress.com

ISBN
978-1-03-913651-9 (Hardcover)
978-1-03-913650-2 (Paperback)
978-1-03-913652-6 (eBook)

1. ADULT FICTION, ANIMALS

Distributed to the trade by The Ingram Book Company

TABLE OF CONTENTS

"*I own that I cannot see as plainly as others do, and as I should wish to do, evidence of design and beneficence on all sides of us. There seems to me too much misery in the world. I cannot persuade myself that a beneficent and Omnipotent God would have designedly created the 'Ichneumonidae' with the express intention of their feeding within the living bodies of Caterpillars, or that a cat should play with mice.*" – Charles Robert Darwin

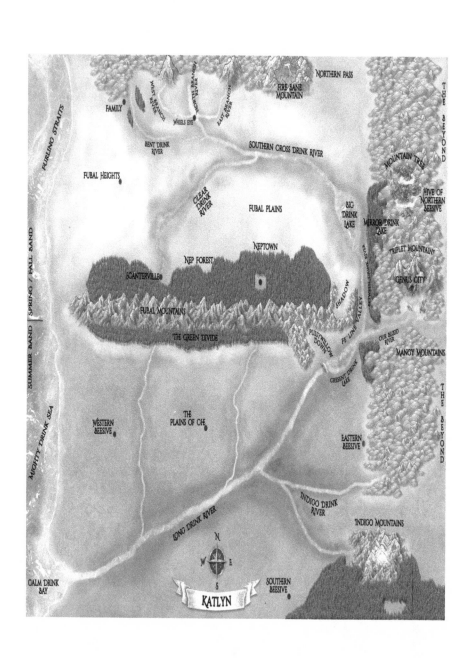

KATLYN

Chapter 1

TAILEY

Barry Newman Perkins—or more accurately, Ichneumon, the Possessor of Souls—hid in the bushes along the driveway of the Simms' home. He (or again, more accurately, *they*) watched the area around the home, spying on the family that resided there. "We can't miss this time. Yes, this little girl has the right eyes—eyes that are full of magic." The voice of Ichneumon was low and coarse, tearing from Barry's throat against his will. "Not like the other girl who made us so mad we had to rip her apart."

Oh God, no ... please ... I don't want to remember, Barry thought, fighting the internal monster that had possession over him.

"Yes, yes, we did have to do that. Murder! Oh, lovely murder!"

Barry still remembered the night when everything had changed. It was after work at the Blue Lantern Bar, and he had been lounging in his car with the window down, enjoying the soft breeze across his face as rock music played on the radio. He'd been drumming his fingers on the door of the Chevy and savoring the short break before he would fire up the old beater and head to the other side of Alba, to the decrepit trailer he called home. With his head leaning against the head rest, Barry had found himself, once again, wondering why he didn't just join the Navy and "ride the waves," as they touted on the television commercials.

He'd sighed ruefully, slouching down in the driver's seat, when all at once, he'd felt a small, sharp prick at the base of his neck and an uncomfortable warmth spreading up to his skull. He had reached back to investigate and found that a welt had already begun to form.

"Damned mosquito," he'd muttered.

He'd wondered if the warmth in his head was really from the insect bite or from the beers he'd consumed earlier. Judging from his overwhelming desire to take a nap, he had suspected it was the beers, surrendering himself immediately...

... and he never had complete control of himself again.

* * *

A couple of nights later, Barry had watched himself murder a little girl. *A little girl!* After she lay dead, the monster in his mind had quickly started screaming at itself for getting "the wrong one." His own mind had ranted in horror at the act, with such venom and for so long that he felt completely out of control, and yet his body was numb and unmoving. The next morning, the local sheriff deputies had stumbled onto him while answering a trespasser call.

He had been locked away ever since, and though Barry had found comfort in the incarceration, which kept him from hurting anyone else against his will, the monster had other plans. They had escaped, and now they were free again. "Finally."

God, no...

This child was for sure the carrier of magic that could stop its dark intentions. Back in the shadows of this new girl's house, the monster shut down any more noise from Barry, locking him away in a dark corner and taking control of his thoughts as well as his body once more. This child was surely the carrier of magic that could stop its dark intentions. "She can never leave this world alive!"

* * *

Across the valley, yellow and crimson hardwood trees traced the outline of ancient hemlocks and pine trees that grew randomly across the slopes, vast and unchanged since the early part of the nineteenth century, when the loggers gave up trying to harvest the trees on the steep ridges of the valley.

It was a bountiful land rich with deer, grazing in the small meadows that dotted the valley floor. Bobcats, coyotes, and black bears still foraged in the shadows of the forest. Ruffled grouse dusted their feathers on the old two-track road that followed the river. Squirrels gathered nuts from the giant nut-bearing trees. Birds of prey like eagles, hawks, and owls hunted upon the air currents both day and night.

Along the valley floor, the Jordan River rushed down in twists and turns toward the southern arm of Lake Charlevoix, which eventually emptied into the chilled waters of Lake Michigan. High in the valley, the river bubbled out of a spring at the base of an enormous willow tree. Further down the valley, the beavers had dammed off the stream, which created a pond thriving with waterfowl and trout. On any sweltering summer day, it was common to find otters gaming in the cool water. Tourist described the land a majestic, harmonious landscape.

On top of the eastern ridge, stood alone A-frame-style home, around which landscapers had outdone themselves, planting many species of pine and maple trees. At the rear of the home, builders had erected an open porch that spanned the length of the building and beyond, overlooking the south end of the valley.

On the wide wooden railing, a large gray tomcat lay in a deep slumber. The light of the yellow sun warmed his belly as the cool breeze of September gently ruffled his short hair. As if it had a life separate from its owner, the cat's long tail danced about the inert body. Close to the full length of the cat's body, the tail swayed like a cobra to the music of a snake charmer's pipe.

Smooth music accompanied the aroma of food through the half-opened kitchen window.

"This is Martini Que of WTPM radio. We interrupt this program to bring the following update." The announcer's voice was flat and uncommitted as she continued her narration. *"Authorities of the State Police have issued a statewide alert to warn all residents to be on the lookout for an inmate who escaped from the state prison in Jackson, Michigan, Wednesday of last week."*

The deejay paused to shuffle papers and confer with someone in the background.

"Barry Newman Perkins, the escapee, is described as Caucasian, six-foot-tall, 175 pounds, with a slim frame, dark complexion, and close-cropped jet-black hair…"

The ears of the drowsy cat rotated toward the voice of the woman on the radio.

"Prior to his escape, Perkins was serving a life sentence for the gruesome murder of fourteen-year-old Ann Marie Coon of Alba, Michigan, four years ago. Perkins was last sighted heading north in a late model brown ford truck on U.S. Route 127 wearing hiking boots with loose fitting dark pants, shirt, and a black stocking cap and felt peacoat. Perkins should be considered extremely dangerous. Authorities advise that anyone locating Perkins should not approach him; instead, they should contact their local or state pol—"

The hiss of air brakes off in the distance brought the cat to full alert.

My Megan is home early! thought the cat, as he hurried off the deck and down the driveway beside the house.

Up the long drive skipped the little girl with long curly brunette hair in a green with lavender polka dot dress with a green backpack who was the object of the cat's attention.

The kindergartner was unaware of the sickened eyes that glared at her from the tall bushes that ran the length of the driveway.

At the top of the sloping drive, the cat stopped to watch his Megan as she paused to admire the late-blooming flowers. Suddenly, his sixth sense detected movement; there was danger off to her left.

Recently, he had been feeling a darkness growing in the deep hardwoods that bordered the Simms' home. He'd given that darkness a name. He called it the Nightman, because it did not feel familiar—not feline nor any other animal he could identify. Yet the darkness seemed not to be completely human either, except perhaps as a means to a horrible end.

Without thought or fear for himself, the cat bolted along the bushes to intercept the darkness that was stalking the shadows. In a final bound, the cat sprung high through the air and landed on the head and shoulders of the Nightman. The claws of the tomcat ripped into his face and neck; teeth biting into his ear.

"Rotten cat!" the Nightman hissed, prying him off his head. The man moaned from the pain as he cast the cat from him. The Nightman could feel his blood running down his body. Fearful of being heard, paranoia compelled the Nightman to run off into the shadowy forest.

Briars and low shrubs ripped at his exposed flesh and his dark garments as he ran deeper into the cover of the shadowy forest. *That annoying cat knows our every move, but how? We MUST have the power that dwells in her special blue eyes!*

From the dark corners of his own mind, Barry listened intently, desperate to understand what drove this creature—desperate to break free.

"Yes, we must destroy the magic before its influence reaches Katlyn where her power will become absolute and spell our end!"

In that moment, Barry regained control over his own mind long enough to scream, *Help! Help!* But the words never reached his lips. The darkness regained control, shoving his consciousness back down into the deepest corners of their shared mind.

The Nightman grunted, wiping away a trail of blood from his cheek, and continued his retreat into the shadows. For now, it would find a hiding place and wait for a better opportunity to reach that little girl, with her magical true-blue eyes. Then he would end her life and possess her soul as he had with so many others in the past.

Although their encounter was brief, it still took a couple of minutes for the cat to get his bearings after the Nightman had slammed him hard onto the ground. Glancing up at the house, the cat caught a glimpse of the little girl as she passed through the front door.

On shaky legs, the cat made his way back up to the house and went around back to his private door, which opened into the kitchen. Before entering, the cat stopped for a quick bath.

Must be neat or the bosses will not let me stay, the cat thought to himself. When everything was in order, the cat pushed up the door flap and made his way into the warm interior.

"So, you're going to join us after all, Tailey," Megan's mother, Clara, called out, as the cat made his way into the room. "You usually come in with Megan. I bet you didn't know she was coming home from school early today and were out hunting mice or something cat-like, right? Hurry to your chair. Megan's expecting you."

Clara had said all this kindly, but her body language told Tailey that something was bothering her.

If she only knew, he thought to himself.

Tailey moved toward Megan, needing to pass by Clara on his way. The woman was in her mid-twenties, with shoulder-length brown hair and an average shape. Although he generally did not pay Megan's mother much attention, Tailey liked her well enough. She had a warm, welcoming smile and a strong protective personality. Brushing past the woman, he jumped up into his chair next to Megan.

Tailey was met by Megan's soft arms as she pulled him into a huge hug. From her folded arms, the cat peered up at her. Megan's shoulder-length curly brown hair was subtly streaked with wisps of red, black, and blonde. *My calico human*, he thought, staring at her fondly.

Over the top of Megan's pouting lips and still-developing nose was a pair of true-blue eyes. Not dark blue like his own, or hazel, but true blue. Deep and pure. The kind that shines in and out of the light.

Four seasons ago, Tailey had come to live with the Simms family as a kitten. Miles down the dirt road from the Simms' home was the Ketchen Potato Farms. Up in the hayloft of the barn, a mother calico cat had given birth to four kittens, one of which was Tailey. For the first eight weeks of his life, Tailey and his three sisters had nursed on mother's milk and learned the ways of cats.

Mother had told them stories, all of which centered on the hunt, and the skills that they would have to acquire to keep the humans (whom she referred to as "bosses") happy with their presence.

"You'll know when the boss is pleased with you when he no longer refers to you as just 'cat' and gives you a name, as he gave one to your father and me: King Moe and his Queen Bonnie."

One night, King Moe came to the barn and motioned Tailey out into the darkness. His father led him out to the middle of the large hay field to the lone apple tree that stood watch over the farm.

At the foot of the apple tree, the father and son sat side-by-side in silence. Around them, the land was bathed in light from the full harvest moon. From the dark woods beyond, cicadas honored the coming of winter with their steady droning song. Then came the mournful hooting of a great horned owl on its nocturnal hunt.

Turning to each other, the father and son joined minds.

The senior cat's green eyes gazed into the eyes of his future with pride. "Son, you have the looks of my father. He also had gray fur and your dark blue eyes, but he lacked your incredibly long and powerful tail."

Tailey noted an unusual gentleness in his father's mind-voice.

"Humans once believed that our kinfolk were agents of evil, but that has never been true. Since the time when the great long fangs hunted the giant mammoths, cats have been the guardians of all that is good," King Moe stated proudly.

"In that beginning time, some cats—those with fangs as long as you— were the users of magic. The greatest of these wizards was Lars, the Shield. Lars and his cohorts, the Gray Circle, battled for the ancient world against the dark evil of Ichneumon, the Possessor of Souls." King Moe's mind-voice now held an icy edge.

"Mighty were these wizards of old. Yet with all their combined powers, they could not stop Ichneumon from draining the life force from many of our people." Gloom clutched the moment.

As if on cue, a passing nighthawk screeched into the dark air above them. The hackles on Tailey's back rose, and his long tail expanded to resemble a long pipe-cleaning brush.

"In their darkest hour, when only a small number of our kind remained, the Wizard Lars summoned the magic buried deep within a talisman of power: the Gray Cat's Eye Stone!

It was in the last circle of battle when the great Lars called upon the powers of the stone. In a blinding whirl of light, Lars, and the other wizards, along with Ichneumon, the Possessor of Souls, vanished and were not seen again. The remaining long fangs witnessed this episode and passed their testimony down through thousands of generations, and to all the felines of the earth, as a warning should the evil one ever return. You must remember these tales of old and pass them on to your own young one day," King Moe said to his confused son.

There was silence between them for several moments.

"In my youth," King Moe stated next, his mind-voice oddly blunted, "I heard a voice in my mind that prophesied that I would one day have a son who would grow up to become a great soldier against an evil so terrible I fear I don't have words to describe it." Tailey was not comfortable hearing flatness in the mind-voice of his father.

"I believe you might be the son that voice spoke of, because you are so different from any of your past siblings." Tailey thought his father sounded almost sad.

"It is time now that you leave us to find your own place in the world. Goodbye, my son, and may Lars, the Shield, protect you always." Upon finishing, the orange tiger-striped cat brushed fondly against his son's side, then turned back towards the barnyard and walked off into the night.

"Goodbye, King Moe."

Throughout the night, Tailey sat under the apple tree, thinking of what to do next. When the morning came, the young cat decided that he must follow the path described to his father by the mind-voice and fight against any evil that might one day come. *Though surely*, he thought, somewhat bemused, *I would have done so at any rate.*

He turned his back on the potato farm then and headed westward, feeling pulled in that direction as if by some powerful magnet. Before too long, he came upon the Simms' home.

And it had been in a moment just like this, nestled in her loving arms and staring into her special blue eyes, that Tailey had realized that Megan was different from the other humans he had encountered in the past and vowed to be her companion and guardian for the rest of his life.

Winter in Michigan could be described as a sanitary-white prison in the cold, deep snow. Few beings ventured about unless it was necessary. Throughout that long winter, the relationship between girl and cat grew past the sort between master and pet and into honest love and enjoyment of each other's company. Tailey found it strange that his Megan never spoke to him like the bosses Clara and Lennie did. She talked with her eyes, and in time, he found that he could communicate with her the way he did with other cats: with his mind-voice.

This would be a special time for them. They spent long hours in front of the television, which showed pictures of other places, things, and people. Sometimes she would bring him upstairs to play with the fake mini human dolls. This game Tailey found tiresome, but Megan loved it, so he would play along for her.

After lunch each day, Megan would join Tailey for a nap upstairs in her bedroom. Sometimes she would just lay there, petting his fur while he slept, ever so careful not to wake her friend.

After nap time, one or both bosses would take Megan into the chair room and teach her to speak to them with her hands and to read the movements of their lips. She told Tailey it was because she could not hear sounds. Megan's father, Lennie, most often did the training. In his early thirties, Lennie was tall with a strong, sturdy build, but he was a quiet gentle man with deep patience. He always wore a light-green uniform with a matching hat, except for special occasions, of course.

"My ears are broken," Megan had once told him. Megan's handicap only strengthened her willpower and determination to learn. Tailey was a great aid to her because he understood human speech fluently. Time moved on, and one spring day, the bosses announced that Megan would be able to attend school in the fall.

Spring had come suddenly, and with it came new adventures for both Megan and Tailey. Always together, the cat would accompany her on short walks; Megan gently held the tip of his extremely long tail, which he would hold straight up, reaching well over her head. They picked wildflowers, looked under logs for salamanders, and took turns chasing each other in games of tag—always with the watchful eyes of Megan's mother not far off.

At the start of September, school began, separating the pair for most of each day. Like clockwork, he would wake her to join him for breakfast. Then he faithfully walked her down the long driveway to wait for the school bus. Shortly before she would return home, Tailey would make for the end of the driveway to await her arrival.

Over the last few days though, Tailey had become increasingly aware of the presence of a dark menace: the Nightman. Today hadn't been the first time the Nightman had started for Megan only to be met by hissing, screaming fury, but Tailey knew that, sooner or later, the monster would grow bolder and ignore his defiant warnings instead of retreating to the woods. Fear made a bed in Tailey's heart.

The rest of the day went by with no further incidents, but that night, while Tailey rested at the foot of Megan's bed, he became aware of a new feeling stirring deep in his young soul. The recent battles with the Nightman had awakened a new sense in him. Urgent … primitive … He needed to hunt! The need came suddenly upon Tailey, and unable to stop himself, the cat made his way carefully down the stairs to the kitchen and out his private door.

On the way out, he heard Megan's parents talking in the chair room.

"Lennie, dear, some concerning things happened today. Tailey didn't come in with Megan after school. He always meets her at the bus stop. And before he came inside, I thought I heard some sort of struggle in the woods. Not for the first time either. Did you hear that report today on the radio? About the escaped prisoner who…"

The sound of their conversation melted away as Tailey passed into the night.

Chapter 2

SPACED

Tailey ventured off into the night. The primordial feline in him was alive for the first time in his life. All his senses were on fire.

Tailey's dilated pupils collected the images of the night. His whiskers were held forward, helping to navigate him through the tall grass to the forest beyond. His ears rotated like radar dishes to catch every squeak, creak, and groan. The hunt!

Not far into the woods, Tailey came upon the fresh scent of what would prove to be a mouse. This excitement carried Tailey over the brink between pet and predator. He suddenly craved the taste of blood from a fresh kill.

The trail to the mouse proved to be short yet somewhat dangerous. The scent drew Tailey through a thicket of wild roses. Here, the cat took a nasty rip down his left side from one of the barbed thorns. Heedless of the pain, which simply added to the cat's lust for the hunt, he moved on.

Hot on the mouse's trail, Tailey came to a stop at the opening of a hollow log. Deep inside, he detected movement. Hunched down low, the cat crept into the log one painstaking step at a time.

Unfortunately for Tailey, the mouse happened to be a veteran of many spoiled hunts and had spied the cat. With its back up against what appeared to be a dead end—the side of a tree stump blocking the opening in the far end of the hollow log—it was preparing a move of its own.

Collecting his legs under him, Tailey launched himself at the mouse just as it bolted through a small crack in the stump behind him. Unable to stop himself mid-leap, Tailey arrived violently in the spot where the mouse had disappeared, his momentum carrying him headfirst into the side of the stump.

For the second time this day, Tailey's eyes spun in their sockets, and it took many seconds for him to regain his balance. Upon recovery, the cat could sense his prey out of reach in the next chamber. To have food so close, yet so far away, left him outraged!

Dashing back out of the opening at the other end, and then springing up on top of the log, the cat ran the length of it to where the stump stood, a couple of feet higher than the log. In one bound, Tailey landed on the thin edge at the top of the hollow stump, nearly falling into its dark cavity.

Peering closely, he again saw the mouse. Again, the mouse saw the cat. Tailey launched himself headfirst down into the wooden hollow. Again, the mouse went nicely back out through the crack, avoiding ending up as the cat's meal.

The cat saw the pain long before he felt it. *Not again!*

Thud!

For the third time that day, the cat found himself knocked half out of his wits. Coming back to himself, he remained where he was, lying motionless inside the tree stump, the need to hunt knocked entirely out of him. Looking around the stump's interior, Tailey spied a golden-brown eye staring at him, which appeared to be streaked with blood. Sensing no danger from it, Tailey suddenly grew very tired and tranquil. Through the trance-like haze, he watched as the golden-brown eye seemed to brighten and then grow dim, over and over, and with every pulse, its brightness grew. Then sleep overtook him.

* * *

Motion ... within absolute darkness...

Tailey could sense his body moving, yet his eyes could not focus on any source of light. *Is this a dream?* Maybe, but doubtful. Unlike humans, cats are not fooled by questions of reality. The world is what it seems; the bird is there, or it never was there. Simple. Humans see the bird, or they may imagine that the bird had been there in the past, or that maybe the bird would be there in the future. Humans were always mixed up with imagination and emotion, not like the feline world of absolutes.

So, Tailey found it easy to accept the fact that his body, while in slumber, was traveling through some darkness, perhaps a void or abyss. His mind was alert to the facts as they developed around him. Tailey tried to rouse himself but failed. Then he focused his efforts on just opening his eyes and was shocked to find what he had accomplished: It was indeed sight, but he was seeing through the eyes of his spirit body. Below him, his body and the pulsing golden-brown stone hovered in a clear bubble-like vessel. All around it, lines of light streaked past him at an amazing rate of speed. Still, he felt no fear of the experience.

He willed his view to change to the field before him. Dots of light appeared and grew bolder as they neared. Then the lights streaked by at a distance and disappeared behind him.

What is happening to me? Tailey asked of himself, knowing he had no answers to offer. Still, he searched his past for an answer.

The dots of light varied in color and size. There were bright whites, blues, greens, reds, and ambers, but several yellow hues dominated the light show.

Further in the distance, an arrangement of lights appeared, shaped like a backward question mark, and as it got closer, he had the impression of deceleration. Yet physical sensation still escaped him.

How long have I been like this? Tailey thought to himself, believing it was another unanswerable question. Time had no meaning to his spiritual body. For all he knew, he may have been traveling for centuries or for seconds; somehow, it did not seem to matter.

Gradually, his path seemed to alter toward the bottom light of the pattern before him, which also was the biggest and brightest of the grouping. The orb appeared to have a pale-blue radiance, and as the space between himself and the light closed, Tailey realized that what he beheld was a sun, like the one that had warmed his belly so many times in the past.

To add to Tailey's confusion, the lines of light stopped passing him by and became points. He'd heard the bosses refer to them as stars. He was now near the pale-blue sun. It was here that another object caught his attention. *A planet, perhaps?* Its shape reminded Tailey of something he had seen before on a shelf in the chair room. Megan's father had called it a "football," or "the old pig skin," but the coloring was not the same.

Danger! The sense came upon him suddenly, and without direction, drawing his attention away from the strange football-shaped object in the distance. A strange evil seemed to be all around him—strange, yet also oddly, frightfully familiar to him.

Out of the ink-black space, a shadow took form, attaching itself to the dome encircling him.

"Yes! A Cat's Eye Stone. I will take it and add its powers to our own." Sickness seemed to drip from every word that invaded Tailey's mind. "What's this? A soul?" The creature's attention turned fully on Tailey then. "We, Ichneumon, will possess you, Cat's Eye Stone, and your passenger as well."

These words struck fear in Tailey's heart—a fear so intense that he saw his sleeping body twitch and quake. The shell around him began to bulge inward at different points, as if the shadow outside were probing it for a weak spot.

Panic spread through Tailey's spirit form. His mind shouted, *No! No! No!* Nothingness again subdued him.

* * *

Barry Newman Perkins hid in the shadows of a dense pine forest, not far from the Blue River Store located along M-66 not far from the Alba Highway. The monster inside his head was pushing him into seclusion as its pursuers stomped through the brush and muck of the swampy lowland that followed the Jordan River.

Somehow, something or someone had alerted the authorities of their presence.

"We must run! We must hide! We must avoid the authorities until we destroy the powers that hide in her eyes! Yes, we must!" Ichneumon, Possessor of Souls urged Barry under low-growing pine boughs and forced him to lay still as the police approached their location.

Suddenly, from deep within his own mind, for no reason he could comprehend, Barry felt the monster's control weaken and then disappear.

"HERE!" he screamed, desperate to be caught and contained before the monster returned. "HERE I AM! OVER HERE! COME QUICK!!"

The state police converged on his location, and in moments, had him in handcuffs. "Shoot me!" Barry yelled. "You HAVE TO shoot me!! PLEASE!" He looked at them frantically as they ignored his pleading and started reading him his rights. "You don't understand! You have to save her from me! I don't want to kill her! Please! I'll do it if you don't stop me!" He wanted to die. He needed to. The horrors of ripping the first little girl to pieces ate at his soul. "PLEASE! YOU HAVE TO—"

"NO!" said the monster then, as it suddenly regained control, snapping Barry's jaws closed as tightly as the cuffs on his wrists. *"Not yet."* Quickly assessing its new situation, it cursed inside Barry's mind. *"What have you done to us?"*

Please ... Shoot me...

"Fear not. Your death will come soon enough ... but not now."

The officers loaded them into a squad car and brought him to the local police department in Bellaire, where he would be kept under constant surveillance until his transport back to the Jackson prison. There he would finish his life sentence and face additional charges, included escaping prison and the attempted murder of a minor.

Chapter 3

KLAWED

The trip out of darkness was so gradual, so unannounced, that Tailey barely realized that he could feel cool stone under his body. The air smelled stale from the lack of movement, its moisture carrying the aroma of ancient mold spores. A drop of water echoed in the distance, and then the silence of a tomb settled upon him.

Tailey wrestled with the idea of opening his eyes, but he refused to succumb to the urge. He preferred to lie there, absorbing the tranquility that surrounded him. The peace reminded Tailey of when he was a kitten, too young to open his eyes. He remembered the warm touch of mother's stomach against his head while he rested with his sisters snuggled about him. These comforting thoughts put his purring machine on high, the vibrations rumbling through his body in waves of pleasure.

A mental voice invaded his dream world. "Comfy?"

Responding to the sudden presence launched Tailey straight up into the air.

Thud!

Out went the lights again.

The journey back from darkness was not as pleasant as before. This time, the first thing he became aware of was a heavy weight on his back, warm air passing over him, and the nagging presence of watching eyes.

Cracking his eyes open to thin slits allowed the pale-golden light to flood his retinas. The first true image that took form was the large head of a Panther at an awful proximity to his own.

"There isn't any cannibalism on your side of the family tree, is there, cousin?" Tailey asked, meekly.

The weight slipped from his back as the head dropped from view. He heard howls and grunts coming from somewhere below him. Tailey realized the weight had been one of the massive paws of the Panther on his back, restraining him from further self-injury.

Crawling to the edge of the shelf on which he found himself, Tailey beheld a sight that confused him further. On the floor below him, a huge Panther and some other creature rolled back and forth. The Panther pounded on the stone beneath him while emitting a series of grunts and howls.

The other party also rolled about, chirping and hooting. Tailey noticed that its hands and feet closely resembled Megan's, but with long fingernails.

"They're laughing at me!" Tailey stated, in flat disbelief.

These words seemed to sober the monster-size cat. "Forgive me. Are you all right?" he asked, as he gained his paws under him. Without waiting for an answer, the Panther continued. "We had been exploring this cave system in search of the Northern Beesive Hive when we came upon you sleeping."

"Sleeping! Cave! How can this be?" Tailey asked. "I was hunting a mouse in an old hollowed-out tree stump, bumped my head, and woke up with you staring at me." Tailey's brain raced to unscramble the mystery of his coming to this ... location.

Tailey glanced around the chamber in which he found himself a visitor. The area was about twice as long and wide as the boss's truck. Softly glowing golden moss grew in the small cracks and crevices about the vaulted chamber.

"Mouse? What is a mouse?" the Panther asked. It was his turn to be confused.

"A mouse, well ... A mouse, you see, is a small creature. I heard the bosses refer to them as 'rodents.' They are good to eat, I hear..." Tailey stumbled for words. "It doesn't matter really."

Looking past the big cat, Tailey spied the other, much smaller creature climbing to its feet, holding its stomach. Shaped something like one of Megan's dolls mixed with a squirrel, though it had no tail that he could see, the small creature was covered with low-piled hair, grayish brown on its back, blending to a golden-orange in the front. Tailey got the vague impression that it was a male of its race. It had soft secondary hair on its pinkish, oval-shaped face. Its eyes were the shape of almonds and completely black, situated close above a small, rounded nose with two nostrils. The nose tapered up between its eyes and then smoothed out onto its forehead. Slightly visible between its brownish-pink lips, Tailey could see its teeth, which seemed sharp and slightly pointed in the front. It wore a dark red cloth swathed around its lower body, fastened in place with a brown cloth belt around its waist.

The Panther noticed that Tailey was watching his companion in wonderment. "Where are my manners? This is my life-companion and friend, Nep, of the Neptunian race. He and his people came to our planet, Katlyn, as refugees long before the first War of the Woods, which is another story for another time. Me? Well … I am Klawed. I am an explorer for the Panther Kingdom, residing in the City of Shadow."

"I am called Tailey," he said in turn. "But I don't have time for more of these pleasantries I am afraid. I am Megan's life-guardian and companion, and I must go to her. She is in great danger from the Nightman, who lurks in the shadows in the forest near our home! Now please, show me the way out of here, and I'll be on my way."

Tailey jumped down toward the flat smooth stone of the floor. *What is going on?* It seemed to take forever to reach the ground. If "Nep" had not been a clue enough, now he knew for certain that he was no longer on earth. It was like the internal pull of this world was weaker.

Without another word, Klawed turned to lead the way out of the cave. As they neared the tunnel exiting the small chamber, the being Klawed had referred to as Nep sprang onto the back of the Panther with surprising agility. Once there, the Nep strapped himself to the black leather saddle Klawed was wearing, which was part of a fine tooled harness. Attached to the harness rings was a long-black cylindrical tube, with something round and silver extending out from its uppermost end. Tailey was tempted to ask about this, but he did not want to waste time. He had to get back to his Megan.

The passage through which Klawed led Tailey was not at all small. The bosses could easily walk here without ducking their heads. The vaulted passage floor was flat and smooth, with only small bits of debris scattered about.

Gazing at the golden glow from the moss that lined the tunnel, many questions assaulted Tailey's mind as his journey through the light-streaked void started to come back to him, along with the attack of the dark creature on his spirit form, and the mysterious blinking golden-brown eye in the tree stump back home. And now he was travelling with a huge Panther and his enigmatic rider.

Is this real? Is this really happening to me? Am I dreaming all of this? Tailey asked himself.

Holy Lars! I sound like a human!

Coming to a stop, Klawed turned back to Tailey. "Your thoughts are leaking! We hear your words, and no, you are not dreaming. And what is a hue-man?"

These words struck a new fear and utter disbelief in Tailey that he had never known before in his life. *'What is a human?'* Suddenly, his Megan seemed far away.

"A human…" He paused, considering how to explain. "A human is like your friend there on the saddle, except humans are much taller, taller than you, with only fine secondary hair on their bodies. Their heads, other than the area around their faces, have primary hair, and some males have primary hair bordering their faces, which they refer to as beards. They wear clothes on their bodies and leather shoes on their feet to protect them."

The huge Panther did not seem to know how to respond to that information and continued up the passage.

"We will be outside soon," Klawed said soothingly. "The sunlight will help to balance you." He turned to continue up the passage, which ran straight for some time before turning sharply to the left. Around the turn, streamers of daylight and cool fresh air filtered through an opening up ahead. The Panther slowed his pace to allow their eyes time to adjust to the growing brilliance.

Outside the entrance, Tailey had to squint for a moment to finish the process of getting used to the full daylight.

The world he saw around him was indeed different. Instead of the lush forest of home he had expected to emerge into, Tailey found himself surrounded by tall sharp mountains virtually barren of trees. The highlands below the overlook had only a few patches of dense woods scattered about.

Further on past the highlands, Tailey could make out rolling plains with mountain ranges deep in the background.

On each side of the tunnel's entrance on the mountainside stood stone giants that resemble great bear-like creatures. The stone figures had large hands with two opposable thumbs on each hand with three fingers in between them. The uplifted hand of one statue held a huge hammer, while the other statue held up a tree limb. The faces of the giants looked smooth, framed by a long mane or beard. Somehow the faces seemed kind and gentle, but also sad, like they were grieving some lost memory.

The full truth came by way of the soft, pale-blue light that radiated from the sun. This wasn't Earth. It wasn't his home.

The weight of this burden tore at his heart.

My dear Megan, Tailey thought, his head hanging low. *How can I protect you from the Nightman now?*

* * *

Back in the cave, a dark form glided into the chamber where Klawed and Nep had found the dazed and confused Tailey. The figure was very tall and powerful, at least seven feet tall, its body covered with thick brown hair except its face, hands, and feet. It wore only brown leather boots and a brown loin cloth. It was Yahmond Yah, who was living for a cycle in the deserted ancient city to prepare for his upcoming marriage to Yana, as Animond tradition required of all males of their race.

Deep on the stone shelf where Tailey had lain, a golden-brown eye-shaped stone glowed in long, even pulses, beckoning the Animond to it. Answering the call, Yahmond Yah took the stone from its resting place and held it in its massive hairless palm. As if completing a mission, the pulsing golden radiance of the stone faded back into itself.

Locking the stone in a tight, vise-like grip, the creature turned to another passage and disappeared into the faint golden glow.

Chapter 4

JUMP JOUSTING

In a grove of trees below the abandoned caves, the trio lay about a small fire provided by the Neptunian. It had been incredible how the Neptunian had called on magic to ignite the flames. It had first gathered some dead limbs from the small stand of trees. One-by-one, Nep had carefully arranged each stick to form a horseshoe-shaped pile with a small opening to the interior.

Then Nep had stood back from the pile of wood, with his arms spread wide, and faced the setting sun, then clapped his hands once over his head, which had summoned many rays of sunlight to condense in the space between his hands, creating a swirling sphere—a seemingly endless kaleidoscope of various colored lights. At just the right moment, Nep had performed a perfect forward somersault, slapping the ball of light with the bottoms of his feet, and launching the fireball into a cup-shaped area of the wood pile, igniting it on impact.

"Show off," Klawed said to no one in particular, before looking at his new companion. "Come close to the fire, Tailey. The heat will help to stay your nerves after such a trying day in a new place. I can see you are not of this world." Without pausing for a reply, he continued. "I've traveled our world quite a bit, and I don't recall ever seeing a cat of your type or size."

"The sun … it's not the same!" Tailey had said, trying not to sound naive.

"Nep, my friend," Klawed said, calling for his attention, "we have a story to hear. Please entertain us with your tale, Tailey. With better knowledge, we can perhaps find aid for you."

Across the fire, Tailey surveyed the pair. The Panther appeared to be many times the size of the ones he and Megan had viewed in the television. This was not any dark-phase Leopard. No, a black pelt covered the enormous Panther from his wedge-shaped head to the tip of his thick, muscular tail.

Nep sat next to Klawed, leaning against him, and staring intently at Tailey with dark, white-less eyes. The Neptunian—slimmer of build than Tailey, though much taller when standing upright—had tufted cat-like ears that rotated to the sounds of the surrounding world during the changing shifts, and were perked forward now, seemingly eager to hear what he had to say.

Tailey considered how much he should share with them. It had been early afternoon when the trio had emerged from the caves. Throughout the rest of the day, they'd picked their way down the mountain to the valley below. Although the way had held little danger, it had still required a considerable amount of time to find their way through the maze of boulders that littered their descent. Klawed had said that they had approached the caves from another direction, so several times, the travelers had needed to detour around unforeseen obstacles that had impeded their progress. Along the way, Tailey had said little about himself, limiting his conversation to comments on passing birds or small animals that scurried from view when they passed. Over the course of their journey, Tailey found that he had gained a certain amount of trust for the two beings and so decided to give them a complete recounting of his past at the fireside that night...

When Tailey reached the part about being attacked on his voyage through the darkness by the entity proclaiming itself to be Ichneumon, Possessor of Souls, the pair sat bolt upright in recognition of the name but remained quiet throughout the remainder of the narration. Upon the completion of the story, Nep climbed to his feet and faced Klawed. Whatever was said between them was kept private, with them apparently able to channel their mind-voices without broadcasting them to others. When they were done, Nep dashed off into the darkness.

"Where did he go?" Tailey asked.

"He has gone back to the cave," Klawed answered.

"Why?" asked the bewildered cat.

"To find the Golden-Brown Cat's Eye Stone you saw in the tree stump," Clawed replied. "We hope to find it and deliver it to the Kittoehee."

"Kittoehee? What is a Kittoehee?"

"Kittoehee is the title given to cats who study magic. The Panther Seeker has been the only Kittoehee I have known. He resides in a chamber deep under Shadow City."

This puzzled Tailey further.

"Try not to be confused. You see, the eye you saw, and the stone Ichneumon referred to, are one in the same, or at least one of the seven. There are seven known Cat's Eye Stones on Katlyn."

"Again... What?"

"Tailey, it is hard to understand a story when the teller begins in the middle, so let me start over." Klawed closed his eyes as if to collect his thoughts.

Overhead, the waxing, gibbous red moon silently traveled across the ink-black sky.

Klawed started his story without warning.

"Our world, as I have told you, is called Katlyn, for reasons no cat is sure of anymore. Here is a tale from our deepest past—the tale of the coming of the Animond, the Gray Circle, and a Great Evil.

It was a time almost beyond memory, when all the cats of Katlyn lived together in peace near the base of the mountain known as the Circles of Indigo. We, the cats, the Neptunians, and the Scantians were the tenders of the flowers of the Plains of Che and the Fubal Plains.

It was on the first night of the full moon when the silver streak fell from the sky and splashed down into the Mighty Drink Sea near Calm Drink Bay."

"Why name both the sea and a bay 'Drink'?" Tailey asked, interrupting.

"We, the cats on Katlyn, see water as something one drinks, so I assume it was natural for the cats of that time to refer to water, whether lake, river, or sea, as 'drink' when naming them," Klawed answered. "Don't the cats drink water on your world?" Klawed asked with feigned incredulity, then continued without waiting for an answer.

"The cats found the silver vessel on the beach, an Ark, as they called it, and from it came a race of people who called themselves the Animond. They were peaceful creatures whom we would soon befriend. And so, it came to be that the

Animond lived among us. They shared in the tending of the flowers until the day they announced that they would find a place on our Katlyn to call their own. So, the Animond left us in pursuit of their own futures. Still, the Animond knew that they would always play a part in the lives of the cats of Katlyn.

In time, the Animond found their home in the catacombs under the Low Jaw Mountain. There, they built the first city of the Animond, which they called 'Family.' In their new home, the Animond people honed their skills as leatherworkers, tanning the hides of the prey animals of the great cats. They fashioned the leather into fine harnesses and clothing.

Other Animond sought the skills of metal smithing deeper in the mountain. These created tools to work the ground for farming grains and tending fruit-bearing trees and bushes, as well as other fixtures that eased the Animond lifestyle.

But the next cycle of the red moon brought evil to our Katlyn. From the depths of the Indigo Mountains, waves of a magical war spewed high into the air and rained down upon the cats, Neptunians, and Scantians—who had also come as refugees from another world—for many days and nights. Then, as suddenly as the battle had started, all became quiet, and from the mountain came the cat wizards—bearers of the mother of all Cat's Eye Stones: the Gray Cat's Eye Stone. They called themselves the Gray Circle and told a story of having come to Katlyn unexpectedly from another world. The Gray Circle gave warning of an evil creature, as old as time itself, which had plagued the world from which they had come. In heated battle with this evil one, their magic had somehow brought them here, and that same evil creature along with them. Although their battle had continued deep within Katlyn's maze-like catacombs, victory once had again eluded them."

After a brief pause, Klawed continued his tale. "To our dismay, they looked afraid. 'The evil host has not been destroyed, and its powerful black magic has escaped! Beware! There will be many more hosts, both on Katlyn and the world from which we've come, as this evil has a reach that spans the distance even between stars!'

News of this evil spread, but though we remained vigilant, time continued to pass as it does, days and cycles progressing ever forward. Eventually, the cats of Katlyn left our home at the base of the mountain, the Circles of Indigo, separating and venturing off to make new homes for themselves. We, the Panthers, traveled with the Neptunians and Scantians to the northern edge of the Fubal Mountains. We made our home under a large overhang we now call the Shadow City, while the Neptunians and the Scanters made their homes in what we call the Nep Forest. The Cougars went further north to the Fubal Highlands. The Lynx went to what is now known as Pussywillow Down, while the swift Cheetahs stayed upon the Plains of Che. All the other big cats, like the Leopards, Tigers, Lions, and Jaguars, as well as the Gray Circle themselves, have since disappeared to the far south and east.

But though we never forgot the threat of the evil one the Gray Circle had named Ichneumon, the Possessor of Souls, and readied ourselves as much as we were able for its eventual return, throughout this time of preparation, an evil shadow fell over the land.

In this ancient time, our world had four seasons per cycle, as our sun travelled different paths across the sky, winter, spring, summer, and fall—"

"You don't have four seasons now?" Tailey asked.

"Well, yes … there are still four seasons, but they no longer change. Do you understand?" Klawed seemed hesitant to elaborate.

"Nope!" Tailey answered.

Seeming uncomfortable with the subject, Klawed pressed onward. "There is another story you should be told about how that came about, another time perhaps, but what matters to this story is that Katlyn's seasons were not fixed as they are now to specific areas. For example, the three of us are in a seasonal band at the moment where it is always spring in the morning and fall in the evening—warm during the day and cold at night."

That puzzled Tailey's mind even more.

Tailey's silence encouraged Klawed to continue with his original story. "In any case, the Beesives of old lived in four great Hives, called the Queendoms of the North, South, East, and West. In those times, all the Beesives were the bearers of a great magic. This magic they used to fortify the life-force of the plants that provided them with nectar.

When the great cats left our home at the base of the mountain, spreading out across Katlyn, the Beesives took over the care of the flowers of Katlyn. The Southern Hive was the largest of the four Queendoms, deep in what now is called the Plains of Che. The Beesives thrived on the vast abundance of flowers of the region.

During one fall cycle, one of the male-drones dreamed of a world where males ruled over the population of the Hive. His dream became an obsession, and his hatred for the queen and her order possessed his soul.

Driven by insanity, the drone waylaid one of the workers who was carrying a full load of raw nectar from the strelitzia flower, also called the bird of paradise flower. This special nectar was used to make royal foods, which was only fed to queen larvae. The nectar in its raw form was pure magic, and only once diluted into royal jelly, or royal bread, could it be consumed safely in large quantities.

As the drone had lost his stinger in his attack on the worker, it knew his own life would soon end. So, in the last moments of his life, the drone took the nectar from the worker's storage stomach and fed it to a male drone larva in a nearby hatching cell, which he carefully sealed so that his treachery would go unnoticed. In the moment of his dying, the drone watched as a strange, wasp-like creature approached, piercing the seal of that same cell, and planting a single egg within the larva he had fed.

That winter the monster-larva emerged from the cell and fed on the souls of the Southern Beesives, one by one. The legend claims that, in the spring, only *it* remained alive, calling itself Ichneumon, the Possessor of Souls."

Chills racked Tailey's body upon hearing the name. "How old is this legend?" Tailey asked disrupting Klawed's narration. "My father told me of the wizard Lars and the Gray Circle, *and* of Ichneumon! How could this Ichneumon have been born after—"

"Tailey, the evil you encountered is thousands of cycles old, and has taken on many forms. This magically corrupted drone was just its most recent iteration, and one with more power than any of its predecessors. Fear, at this time, *is* in order, but you should know that there will come a time when fear has no place—when only the strong will survive."

A long silence fell between them then, and pondering the passage of time, Tailey found himself once again fixated on the earlier issue of this planet's seasons being "fixed."

"Let me get something straight," he said. "With the seasons being fixed, as you described it, how do you know when one year/cycle begins or ends?"

Klawed gave the matter some thought before answering. "Well, it was explained to me like this: There are thirteen moons in a cycle, or twelve months. That means that there is one moon each month, except on the sixth month of the cycle, when you get two moons. The second moon of that sixth month is a red or Blood Moon. There are thirty-six days in a month, which totals four hundred thirty-two days in a cycle."

"The months are just numbered?" asked Tailey. "Not named?"

"Why should we give them names?" Klawed said. "Most cats don't care what day it is, or even what *time* of the day it is."

Briefly, the Panther paused to gather his story legs under him, and then picked up where he had left off. "After departing the murdered Hive, Ichneumon began to build a realm of its own with the help of his possessed hosts, whose spirits watched through their own eyes, unable to stop themselves from the horrible actions they were made to commit.

The evil magic of Ichneumon brought havoc and darkness to Katlyn. The Green Nation invaded the Nep Forest and enslaved the Neptunians and Scanters."

Off in the distance, a mournful howl rang out, bringing the Panther to a defensive crouch.

"Nightwolves! Quickly, up that tree, Tailey!'

Tailey hesitated.

"Now!" Klawed ordered.

Compelled into action, Tailey made for the tree. Several bounds and a few scrapes later, Tailey found himself on a low limb that overlooked the camp. He noted again that the pull of gravity seemed weaker here on Katlyn, making climbing a lot easier.

With one massive front paw, Klawed scraped dirt onto the embers of the low fire. In Tailey's night vision, he saw the tail of Klawed coil around and back—into the dark object on his harness, which Tailey had forgot to ask about. With one fluid motion, the Panther's tail uncoiled with a silvery object on its end. Extending from the silver tube it was now wearing was more silver, quite thin.

What is that? Tailey asked himself.

"A tail-rapier. Now, be still!" Klawed's unexpected mind-voice answered.

Seconds later, Nep returned. From what direction, Tailey had no idea. One minute, the Panther stood alone, and then suddenly, Nep was vaulting up into the saddle.

As one of five shadowy forms emerged from the trees, Tailey remembered his former life on the Ketchen Farms. Though his memory of it was a bit fuzzy and vague, he thought that these ghost-like figures resembled the bosses' dog. Queen Bonnie had called it a German Shepherd when she'd warned Tailey to stay clear of it ... yet these were much larger, though not as big as Klawed.

In staggered timing, the Nightwolves wove back and forth in a half-moon arc, snarling and displaying their fearsome fangs. From somewhere below and behind Tailey, a twig snapped. The sound seemed so out of tune with the happenings below that Tailey could not resist the urge to turn and search for its source.

Slowly, from behind them, came a lone Nightwolf. Their pack's plan became all too clear to Tailey then. The five Nightwolves would distract the Panther and Nep long enough to give their comrade time for a clear lunge at the throat of the Panther.

If I call out to Klawed, he might turn and leave an opening for the larger body of attackers, Tailey thought to himself, knowing all too well what must be done. Tailey would wait for the Nightwolf to pass beneath him.

Time seemed to stand still, and each step the Nightwolf took lasted for what seemed like an eternity. Fear of what he was about to do tightened the cords of his throat to the point where he felt himself about to choke. It was then that the words of Klawed returned to him: *"There will come a time when fear has no place—only the strong will survive."*

The words raised the hackles on his arched back. His snake-like tail rose straight up and the hair on it expanded, making it look twice as thick and strong. Summoning all his courage, Tailey leapt at the head of the unaware ambusher.

Tailey felt like he was floating down toward the Nightwolf. For a second, he worried that he had misjudged his attack. Then his claws and teeth were ripping at the face of the Nightwolf. Howling in pain, the Nightwolf ran in circles, trying desperately to dislodge the hissing gray fury. In a mighty effort, the Nightwolf ran forward and then suddenly stopped, bucking its back, and snapping down its neck. This action launched Tailey like a missile through the air and into the side of a tree, releasing him once more into cool, peaceful blackness.

Chapter 5

GENUS CITY

The way back to the cave proved to be much easier than the trip down to the valley. Nep was quick and could fit through places where Klawed and Tailey could not possibly have hoped to pass.

Nep had spent most of his life with Klawed, and he could tell when the Panther was building toward the telling of another story. *The big blowhard will go on for hours,* Nep thought to himself as he made his way up the mountain. *I hope Tailey is a patient listener!*

Neptunians were not an overly gabby race. Instead, they had built their whole society here on Katlyn with the idea that the greatest knowledge could be gained by listening to the elements that made up their new home.

"Knowledge is power, and power is knowledge. The greatest knowledge of all can be found in the light of the maker. Not through the control of others, but rather through letting the light flow through the soul." The Spring of Truth had said as much. By listening to the words of the Spring of Truth, the Neptunians had been shown the way to free themselves from the evil host that had possessed the Green Nation.

Nep remembered the stories the Elders told of Neptune, their old home planet. A giant forest planet, Neptune had orbited a blue-white sun named Denebola. Other planets in the system were the desert world of Tiviania, the water world of Watartar, the stone world of Firmatia, and the farming world of Scanton, with its fertile soil.

At first sight from afar, Neptune appeared wild and primitive. But under its dense canopy, a complex society had evolved—a society that had cared little for the natural world around them. In time, the population had outgrown the planets' ability to feed them all. So, in desperation, the Neptunians had built vessels that could travel across the expanse to other worlds where they could continue their search for resources.

The Neptunians first traveled to the other giant-sized planets of Tiviania, Watartar, and Firmatia. What they found were three more worlds that had also abused their resources and were ready to join Neptune in their search.

Together, the ambassadors of the four giant worlds traveled to their smaller neighbor world, called Scanton, and what they found was a world with the capacity to feed both themselves and all four of the giant planets as well.

The occupants of Scanton were more than willing to help, and in time, a trade agreement was reached. The ambassadors returned to their home-worlds to begin the process of building vessels to transport goods back and forth between the planets.

Meanwhile, the Scantians used their own technology to grow more food, and soon their whole planet was a farming enterprise, with their capital city, Plenty, evolving to become the trading capital of the surrounding solar system.

The Scantian government had been founded on strong religious beliefs. Still, even they were corrupted by the power of controlling so many lives. A different evil had found its foothold in the political arena, and its name was Devastator.

There was a small period of peaceful relations, but then small squabbles started and developed into full-blown confrontations, which the Scantians won because they had control of the food supplies.

Over time, the Neptunians and Scantians became close friends outside the government. They shared beliefs in the existence of a god, and with the Scanters' guidance, the Neptunians learned about the conservation of resources and absorbed the Scanters' love for natural things that had once been taken for granted. The Neptunians had learned from both their past and their new friendship. Instead of being slaves to their hunger, they built other starships that could search the stars for other worlds to call their own, thus lowering the burden on their home-world.

Many cycles after first contact, the war machines of Tiviania, Watartar, and Firmatia were launched and enroute toward the planet Scanton, following in the wake of two Neptunian transport vessels, christened *Salvation,* and *The Light*—the empty *Salvation* having landed on Scanton and gathered up all the would-be refugees of the coming war who were willing to leave.

Nep stopped outside the cave entrance and gazed out at the stars and the world around him. He could not help wondering, as he often did, if there were any other survivors of that war, and where were they now.

Putting the matter aside, Nep called to his light magic. With a small ball of light cupped in one hand, Nep investigated the chamber where they had found Tailey. Nep was surprised when he was unable to locate the stone.

There was a scent in the air, so weak that Nep was not able to identify its source. The stone floor left no footprints. Klawed and himself had stirred the dust to the point that, if something had come and taken the stone, any clues as to their identity, or even presence, would be safely hidden.

Nep gave up the search for the missing stone, remembering that these magical stones had a mind of their own and often disappeared for no apparent reason. He returned to the surface.

Surely, Klawed must be done with his story by now, Nep thought, as he looked for a suitable place to rest. *But why take chances?* Nep could not suppress the urge to chuckle.

Nep dearly enjoyed being life-companion to Klawed, but he also enjoyed some time alone or with others of his own kind. Those moments seemed so few and far in between. It was true that Klawed could not be matched when it came to bravery and loyalty. But it was well known in the Kingdom of the Panthers, and in all the known lands, that Klawed was fond of long-winded tales—both giving and receiving.

Nep remembered the last reunion between Klawed and Onlooker Jib. The entire clearing below Shadow was full of spectators who'd come to enjoy the Festival of Joining. At the festival, young Neptunians chose between two pathways: choosing a newborn Panther to be companioned to for life or be named and begin courtship with a future spouse.

Those spectators that could not sneak away were fast asleep by the time the two windbags had finally talked themselves silent. The wife of one of the many Scantian ambassadors slept with her head on his shoulder, but her husband, Ambassador Conifert Dew, hung onto every word that was said. Although he had little to add to the conversation, it was plain to see he was enjoying himself.

"Hey, where did everybody go?" Klawed had asked. Timing was everything, and Klawed was the master tale-weaver. Whoever was still awake was taken by the moment, and laughter fell like rain about the clearing.

As Nep got to his feet and started his decent back to the camp, he wondered how his life would have been if he had chosen to be named and pursued a bride over joining with Klawed.

It was hard to imagine. He had only stayed in the Neptunian family environment a brief time before joining with the Panther.

For the most part, Klawed was the only family he knew. They'd grown up together and shared every aspect of a family lifestyle. The Panther and the Neptunian were bonded as brothers, a perfect union of hunter and warrior.

But there was more than just warring and hunting to their bond. The station of being a Panther's Neptunian was to be a collector of knowledge. In this way, the colony of Neptown could gather information from afar under the protection of the Panthers who had always resided on Katlyn.

The Neptunians of old would not abuse this world as they had their own. Certain technologies had been quickly scrapped and replaced with the natural, elemental magic that they'd found inside themselves here, and in the world around them. To use this magic wisely without abuse required profound knowledge, and even after countless cycles, there was so much more of Katlyn to learn about.

The Forest of Nep had accepted and welcomed both Neptunians and Scantians, providing them with a place they could call their home. The spirit given to the forest by the maker would never be forgotten nor abused.

As Nep moved through the maze of boulders, a thought occurred to him: Katlyn had become a planet of refugees, and would now, perhaps, be the last stand against evil. Failure would mean it would become just another link in a chain of evil that seemed to cross both time and space.

Nep was closing in on the location of their camp when he happened on the small band of Nightwolves. They were standing in the shadows observing Klawed and Tailey around a low fire.

Klawed and Tailey were flapping mind-gums, completely unaware of their surroundings. *Klawed is getting reckless in his old age*, Nep thought to himself, as he crept closer to the Nightwolves.

"You two," the Nightwolves platoon leader said to the pair that stood slightly apart from the rest, "Return to the main pack. Inform the Den Mother of the Green Nation that we will be bringing in two cats for her pleasure."

As the two Nightwolves disappeared into the night, the leader turned back to the rest of the platoon.

"Give me a couple of minutes to work my way behind them. Then fan out and approach them quietly. We'll be on them before they even know we're here!"

Nep knew the Nightwolves platoon leader was right. What he had to do was warn Klawed and Tailey. How to do that was not noticeably clear though. His mind-voice would not carry that far. His light magic would warn them, but in using it, he would most likely end up as a wolf snack. Nep concluded that all he could do was wait and hopefully be inspired by the time the need for action could no longer be avoided. The wait was short. The Nightwolves followed their orders and silently spread out just beyond the view of the cats.

Nep picked up the jagged rock he had just stepped on and approached the Nightwolves before him, then charged the Nightwolf at the same time as he hurtled the rock at the base of its tail. The Nightwolf let out a mournful howl from the sharp pain that shot from up its rear-end.

* * *

Southeast of the travelers, deep in the Mangy Mountains, stood three almost identical mountains, collectively called the Triplets: The Northern, Western, and Eastern Spires. Thousands of feet above sea level, their sharp peaks and sheer cliffs marked them as newly formed in comparison to the rest of the mountain range around them. Smoke and steam bellowed out of the volcanic exhaust ports scattered across the heights of the three monoliths.

All around the Triplets, the Mangy Mountains spread out as far as the eye could see, tall yet blunted from centuries of wind and rain erosion that had consumed their once vivid details. Patches of ragged vegetation growing randomly across their faces, and the haggard groupings of trees that dotted the valleys between them, gave the visual impression of mange, as the name of the mountain range implied.

Rising from the planet in a triangular grouping, the Triplets bordered a valley. The three sides facing inwards were sheer granite, but about a hundred feet up on the Northern Spire, an enormous stone shelf jutted out. Under this natural shelter, a massive cavern had been carved out of the stone.

From the center of the cavern, a river flowed out and over the edge into the valley floor below. The water gathered in a deep pool there before traveling through the heart of the valley.

Inside the broad cavern were polished avenues, lined by buildings, all carved out of the mother stone of the mountain and artfully arranged across the expanse of the cavern's floor. The buildings were not simple dwellings hammered out of boulders. No, each structure was intricately etched with rune symbols that described the families of residence. The huge doors and hinges were carved of stone, and above each doorway, the residents' Home Stone was carefully set, some held in sculpted, outstretched claws or hands, but most appearing to have been woven into the very pattern of the house.

Many feet over the rooftops, the domed ceiling had also been decorated by these tailors of stone. The designs were much different from those on the buildings of the city. These portrayed images of the cats of ancient Katlyn: A Lion poised to hurtle itself forward; a saber-toothed Tiger hunched in the moment of pouncing; a Panther brandishing its tail-rapier over its head; a Cheetah frozen in an open stride ... and so many others. Cats of Katlyn, big and small, each posed in some fashion of battle or act of hunting.

In the center of the cavern, along the back wall, was the largest structure of the city, and above its flat roof was carved the titan-sized likeness of the angelic Cloud Leopard—its proper name lost in the annals of time—floating above an intricately carved rune that looked much like a dove-winged letter "G," the Animond's seal for "Genus." Here the sculptors did their greatest work. Every detail of the Cloud Leopard was bold, from the cloud-like patches on her fur, to the white feathers of her outstretched wings. The crafters had spent many cycles mining the gems and other precious stones to give her true image color. One gray stone in the shape of a cat's eye, and placed accordingly, gave the whole creation a lifelike appearance.

Through the arena-sized structure, built toward the back of the city, there were tunnels that led into the mountains. Many were lined with work stalls, where the crafters of metal hammered-out tools and weapons for trade.

A thick rampart lined the outer limits of the city. It was made of polished stone but lacked any protective projections along the top. It was designed to protect the homes from the elements rather than an enemy invasion. On each end of the rampart, massive stone gates opened to wide ramps hewn from the granite, which led to the valley floor below. From the ramps, crushed-stone roads met at a stone bridge at the head of the river. Along the east side of the river, the road branched and followed the river out through a narrow pass to the Mangy Mountains beyond, then under the bridge that crossed the Long Drink River just after it flowed out of Crescent Drink Lake.

From the rich fertile soil of the valley grew the fruit trees, bushes, and vineyards, along with grain fields, which fed the population of the city.

It was the city of the Animond, named Genus to honor the planet from which the maker had created their race.

In a work stall in the city, Yahmond Yah knocked molding sand off a small blade with a blunted hammer he held in his three-fingered, two-thumbed hand. With just a small effort, his grip could crush bone.

The hammer blows he delivered were sure and on target. The packed sand spattered on his leather apron and gloves, which protected the long brown hair that covered his limbs and body.

On a shelf above his worktable, a Golden-Brown Cat's Eye Stone pulsed as it sent instructions to the Animond on exactly how to create the small blade and the structure in which the stone itself, would be set—waiting to be placed in its destiny.

Chapter 6

GONE FISHING

The throbbing pain in his head slowly drummed Tailey back from the valley of darkness, the creaking sound of leather in his ear almost unbearable. The air held a faint tinge of sweat, yet the purity of the air diluted the smell to a tolerable level.

Cracking his eyes open, Tailey found himself being carried through tall grass. Ahead was the powerful neck and head of Klawed. Behind was the spike-toothed grin of Nep, strapped into his saddle harness.

Making an effort to move, Tailey found that both his front and back legs were bound to the Panther's harness like a sack of grain across the back of a donkey.

The mind-voice of the Panther flooded his still-ringing head. "Top of the afternoon, young Tailey!"

"What in the name of the Great Lars…" Tailey groaned as reality poured back over him. "Klawed, I have to find my way back to Megan. She needs my protection."

The trio made a sharp turn to the left and soon came to the edge of a river. Here the Panther crouched low so that Tailey could slide off after Nep released the knots that held him in place.

The pain from his stiff muscles equally matched the pulsing of his head-ache. It took several moments of stretching to work out the knots and cramps. Together, the three went to drink from the river.

Tailey paused to admire how clear the water appeared. *It's like flowing glass.* The water was cool and pure with no hint of chemicals or waste. He could not fight the urge to submerge his head, and found the cool water soothing to his sore, abused crown.

Of course, a wet head was a sure signal that it was time to bathe, which was long overdue. During his grooming, Tailey was reminded of his hunt for the mouse when he found the wound along his left side, from the rose thorn, which was well on its way to healing. In this moment, his fear for Megan overwhelmed his throbbing head, which hung low in defeat.

"Will you come with Nep and I to Shadow City, the Kingdom of the Panthers?" Klawed asked. "If anyone can help you find a way to your home, it would be the Kittoehee, who has much wisdom and the use of magic."

Lifting his head, Tailey looked to the big cat, who had also completed his bath. The Panther's jet-black fur shimmered with a healthy sheen, licked clean of the trail's dust.

"At this point, I don't have many choices."

"Be strong, Tailey! All is not lost—not yet at least!"

In a blinding flash, the tail of Klawed pulled the tail-rapier free of its scabbard, and he launched himself at Tailey. In the last bound, the Panther turned himself sideways, whipping the tail-rapier in an arc. Taken completely off guard, Tailey stood frozen, his eyes wide with horror, as the blade slashed toward him.

Fortunately, the blade traveled riverside of Tailey, doing so and then snapping back behind its wielder. At the same moment, a dagger-shaped head fell to the sand next to him. Over Tailey's head, a long-tubular body—absent of its head—flew neatly over his back and dropped lifeless to the ground on the other side of him.

"Time to eat!" Klawed announced, with a humorous tone that Tailey found to be a trademark of the big cat. "You need to show much care when traveling close to the waterways of Katlyn. There are fish that will launch from the water and skewer you, my small friend!"

Up in the trees that lined the river, the Nep's chattering and sharp hoots echoed the enjoyment of his companion.

"Seems that I have a lot to learn, if I am to survive here on Katlyn," Tailey said to no one in particular.

Grabbing the hard-shelled body of the fish in his jaws, the Panther dragged the carcass just out of sight of the river. There, he cracked the outside husk with several blows of his huge paw.

The boneless pink meat had a sweet taste, which Tailey found most excellent, and he ate his fill while the Panther stood guard.

In his turn, Tailey stood watch as Klawed finished off the fish. Considering the length of the thing, the fish easily provided full bellies for both cats.

"What about Nep?" Tailey asked.

"Oh, Nep doesn't eat meat. Strictly nuts, berries, and some types of grass."

Leading the way, Klawed turned away from the river and headed away from the rising sun.

Away from the river, the tall grass gave way to short plush ground cover. Here the cats were able to travel side by side. Many hours later, they stopped for a rest at the edge of a gradual descent, overlooking a broad expanse.

Klawed's mind-voice intruded on Tailey's silent contemplation of the world before him. "The Fubal Plains, land of the Green Nation. We must travel with caution."

"What happened to the Nightwolves?" Tailey asked, while his mind played out his role in the fight from the previous night.

"You were brave to attack a beast so many times your size, but it wasn't necessary. They were attempting the oldest trick known to cat kind. Nep gave me warning of the approaching ambush. Still, it gave Nep and I much to laugh about as we traveled last night. Your attack came as such a surprise to the Nightwolves that it sent the whole bunch of cowards fleeing for the plains! Back to the Green Nation, with whom I've heard the Black Nation has joined in recent times."

The Panther emitted several grunts, which Tailey now recognized as the Panther's laughter. Humor in cats was something Tailey found difficult to understand. When you are happy, you purr. When you are comfortable, you purr. Simple... When you are mad, you hiss, spit, and scream. In Tailey's world, laughter in cats was practically unknown.

"What are these nations I keep hearing about?" Tailey took the opportunity to find clarification of the massive canines they had encountered last night.

The Green Nation is a joining of the many Greenwolf Packs that litter the Fubal Plains. The Black Nation is a joining of Nightwolf Packs and the Nightwolves are somewhat smaller than the Greenwolves. The Nightwolves reside in and along the Mangey Mountains. Although, the Nightwolves are not cursed from the sun as are the Greenwolves. They have had joint efforts in the past.

"Where did Nep make off to?" Tailey asked, suddenly realizing that the Neptunian had not rejoined them after the river.

"He is scouting ahead for a place to rest tonight. It's not safe to journey on the Fubal Plains at night, especially with a full Blood Moon not far off."

Chapter 7

NUTS!

Below the pale-blue sun, the Fubal Plains stand as a broad rolling plain leading up to the highlands of both the Low Jaw Mountains and the upper reaches of the Mangy Mountains. Rainstorms pass from the heights of the Low Jaw Mountains and gently sweep across the shifting sea of grass and flowers. Between each storm, whole days of sunlight produce a greenhouse of growth, which support the herds of beasts that thrive across its face.

Great circles of the three-horned xantelopes, thundering lines of massive bison, clusters of wild goats, shimmering streams of mirror deer, and other herd beast move about the Fubal Plains in cadence to the rainfall, both day and night.

By spring/day, the Fubal Plains is a peaceful symphony of renewed life. Fawns born in the first rays of sunlight gather their legs under them for their first steps. By afternoon, these young mammals will almost have the agility and speed of their parents. In this way of nature, the fawns now stand a good chance of surviving the coming of fall/night.

The coming of night paints a new face upon this tranquil setting, as intense winds come out of the north, carrying with it the frigid air of fall. The rainstorms change to snow flurries then, and any standing pool of water crust over with ice.

Harmony turns to chaos when the agents of the Green Nation take to the plains. In the darkness, these predators generally weed out the lesser members of the herds. Yet nothing was safe when the Greenwolves of the Fubal Plains were afoot. Nothing!

* * *

The moon overhead held only a slight hint of red, as it traveled across the ink-black sky. The outline of a giant bird of prey floated across the eerie glow of the lunar surface. The mournful screech of the bird drifted upon the chilly air currents of the night in the Spring/Fall Band, and slowly faded into the distance.

The chilly air out of the north carried little scent of the herd beasts, as the wind swept the top of the grasses across the highlands that skirted the fringe of the Mangy Mountains.

Tailey absorbed this new world in a way that he found startling. Human influence had made his old world seem friendly and tame when compared to this wilderness devoid of mankind. Technically, the Nep had a lot of the same features as the human bosses back home, but there seemed to be many differences as well. In the small amount of time that he had been on Katlyn, Tailey found that the wild in him loved this world. It was pure. The air, the water, the rich fertile soil underfoot… The very food he consumed was free of pollution or chemical enhancement. Yet, there was something more … something just under the surface of Katlyn that Tailey found appealing.

Then there was the feeling of having less pull on his body from the world around him. Here on Katlyn, he could do acrobatic jumps and twists with his body that he could never do back home. Leaps into the air felt like slow motion as he traveled from one bound to another. *What an amazing world!* Tailey thought as they traveled along.

Staring out over the Fubal Plains, Tailey's thoughts returned to his Megan. His body gently vibrated to the rhythm of his purr, as warm memories of times past reeled through his mind: the long winter nights that they snuggled together watching the pictures on the television; guiding her as she learned to speak human; and then the most special moments: when he lost himself in the depths of her amazing blue eyes.

On my father's name, King Moe, I vow that I will never give up on finding my way back to you, dearest Megan.

He felt a light pressure on his left shoulders and turned his head to find Nep standing beside him, resting his hand gently on Tailey's fur, his white-less eyes wet with tears. No words were spoken, yet Tailey could sense that Nep felt his pain.

"Nep hears your mind-thoughts, even though it is not your intent to share them."

Tailey turned back to the plains to find Klawed coming up the slope toward them with a generous portion of meat gripped in his jaws.

"The wonderful thing about mind-voice is that one may speak with his mouth-full!" Klawed joked.

Quickly, Nep's dark composure brightened, and he scampered off into the darkness to search for food for himself. Light hoots and chirps echoed back to Tailey and Klawed. Soon, these sounds faded into the distance, and the natural tone of Katlyn's night resumed.

Klawed dropped the meat in the grass before Tailey.

"You must concentrate on muting your thoughts if you're ever to have any privacy on Katlyn," Klawed said, then moved beside Tailey, plopping down to rest his full stomach while Tailey gently nuzzled the meat to guess its origin.

"Wild goat. It usually takes almost two of the little beasts to fill me up. I saved a tender strap off the back for you, my friend. Now eat, and I will finish the tale of Katlyn."

Upon the end of his inspection, Tailey began consuming the savory meat. Rich and still plump with blood, Tailey found the meal to be the best he had ever eaten.

"Now where were we? Oh, yes. Ichneumon, the Possessor of Souls, had just destroyed the colony of the Southern Beesives."

Just the mention of that horrible event caused Klawed to pause.

Klawed chose his next words carefully. "Most of Ichneumon's evil was focused on the Green Nation—the Greenwolves of the Fubal Plains—who, under his sway, had invaded the Great Forest of Nep, enslaving the Neptunians and the Scantians who resided therein."

"So, how does this all tie in with the Cat's Eye Stone that brought me here? And why me?" Tailey interrupted.

Out of the night, the Nep returned, carrying two nuts half his own size. Changing the course of the conversation.

"You found some bushnuts? Those look to be healthy specimens. I hope they'll be good for seeding," Klawed said.

After carefully setting the nuts down, the Nep went to Klawed and removed a leather pouch from the saddle bag attached to his harness. Working loose the drawstrings with a gentle shake revealed that the pouch was actually two pouches joined by a wide leather band. In these pouches, the Nep placed the bushnuts with great care and then knotted the drawstrings shut.

Drawing the acorn-like nuts up with him into the riding saddle, the Neptunian secured the packages and himself in place. Nestling his head between the nuts then, like an infant between its mother's breasts, Nep fell off quickly into slumber.

Klawed read the curiosity in Tailey's watchful eyes. "There is only one such tree in all the Forest of Nep, and there must be at least two for the plants to reproduce. The Neptunians hold the bushnut as sacred food. For the rest of our journey back to Shadow and the Nep Forest, Nep will guard this treasure with his life."

Klawed again shifted back to his tale. "Alright so … for a hundred cycles, the Green Nation ruled over all that dwelt in the Forest of Nep and the Fubal Plains. During this time, two events shaped the future of the Neptunians, Scantians, and Panthers:

"First, the Neptunians and Scantians found the Crying Tree, which held the Spring of Truth in its womb. The Neptunians learned the truth of their own abilities to use the magic of the pale-blue light, and the Scanters increased their folklore of the forest.

"Second, a Panther named Katanna found six Cat's Eye Stones, deep in the heart of Shadow. Katanna mastered the powers of the stones and became the first Kittoehee of the Panthers to hold such a great authority.

"And so, the Neptunians and the Scantians began the long fight to free themselves from the Green Nation, but their newness to the ways of magic left them poorly equipped for battle. Still, they refused to yield to the dark inherent magic of the Greenwolves. For many cycles, guerrilla-warfare raged across the forest.

"The Panthers entered the fray when Katannon, son of Katanna and second of the Kittoehee, foresaw our own doom if we failed to aid the forces of light. So, my people joined the battle, tooth, and claw. Our tail-rapiers, a Panther's preferred weapon, turned the tide of the war. But the war was far from over. The dark magic that possessed the Green Nation drove the Greenwolves insane. No longer was it a war between the minds of generals. No! The Greenwolves attacked in an all-out frenzy. Much blood was lost in the maddened melee.

"In the heat of this nightmare, the Northern Beesives launched a magical attack on the Greenwolves' Den Mother, the queen of her kind, and destroyed her. The Green Nation were then easily routed from the forest.

"Katannon looked about him then and saw all the death and misery the Greenwolves had caused. Once again, he called on the magic of the Cat's Eye Stones and cursed the Green Nation from ever again seeing the light of day. But the curse was much more powerful then Katannon had realized. The backlash of the curse affected our whole world. The changing seasons gradually slowed and finally stopped, becoming fixed as they are today, with the region of the Plains of Che trapped in eternal summer, and here on the Fubal Plains, there is perpetual fall in the evening and night. With the chilling cold, rides terror and chaos. When the morning sun climbs above the Mangy Mountains, it acts as a signal to the wind to shift from north to south, carrying the warmth of spring back into the region for the day. With the warm air currents lie the promise of new life and hope."

"Klawed, I get the impression that there was more to your visit to the caves where you found me than what you've already said. Why were you searching for the Northern Beesives?"

"Evil has grown powerful once more, after so many cycles," Klawed said. "Tomorrow, we will not stop until we are across the Clear Drink River and the upper plains, and into the Forest of Nep. It shall be a long day. You should rest now," Klawed said, cutting off any further questions.

Sleep avoided Tailey for some time. The world around him seemed in chaos. Sounds of terror and panic carried on the wind as steel jaws locked on the throats of the night's victims. Through it all, the Panther and Nep slept as if they felt nothing of the feeding frenzy that rampaged below them. When sleep did arrive for Tailey, it brought with it dreams of his home back at the Ketchen Farms. The vivid picture of King Moe and his mother, Queen Bonnie, remained clear in his mind the next day. King Moe sat under the lone apple tree in the middle of the bosses' hay field, and Queen Bonnie laid with her head resting against his locked front legs.

Together their mind-voices had flooded his dreams: *"You are the one. You will be a great warrior against evil. Grow strong and be brave!"*

Chapter 8

YAHMOND YAH

With dawn approaching, a solitary wasp-like creature took roost on a small ledge, which served as the threshold to a vent hole formed when the volcanoes had pushed up the Low Jaw Mountains from the depths of Katlyn. On the face of the fang-shaped mountain, the vile spawn watched as the Den Mother led her vanguard into the safety of their lair, safe from the killing light of the pale-blue sun.

As the sun rose above the Mangy Mountain, two large males were still hundreds of feet from the cave entrance when the first wide band of blueish light engulfed them. The wolf-like creatures toppled as if hit by a hunter's bullet.

The dark creature watched with glee as the two Greenwolves were overcome with madness, foam flowing from their noses and snapping jaws, blood gushing from their eye sockets, screaming howls of misery welling up from their throats as they thrashed and rolled in a frenzy across the short grass. Suddenly, the two victims of the sunlight found each other. Their claws and teeth of each ripped and shredded the other without mercy.

Time for the two Greenwolves was measured by the pulsing of their blood, which spewed from their many wounds. The dark creature watched intently as life departed the Greenwolves.

The mercy of death brought a sudden realization to the dark creature: "Souls lost!" The dark creature howled its rage. "Come back! Come back, so we may feast on your souls!"

Half off its perch, the dark creature remembered the other Greenwolves who could be watching their failing brothers inside the black shadows of the cave.

"We mustn't give us away to the others," the creature muttered quietly to itself. "No, we must have those souls to fuel our vengeance on the world of Katlyn and its fools!" It turned back to the vent port and disappeared into the darkness of the underworld.

* * *

Yahmond Yah stood before his home, admiring all the work that he and his future wife, Yana, had done in creating another page of their families' history. For many cycles, they had labored to complete their new home, which was their wedding gift to each other—their beginning of a new life together. Everything had been done according to Animond custom. The male hand-carved the dwelling, while the female etched the furnishing of the home from the removed stone. His bride was even now searching the heart of the mountains for the one stone that would become their "Family Stone," which he would set above their doorway—the final seal of their union together.

Before Yana could leave on her seven-day search, Yahmond Yah had needed to complete a cycle in the caves of the Animond's first home on Katlyn: the deserted City of Family. There he'd roamed the passages, listening to the voices of the spirits of the past. It was the hopes of the Animond that future husbands and fathers would not fall into the hands of possession, as the Animond of old had done back on their home planet of Genus. Nor fall to the evil that dwelt deep in the catacombs under the Low Jaw Mountains.

Now, while he waited for Yana, Yahmond made use of his time, fashioning the small tail-rapier he'd been prompted to create, using the instructions that still poured into his mind from the Cat's Eye Stone. After honing the blade razor sharp on both edges, Yahmond set the Golden-Brown eye-shaped stone into the hilt of the blade. He then crafted a scabbard and hid the item in a leather pack in a secret place in his family's workstation.

As the seventh day of Yana's journeying passed, and still Yana had not returned from the depths of the Northern Spire, in Yahmond's heart, the feeling that something was terribly wrong grew to the point of distraction. It was time to go search for her.

The soft leather boots that protected Yahmond Yah's hairless feet made no sound as he made his way down the polished stone avenues to the main hall and the tunnel entrances within. The others he passed remained quiet, for the Animond knew of his plight. In the way of his people, he would go alone to find his missing bride.

In front of the massive stone doors that led into the great hall stood the Spring Fountain, the main water source for the whole city. From the top of the mushroom-shaped pillar flowed the water, which was caught in stone channels, carrying it to aqueducts that fed the flowing water through stone pipes to each home, before completing its journey to the Our Blood River. The river flowed out between the Western and Eastern spires of Triplet Mountains to the Mangy Mountains and out to merge into the Between Drink River before dumping into the Crescent Drink Lake.

At the deep basin around the spring fountain, Yahmond Yah knelt to fill his canteen, and drinking more of the icy water straight from its flow, he listened as air bubbles escaped the vessel. The shock of coldness helped to reinforce his choice as to where he would begin his search for his beloved Yana.

Through the open doors, Yahmond Yah entered the great hall. To his right, the stage where the bishop preached the word of the maker stood in shadows. Only a few of the glow-orbs, which were set at the end of stone stalactites, illuminated the vast chamber. To his left, rows of stone-hewed pews sat empty and quiet. Across the "Hall of Genus" were three sets of smaller stone doors, opening to the work areas and further into the vast maze of mines and tunnels beyond the depths of the catacombs which riddled the stone beneath the Mangy Mountains and the heart of Katlyn.

To the center-most door Yahmond Yah went, pulling the iron ring and opening it with little effort as he had done so many times in the past. The usual wash of hot air seemed out of place without the sounds of the forges bellowing and hammers pounding on steel. Just inside the doorway, he paused to let his eyes get used to the golden glow of the passage as the door gently closed itself behind him.

The closing thud of the door propelled Yahmond Yah into motion once more, and in a few long strides, he found himself at the entrance to his work chamber. With no time to waste, Yahmond Yah went directly to the metal rack along one wall. There hung the tools of his trades: hammers, chisels, and an assorted variety of files for both wood and metal.

Yahmond Yah removed the heavy apron that covered his front then and hung it on the only empty peg on the rack. The weight of his apron activated a hidden latch, which caused the rack to swing out and away from the wall, exposing a hidden locker, from which Yahmond Yah removed a brown leather harness with a large, squared leather pack attached to the back. Brass rings were fixed about it onto which other items could be lashed.

Next, he brought forth a leather sheath with copper bindings holding it together, the hilt protruding from the top of the sheath gleaming of gold between the bands of leather, and its pommel, the largest and purest of rubies, shimmered in the dim light.

With the harness in place, and sheath and canteen strapped to the securing rings, Yahmond Yah turned back to the passage that led deep into the heart of the mountain.

Chapter 9

LOST SOULS

A heavy sleet that fell in the night had swollen the waters of the Clear Drink River and Southern Cross Drink Rivers to the top of their banks. Klawed and Nep led the way southeast along the Southern Cross Drink River, from where the two rivers joined, in hope of finding a place in which to cross over. It was well past midday before they happened onto a place where the water did not appear deep, though the current was swift. It appeared passable, though one bad step could spell doom for the trio.

"Tailey," Klawed said, "you'll have to ride behind Nep and the bushnuts. I cannot ask Nep to dismount with his treasure, leaving them at risk, to come back across for you."

It was obvious to Tailey that the Panther was in turmoil over how to get them all over to the other side safely.

"We could bind you to the harness, "Klawed offered.

"No, I can hang on." Tailey did not like the idea of being tied in place again.

"Are you sure?"

Tailey was sure. "Let's do this!" He could sense the relief in Klawed's mind-voice that they would not be delayed. He sprang up onto Klawed's back behind the Neptunian.

The Panther and crew waded into the churning brown water until Klawed's belly was just inches above the river. His next steps brought the water level with the Panther's back, where Nep held tightly onto the bushnuts, and Tailey gripped the saddle as the raging current tore at its bindings … and his grip.

The current proved to be swifter than Klawed had anticipated, and it soon had him swimming for their lives. Tailey realized all too soon that his hold on the saddle was not going to last long, and sure enough, the water began sweeping him downstream. Suddenly, Tailey felt a long tree limb under his stomach. He grabbed it tightly, wrapping all four legs around it. This would at least keep his head above the water, or so he hoped.

Tailey was shocked to find that the tree limb was instead the tail of Klawed, which whipped him in all directions. Many times, Tailey found himself dunked underwater.

Finally, Klawed used the last of his strength to pull them onto the grass on the far bank. The Neptunian's lower quarters remained tightly secured in the saddle on Klawed's back, and his arms remained locked around his precious bushnuts, which he had wedged his body between in hopes of keeping the pouches from being ripped from their bindings by the raging current.

Exhaustion carried the two cats and Nep into a dreamless slumber, and the hours that they required to cross the Fubal Plains rapidly passed them by. Their doom rose with the setting of the pale-blue sun.

* * *

The blood oozed from the wounds of the TIG-Horde, which lay dead around the feet of Yahmond Yah, as his red blade mowed through his attackers as he moved toward his Yana. Two TIG-Workers held her captive across the subterranean chamber.

The TIG-Horde, armed with a variety of stone-made weapons, strained to keep Yahmond Yah from his bride. Mechanically, Yahmond Yah's ruby sword blade sliced through the jungle of TIG-Horde before him. The red-skin devils, less than half his size, fought the seven-foot giant without fear. Many times, their weapons struck home on Yahmond Yah, but the Animond ignored the blows, his attention focused solely on reaching Yana.

As Yahmond Yah's struggle brought him closer to Yana, the magic wielders among the TIG-Workers restrained her. With their staffs held out before them, the TIG-Workers lips moved together, calling on the powers of darkness to condense in the black onyx orbs set in the top of their staffs.

Yahmond Yah saw the black rays of evil as they streaked past the glowing moss that grew on the wall of the cavern. He leapt at the first TIG-Worker, swinging the ruby blade at its head, but his efforts were in vain. The dark magic peaked, and in a flash, spirited away the two TIG-Workers from the chamber, taking his beloved Yana with them.

Turning back to the TIG-Horde, Yahmond Yah found the last few of them retreating into the tunnels. All that remained were the dead, and himself. "YANA!" Yahmond Yah's scream echoed through the silent underworld. Desperately, he fought to control the rage that boiled within his soul.

* * *

"Sleep, dear Mother," said the voice of the black wasp-like creature, as it flew up from the back of the Den Mother's neck toward the small tunnel that vented air to the large cave at the base of the Low Jaw Mountain range. "Soon you will become one with us again! Yes, we are many!" gloated Ichneumon, the Possessor of Souls.

Around the Den Mother, the main body of the Green Nation slept. The dark magic of Ichneumon would not allow the Greenwolves of the Fubal Plains to wake and spoil its deeply laid plans. So, evil passed from the cave, leaving in its wake thousands of unsuspecting victims that would murder and destroy the Neptunians, the Scantians, and most importantly, the Panthers. All in the name of their Den Mother. "Us is within her!"

All, but one...

* * *

Luna slept near her mother in the place set aside for the females of the Green Nation, one of whom would take the place of the queen should she become too weak or die. Luna, the youngest of the sisters, slept uneasy this day and came fully awake upon hearing the words of an intruder. Her young eyes searched for the source of the voice, locating the dark creature disappearing into an opening in the ceiling. Luna growled the alarm, but no one answered it. The entire population seemed to sleep like the dead.

A strange odor flooded the cave. The smell stung Luna's muzzle, which brought a wash of fear over her. The young pup carefully rose and went to the back wall. There she backed into a small crack between two boulders. Her size allowed her to squeeze into places that a full-grown Greenwolf could barely insert its head.

The vantage from which Luna hid herself had a full view of the Den Mother, lying on the raised stone dais a few short yards away. Luna watched in horror as her mother's body lurched in spasms. Low growls escaped the Den Mother's throat from between her jaws, which snapped at invisible targets about her head. Then she lay still for many moments.

Slowly, the Den Mother climbed to her feet, as if waking after a day's sleep. Luna felt the hackles of her fur along her back rise as she watched her mother stalk around the dais, seeming to see the cave and her people for the first time. Gradually, the Den Mother's pace increased, her body making leaps and twists as though testing her own limits of motion.

Suddenly, the Den Mother wheeled around and locked in a motionless point right at Luna. Her burning red eyes, once green, probed the dark where Luna stood frozen, barely able to breathe.

"Come out, young one, '" the Den Mother's mind-voice invited. "Yes, come to Mothers, we need your soul." For a moment, Luna almost succumbed to the hypnotic eyes of her mother, but deep inside Luna's soul surged a force. An energy, new and unnamed, swelled inside her. At first, she feared the energy. The fingers of her inner mind sorted through it. Energy? The word did not describe the wave of power that washed over her. Magic! Yes, it was the magic that was passed with the death of the elder Den Mother to her successor.

But Mother is not dead! Luna thought, as she stared into the eyes of the Den Mother.

The Den Mother began to stalk toward Luna in short, measured steps until she had closed the gap between them by half. Then the Den Mother launched herself at the opening. Steel jaws with sharp pointed fangs snapped dangerously close to Luna's face. Luna's body locked with fear. The cold stone at her back kept the young pup from retreating from the death that sought to ravage her soul.

The new magic flowed on the blood of Luna's veins and grew at every point of her being. As if knowing the danger to its vessel, the magic went into action on behalf of the pup. The stone at Luna's back split and opened to form a tunnel, then her rear paws dragged her back into the dark gloom.

Luna felt herself being pulled backward for only a short measure of time. Then she found herself in a large space, illuminated by the light of the golden moss that covered its surfaces. The stone that allowed her flight slowly closed then, cutting off the howls of anger from the Den Mother.

Mother! This thought echoed through Luna's mind as she turned to follow the passage. Sad tears ran down onto her fur, with its blending of soft green and red hairs, as she wandered into the depths of the mountains, alone for the first time in her life.

Chapter 10

FLEE

Yahmond Yah sat on a flat stone next to the tunnel opening, like a sentinel before the gates of a castle. His fingers gently traced the double-edge of the ruby sword that sat across his legs. The faultless, diamond-shaped crystal's razor-sharp blade disappeared into the gold of the hilt. The hilt was an amazing piece of work itself. The finger guard had raised dove wings that fanned back toward the ruby sphere that had been set as the pommel. The oval handle, long enough for two hands, and was gnarled and wrapped in leather to improve the user's grip. The sword was the work of a master craftsman of stone and metal.

Gazing into the depths of the crystal blade, Yahmond Yah remembered how this sword, crafted for the hands of the Animond, had come to be...

Ell Yah was Yahmond Yah's first ancestor on Katlyn, having come to the planet—countless cycles earlier, when the world was still at peace—on board the Ark. The great cats, the Neptunians, and the Scantians welcomed all the Animond to Katlyn, but the cats took a special interest in Ell Yah, who had arrived as an orphan. The great cats, though mainly the Panthers, taught him the ways of cat kind: the tending of the flowers, and especially, the skills of the hunt.

As Ell Yah reached his adulthood years, the Animond community felt the need to build a home of their own. Soon, the time came when the elders announced their intentions of finding a place to call their own—a place to call "Family." As much as Ell Yah loved being with the great cats, he knew that his place was with his own people. So, when the Animond left for the mountains, he had departed with them, and with him, he took all the knowledge the great cats had given him.

The Animond found the catacombs below the Low Jaw Mountains, and there they built the city of "Family," their first city on Katlyn, closer to the planet's heart.

Ell Yah found love in the subterranean city. With their new "Home Stone" in hand, Ell married Melo, but when it came time for the couple to recite the Oath of Peace, Ell's voice remained mute. That night an apparition appeared to him. It was a cat with cloud-like patches on its fur, and white, dove-like wings on its back.

"The cats know peace, but we also know its cost," said the gentle mind-voice of the angelic cat. "Ell Yah, you must go deeper into the catacombs to find that which will give peace a chance for the Animond."

So, Ell Yah had gone deep into Katlyn, and after many cycles, returned with the ruby crystal sword—and a secret: There had been two crystal blades forged in the gloomy depths. The first was of black onyx, and its evil had lain dormant as he'd worked it. It was not until Ell Yah had finished polishing the edges of the blade that the evil within had begun rising from its depths. Ell Yah had returned the blade to the fire, not realizing that the blade would not be destroyed so easily and had fallen short of the molten lava.

Ell Yah turned his efforts to another sword, working again to create the sword of peace, this time using the purest of rubies. After fashioning its hilt and sheath, and polishing the crystal ruby blade razor sharp, he hid the sword, concealing its destiny in the passages of time.

One day, as an Animond bride was searching for a Family Stone for her wedding day, she came upon the ebony sword. As she held the blade, her mind, heart, and soul became corrupted, changing even physically until she no longer recognized herself.

Soon many other Animond, both male and female, began to go missing.

Much time passed, and with it passed Ell Yah and his wife into memory.

Eventually, out of the darkest passages came the TIG-Queen, with her ebony sword, and her TIG-Workers, and enslaved the Animond with no clash of arms, nor any other resistance. The Animond's Oath of Peace would not allow it.

Many cycles passed as the TIG ruled over the Animond. Torture, pain, and suffering came to be a way of life for them. At the midpoint of each of those many cycles—the second moon of the sixth month—during the seven nights of the Blood Moon, an Animond was sacrificed to please the TIG-Queen, the victim's remains then devoured by TIG-Workers.

Then the War of the Woods came upon the Nep Forest, and the TIG-Worker's labors shifted to preparations for war. Thousands of cloning cells—like those of the Beesives—were created, in each of which the TIG-Queen laid pieces of Tig-Workers she had sacrificed. From these cells, the TIG-Horde emerged, mindless clones with a single purpose, warped and demented. With her newly born army, the TIG-Queen marched off through the tunnels that led to the Nep Forest. Leaving only a few of the TIG-Workers to oversee what was left of the Animond population.

With the window of opportunity open, Warroad Yah—descendant of Ell and Melo—removed the ruby sword from its hiding place. Remembering the teachings passed down from generations of fathers, Warroad attacked the TIG-Workers left behind. The magic of the ruby sword defeated the dark powers of the TIG-Workers and freed the Animond, just as the vision Ell Yah had received so long ago had foretold when directing him to forge it.

The Animond's freedom from slavery unbalanced the powers of the TIG, and their assault on the surface never came to be. Instead, the TIG-Queen returned to her dark queendom to find it completely abandoned.

Yahmond Yah searched the depths of the ruby sword with his eyes, then carefully returned it to its sheath, which hung across his back. As he climbed to his feet, the weight of the sword and backpack dug the straps of the harness into his shoulders. He stretched his arms above his head in hopes of shaking off the fatigue that knotted his iron-corded muscles. As he moved forward into the massive cavern that had once been called "Family," he could feel the ground's heat through the leather that protected his feet. Lights danced about from the bubbling lava pools that had consumed the once glorious buildings of the ancient city, though the road that had snaked through its heart remained intact. The smooth stone of the road lay dark and fathomless as it meandered between the dark pillars that reached into the midnight darkness above. The eerie silence was absolute as Yahmond Yah traveled along the road in half steps. The air weighed heavy with the scent of sulfur, and the heat seemed almost unbearable at times. Sweat trickled down his arms, matting his fur. He finally stopped at a crossroad and drank sparingly from his canteen.

With his hands resting lightly on his hips, Yahmond Yah slowly rotated to view each direction. The road to the right was as wide as the one he'd already traveled. The way left was more like a small path, leading between two lava pools and disappearing into an opening in the cavern wall.

A pulsing sound built slowly in the ears of the Animond and quickly became more pronounced. It was the sound of a drum ... or many drums beating at once. The stone about Yahmond Yah echoed the sound so it was impossible to tell from which direction it came. Some inner instinct drew him left along the smaller path.

The heat at this proximity encouraged Yahmond Yah to hurry to the opening where the path disappeared into the stone wall of the cavern. As he ventured into the shadows, he was mildly surprised to find that the passage indeed seemed to be where the drumming sound was coming from. Several steps into the gloom, the incline of the path increased steeply, leading him upward toward hellish lights that shone in the passage a hundred feet or more overhead.

The tunnel's surface was smooth as polished glass under the feet of the Animond, as he climbed up toward the summit. Each step would have been impossible if not for the handholds that had been carved into the walls by unknown workers. Yahmond Yah was sure the passage had been built by the hands of the ancient Animond race, but its purpose escaped him.

The tunnel opened to a small shelf, like a balcony, in an enormous chamber. Yahmond Yah crawled to the edge of the shelf for a better view of the surroundings. The ceiling tapered sharply upward, like a funnel with its spout to the sky, rather than the domed ceilings more typical to these caverns. Large demonic faces were carved into the stone walls in random intervals about the chamber, burning gases spewing from their stone mouths, illuminating the bizarre events that were transpiring below his hiding place.

Below and to the right of Yahmond Yah, the bulk of the TIG-Horde danced like bees in a hive. Yet their screams and howls left the impression of a pack of wolves fighting over the rights to a dead carcass.

Three huge drums sat evenly spaced before a stone alter. TIG-Workers circled around it with each beat of the drums, which they struck with what appeared to be leg bones from some fallen creature. Their thin-lipped mouths chanted words that were foreign, yet almost familiar to Yahmond Yah. Chills racked his spine as he realized that it was the stretched red skins of TIG-Workers, attached to the drums' wooden frames, which were echoing with sound.

The stone altar was simple in design from what Yahmond Yah could see of it. A squared stone, with runes etched in the sides—barely visible under the blackened gore that had dripped over them from past sacrifices—sat upon a raised dais.

Yahmond Yah froze his body, heart pounding in his chest, when Yana walked into view from the left of the chamber. Behind her walked the TIG-Queen, with an ebony sword held close to her chest, its point upward. From the tip of the sword rained down a dark aura of evil magic that fell upon Yana. It seemed to control her every move as a puppeteer would work a puppet. In mechanical steps, the TIG-Queen directed Yana to the altar, and she lay upon it without pause or question.

Yahmond Yah's mind raced through different scenarios in which he might rescue his bride, but all of them ended with both of their deaths. Helplessness washed over him. He had no choice but to watch and wait for something—anything—to change, allowing him to act.

Suddenly, the voices in the chamber fell silent, and the countless black, demented eyes turned to the stone altar. Only the drums could be heard now, as the TIG-Workers continued their relentless dance around them. Then the pitch of the drums lowered to a deep bass, and then, as if on some unknown cue, all the TIG-Horde dropped to the stone floor. Their twisted fingers raked the air over their chests. Their bodies shook in spasms. Their legs flinched and kicked without control.

Fear began the long climb up Yahmond Yah's spine as he tried to will his body into motion but failed. He could only watch in horror as a small part of each of the TIG-Horde's souls rose from their chests in slivers of shadow, gathering to create gray spheres—one over each drum. Yahmond Yah stumbled onto the realization that this was not a typical part of their sacrifice ritual, but in terms of what it was instead … his own reasoning escaped him.

Throughout the building of this nightmare, Yana lay upon the stone block, her petite frame relaxed with her entwined fingers resting on the fur of her stomach. Yahmond Yah noted that her head and body hair were neatly brushed and her bare face and hands free of dirt. Yana's gentle brown eyes were open wide, staring intently at the space above her.

The beat of the drums began again, quickening to a rumble, though no one seemed to be making them sound. The TIG-Horde resumed their demonic howling and dancing. Tears stung the eyes of Yahmond Yah as he tried once again to break free of the invisible giant hand that had pinned him to the shelf. His lungs burned from the exertion of trying to breathe under the suffocating weight of the air around him.

The TIG-Queen remained standing behind the altar, her ebony sword now held over Yana's prone body, the sharp edge poised to strike. Still unable to move, Yahmond Yah watched in utter terror as the TIG-Queen raised the blade above her head. Holding the blade high, the TIG-Queen gave Yana a hideous smile, and black gore dripped from between pointed teeth as she gazed down on her intended victim. The ebony sword began to pulse, summoning the three gray spheres to it. The blade drank in the souls as a sponge would absorb water. The muscles of the TIG-Queen bunched under her ancient, wrinkled skin as she chopped down toward the throat of Yana.

Only as the ebony sword fell toward her did Yana's body respond, her eyes falling closed.

As if it had a mind of its own, the ebony sword stopped just as it touched Yana's skin. Yahmond Yah could see only a thin trickle of blood on her throat. Despite how hard the TIG-Queen tried to complete the stroke, the sword refused to budge.

Suddenly, dark magic burst from the hilt, throwing the TIG-Queen to the stone of the dais. The ebony sword, now acting on its own, hovered hilt-down over Yana's throat. Dark liquid dripped from the handle and was absorbed into the scratch on Yana's throat. When the process was complete, there was no sign of blood at all . . . or any wound on her.

With her eyes still closed, Yana reached up and gripped the sword hilt. Black magic radiated from the sword tip, which gripped the limp body of the TIG-Queen and raised her high over the altar. There, the TIG-Queen floated . . . suspended in mid-air. The howls of the TIG-Horde turned to a high-pitched scream, their arms reaching toward the TIG-Queen.

Like a rag doll, the black magic tossed the TIG-Queen out into the masses of TIG-Horde, who ripped her body to pieces.

Yahmond Yah lay upon the shelf wide-eyed with his mouth wide open in horror as he watched the TIG-Horde consume the flesh of the fallen queen. Turning back to Yana, he found her now-black eyes locked onto him. She sat up then and started screaming orders at the TIG-Workers, who reacted to her as though she were the TIG-Queen

The truth of what Yana had become managed to free Yahmond Yah from his invisible bindings. Stone missiles began crashing against the walls around him as he stood looking down at Yana, who continued to meet his gaze with her newly acquired black eyes. He couldn't look away. For a single moment, Yana's eyes seemed to clear, appearing normal and begging for help, but then the darkness returned to claim its prize. Yahmond Yah felt the spider webs of magic trying to bind him and launched himself back down the steep tunnel behind him.

He dragged his hands along the smooth stone floor in hopes of slowing his descent, but it had little effect as he plummeted toward the bottom. At the base of the tunnel, he hit the cupped dip at full speed. Airborne, arms flailing, he flew outwards toward the lava pools, and then over them, his momentum enough to carry him well over the magma and to the intersection beyond.

Landing somehow on his feet, Yahmond Yah quickly looked desperately left and right. From both directions, the TIG-Horde came howling after him. This time, at the crossroad, the choice was made for him, and he hurtled himself forward away from the chaos.

The Animond's long legs quickly outdistanced the TIG. The road he was on twisted back and forth, up, and down as he sped on. Large rocks and boulders blocked his view fore and aft as he went, the sound of the TIG always broadcasting their location, not far behind him. Turning a sharp corner, Yahmond Yah had to come to a sudden stop.

* * *

Luna wandered along what appeared to be a main passageway. She had no idea of where she might be in this subterranean world, but she had to believe in the magic that had invaded her body shortly after her encounter with her mother, the Den Mother of the Green Nation—the magic that had fused to every nerve of her body and soul. Luna was sure it was the magic passed from one Den Mother to another, but something seemed different. The magic felt filtered, cleaner somehow . . . unchained of the evil enhancement that she would normally feel around her mother.

Luna could not guess why the magic acted or felt this way, or why she—being so young—had been chosen to be the next leader of the Green Nation.

The magic guided Luna deep into the heart of Katlyn instead of to another den of her people. The passage ahead was much broader than in the upper reaches. There was also less water to drink and even fewer rodents to feed on. The lack of moisture worked against the growth of the golden glowing moss, which now only grew in cracks and crevices. The lack of light made little difference to Luna though, being a creature of the night.

Luna's thoughts kept straying back to the confrontation with her mother. She felt blind to any reasons why her mother would try to kill her. It was not until she looked at the situation through the eyes of her magic that she was shown the truth. Her mother had been possessed by the creature she had seen exiting the den through the vent hole. Its dark, evil magic was at work there, and it would not just control her mother but rule the entire nation of warriors-hunters. Sadness clung to her heart, but her magic fed strength into her resolve to act on behalf of her people.

The tunnel was level, yet the passage began to snake-turn through the stone before her. The smell of sulfur hung heavy in the air as she traveled through the climbing heat radiating from beneath her paws. Her head and tail hung low as she pushed on into the darkness.

Day and night meant nothing to Luna here in the underworld. She could only measure time by the number of rest stops, and as her strength trickled away with lack of provisions, Luna knew that this measurement would hold no accuracy with her rest stops becoming more frequent.

Strange rays of light ricocheted off the stone of the curve before her, more luminescent even than the brilliant rays of the sun—or so she imagined, having never seem them. Completing the turn, Luna saw that the light was coming from a chamber not far ahead.

The passage she was in opened into an enormous chamber. A polished stone road wormed between lava pools and giant columns. Gas vapors were igniting in various areas, casting shadows that danced about the space as shades in a graveyard.

Luna stood in the entranceway, speculating on her route choices, back away from the chamber, where she felt the heat would kill her, or follow the road into the furnace. While her mind cautioned retreat, her magic urged her to go. Luna had taken several steps back into the passage before the insistence of her magic turned her back into the chamber.

The heat grew rapidly as she ventured along the road. Luna felt her energy leaving her more quickly with every step she took. Stopping to rest was out of the question, for she knew the heat would cook her before she would awake. Still, exhaustion was claiming her, her legs twitching and shaking with each step. Her ears heard only a steady hum; her dry nose smelled only sulfur; her eyes saw only a hazy blur. Luna's mind told her that her legs were done. The small pup knew she was falling. Death was upon her.

Chapter 11

DEFIANCE

The false trail had worked far better than Klawed had anticipated. It was well after midnight when the Greenwolves finally sorted out the trio's hiding place, under the washed-out creek bank. The wash was neither deep nor wide, but Tailey was able to find a niche that could offer some protection should the Panther be overcome.

The small overhang of sod and dirt where Klawed crouched offered little protection from above. The Neptunian remained strapped in his saddle, his bushnuts secured before him—as Klawed had said, he would not leave them. In the tight quarters, Klawed had limited use of the tail-rapier, which remained in its sheath.

Tailey watched over Klawed's back. The red light of the moon showed the shadows of at least two score of the Greenwolves standing along the creek bank. The bulk of the pack centered around a slightly smaller member, whom Klawed had explained earlier was the Pack Mother. In the darkness, it was impossible to identify colors, but it was apparent that the leader's fur was darker than the rest.

The leader nodded her head towards one of the large males next to her.

"Now the test," Klawed's mind-voice said to no one in particular.

The male Greenwolf jumped into the creek before the waiting cat. The receding water ran about its ankles as it hunkered down in a battle-ready pose: ears drawn back, tail, and hind legs coiled for launch. A low growl escaped through its teeth as the Greenwolf displayed its formidable fangs.

Tailey looked on in wonder, amazed again at how large the Greenwolves were in comparison to the wolves he and Megan had watched on the television. Tailey was also able to see, even in the near darkness, that the animal before them was healthy and strong.

The Greenwolf was mistaken if it read Klawed's lack of concern as fear. Hurtling itself at the throat of the Panther, the Greenwolf would never make this mistake again. The reflexes of the Panther were like lightning; his razor-sharp claws and mighty strength slapped the Greenwolf's head clear from its shoulders, and its headless carcass fell twitching into the stream.

The pack was enraged by the sight of their fallen brother, and in no certain order, the Greenwolves charged toward the Panther. At this moment, Nep untied the bindings that held himself and the bushnuts to the harness and bolted back into the crevice beside Tailey. The Neptunian's action came as a surprise to even Klawed, who turned momentarily with eyes full of questions, but only for a moment, because the Greenwolves were almost upon him.

The Neptunian's reasons for retreating from the Panther's back soon became all too clear, as the first rush of the enemy met the Panther in combat. The steep creek bank would only allow four or five of the Greenwolves to advance on the trio's natural bunker. Tailey felt the hair on his back and tail rise as Klawed threw himself on his back across the opening, his tail snatching its rapier from its sheath as he did so. The first five Greenwolves died from the Panther's four raking claws and slicing blade. If Nep had not freed the Panther of himself and the bushnuts, Klawed could not have made that maneuver, which would have meant his life ... and theirs too.

Tailey looked over at Nep and realized just how important the bushnuts were to the small creature, for the Neptunian stood before them even now, braced to die for them. More importantly, Tailey now knew how strong the friendship was between Klawed and Nep. Klawed would not have crushed the Neptunian beneath him even to save his own life. In the shadow of the hero that fought before him, Tailey stepped forward and stood in front of Nep. He would not die a coward hiding in the corner.

Suddenly, Tailey felt the ground fall out from under him, and the familiar darkness that rode aboard unconsciousness traveled through his mind once again.

* * *

Weenep sat upon the oak limb at the top of the tree, looking out over the Fubal Plains. A dwarf from birth, the Neptunian stood not much higher than a newborn Panther kitten, even as an adult. She wore a green sleeveless tunic with a narrow brown belt made of cloth about her waist. Her mind wondered as she gazed through the red moon's light and out over the Fubal Plains that lay on the northern border of the Nep Forest. She knew that, out there amongst the Green Nation, her destiny awaited her … whatever that might be.

The elders had been baffled when Weenep had chosen not to become an honored life companion to one of the newborn Panthers or seek a mate and be named either. Surprisingly, they also respected the fact that it was her choice to make. She was nicknamed "Wee Nep," because of her small size— she certainly was "wee"—and before too long, the community just referred to her as Weenep.

Weenep continued her studies of the magic of the forest and the lure of the bushnut. She enjoyed her own company, so she stayed alone as she traveled about the area.

There was something more that occupied the mind of Weenep though, and she felt that it was the difference between herself and the rest of the Neptunian race: It was her magic. All the Neptunians possessed the magic of calling light to serve their means, but along with that skill, her magic had an additional quality to it, which she practiced in secret. Weenep could call the light to her, and with a lot of concentration, she could become a part of that light. In her practices, she found that she could dissolve into the light and reappear in a different location to which she had affixed her mind.

Weenep was unsure of why she hid her talent in a cloak of secrecy, but some inner voice told her that it was not yet the time to reveal all her magic.

A long mournful howl echoed from the plains before her, as a northern wind sent a chill up her spine.

My destiny approaches, Weenep thought to herself.

* * *

"You are a long way from home, small puppy," Yahmond Yah said as he stroked Luna's fur with his large hand.

Yahmond Yah had just turned a corner, deep in the place once known as "Family," when he had practically stepped on the Greenwolf pup, lying helpless on the hot stone road. With the TIG hot on his heels, Yahmond Yah wasted no time debating the pros and cons of helping the creature, even though it came from as shaded a background as the Green Nation. He tucked the small hairball under his arm and bolted away.

The TIG followed Yahmond Yah relentlessly through the tunnels with their keen sense of smell. Only after reaching the upper passages, where more water could be found and used to hide his scent, did the Animond stop to rest and help the pup.

The Animond sat next to a small stream that trickled down the edge of the tunnel, a boulder blocking him from view of the lower passage. The golden moss glowed brightly around him as he examined the pup for injuries. When no wounds were apparent, he worked some liquid down her parched throat. Then he gently washed her matted fur with the soft sand that had been washed down the stream from above. Once he had done all he knew to do to help her, he leaned back against the cool stone of the wall and let himself sleep, which he desperately needed, the small puppy cradled in his lap.

A numbing sleep took Yahmond Yah immediately upon closing his eyes. At first, dreams scratched at the surface of his unconsciousness but only left hints of what they might have been. Nightmares fared better at disturbing the Animond's slumber, as they always seemed to do. When his eyes popped open, all that he could see was the image of Yana's face, her black eyes piercing his heart, as he fell from the shelf toward the waiting TIG-Horde. He had to shake his head several times to clear his mind of the horror that ripped at his soul, but that horror was replaced by sadness. His hands covered his face, his chest heaved, and his shoulder shook as tears ran through his fingers and down his arms.

After a time, a door in Yahmond Yah's mind quietly opened, and from it, a soft hum gently sought out his pain and slowly eased it away. The humming then started to flow through his body, soothing his knotted muscles, relieving his aches. The humming went to his heart then and sent warmth into his soul, healing the wound that the black arrow of his nightmare had inflicted upon him.

Gradually, his tears subsided, and his body relaxed. When he brought his hands away from his eyes, Yahmond Yah saw the little puppy sitting across from him. Her gentle green eyes were filled with sympathy.

"Thank you," Yahmond Yah said. "Thank you for bringing me back."

"And I should thank you," a delicate mind-voice said, "for bringing me back from the edge of death."

"Strange," Yahmond Yah said, his voice rolling out on a dry tongue, "that you understand the words of an Animond."

Shifting his body so that he was on his hands and knees, he worked his way over to the water. Bending for a drink, he said, "Stranger yet is that you are able to speak my language fluently."

Luna pondered these facts as the Animond drank from the clear stream. The strangest part, which Luna kept to herself, was the fact that she had never heard of an Animond. It had been only a few weeks since she had been weened of her mother's milk; her travels out into the world were numbered to only short trips to eat where another Greenwolf's killed. Luna could only guess that her newly inherited magic had many levels in which it would help her to survive.

Yahmond Yah watched Luna take her turn drinking as he refilled his canteen. He could not imagine how one so small could have survived so long on her own, or how it came to be that she was alone in the hellish underground in the first place.

"Young puppy, I—"

"Luna," she said, interrupting. "I am called Luna among my people."

"Luna, "the Animond said, beginning again, "I am Yahmond Yah of the Animond, of the City of Genus." Feeling foolish for forgetting his manners, he'd offered a formal greeting.

"I am on quest to . . .," he found himself stumbling through the different avenues of how to complete the sentence. He knew in his mind that the quest to rescue Yana from the clutches of the TIG was done, but his heart and soul refused to accept defeat on its present terms. He sighed. "To free my bride." Whether that now meant freeing her from the TIG or from herself remained the question in his mind.

Luna did not offer any explanation for her present situation, and Yahmond Yah chose not to pursue the matter. Instead, he offered Luna some slices of dried fruit from his pack and resumed pondering his next course of action.

In the far distances, a howling scream drifted up the shaft to Luna and Yahmond Yah. She looked up at him with questioning eyes.

"The TIG have found our trail," Yahmond Yah offered, in a low voice.

"What is a TIG?" Luna asked, unaware that she had taken a few steps closer to the Animond.

Yahmond Yah climbed to his feet and started up the passage, reaching the next intersection and moving around the turn in just a few long strides. Luna followed on shaky legs, still weak from the lack of rest and food.

"The TIG hunt me," Yahmond Yah said, as Luna made the turn behind him. He had paused to wait for her. "You should hide while the TIG chase me and then make it to the surface. It isn't too far above us I think."

"No, I would like to stay with you," Luna said without hesitation. "If you'll let me."

"Come!" Yahmond Yah said, as he picked up Luna. "We will make better time this way."

The Animond and his small burden continued down the passage. Around them, the barking and howling screams of the TIG grew closer.

"TIG is what they call those who have been 'Transformed-Into-Ghouls'," Yahmond Yah whispered, as they traveled. "Many cycles ago, a group of Animond were changed by the evil of the ebony sword into the creatures of today. They no longer even resemble the noble beings they once were, with a single exception: their hands."

He flexed his free hand before Luna's face, so that she could easily see the three long digits, bordered by two thick thumbs.

The passage began to turn gradually to the left. Yahmond Yah traveled near to the wall, hoping it would provide some cover, but his efforts were for naught. At the end of the bend, three TIG-Workers blocked their way, their staffs planted before them, calling on the powers of darkness.

"A trap," Yahmond Yah grumbled, as he turned around and ran back the other way. In a few strides, the sounds of the TIG-Horde, coming to box them in, reached his ears.

Yahmond Yah recalled only one small passage in the whole bend, and he pumped his legs with all his might, knowing it was their only chance.

The TIG-Horde was almost on them when they reached the passage.

"Go! Hide!" Yahmond Yah said, as he set Luna down and removed the ruby sword from its sheath on his back. "I'll buy you all the time I can."

Then the TIG-Horde was on him. Yahmond Yah stood before the smaller passage and swept the ruby sword back-and-forth. Body parts flew in all directions, and corpses began stacking up around his feet. The blackened gore made the stone under his boots slippery. Yahmond Yah nearly fell as the vast numbers of the TIG-Horde pushed him back into the smaller passage, where only three or four could attack at a time.

The passage was inclined but not so sharply that he would have to turn his back to climb. The TIG were fearless warriors, and Yahmond Yah dared not to turn his head to see what could be coming at him from behind. He prayed to the maker that the TIG had not blocked this way too.

Luna's mind-voice blasted into his mind: "Move!!"

* * *

Luna forced herself to climb the passage; her legs wobbled, and the pads of her paws were tender still from the heat damage. Her heart sank as she came upon the wall of rocks that blocked the way. She turned back around to check on Yahmond Yah, who had just started backing toward her.

Yahmond Yah was not a warrior. The red sword seemed awkward in his hand; his brute strength helped to offset his lack of skill, but the stone clubs and axes of the TIG were coming closer to their target with every stroke. The narrow passage was no place for using a long sword.

Luna waited until Yahmond Yah had backed closer to her, where the passage widened slightly, and then began calling up her magic. It came quickly to her call as if eager for battle. It pumped from her heart and spread through her body, riding aboard the cells of blood, her muscles absorbing more or its power with every passing moment.

Her weakened state no longer apparent, Luna felt her magic peak and directed it to the wall of rocks and stones, warning Yahmond Yah with her mind-voice as her magic slammed him against the wall and built an invisible shield around him. She let some of her magic ride upon the first large stone she launched down the shaft, which crashed into the chest of the leading TIG and sent its corpse bowling into those who followed behind. There was no ducking the stone hailstorm that followed. Wave after wave of stones fell upon the TIG until the passage below Yahmond Yah was completely sealed.

Silence filled the small chamber as Luna released the magic that had shielded Yahmond Yah. His body shook from unused adrenalin as he replaced the ruby sword in its sheath. His mouth opened and closed several times as he walked toward Luna, the words refusing to form at first.

"Again, thank you, Luna, "he finally managed to say, as he knelt before her.

Moments later, the arch of rock above them—formed by the removal of the rock beneath—collapsed, and bits of debris rolled to the floor around them. On the back of the miniature avalanche, a small gray cat landed at their feet, unconscious to the world.

Chapter 12

MORNING'S LIGHT

The Den Mother and her vanguard reached the summit of Fire Bane Mountain, which lay on the east end of the Low Jaw Mountain Range, just a few short hours before sunrise.

"Good!" she mused. *"We have time; yes we do. It's an old spell. Yes, it is. And we can make it work with the young."*

The eyes of the Den Mother searched the depths of the crater below them and started calling the black magic to her. Her body shook as the dark power filled her body to capacity. She released the energy at the center of the dormant volcano. Red bubbling magma answered the beckoning call of the black magic swirling about the base of the crater, and thus, the Fire Bane flowed once more. Flames danced upon its surface, casting demonic shadows on the steep walls of the mountain container.

The Den Mother watched, pleased with her accomplishments so far, but she could not waste time gloating. No, there was still much more to do to complete the spell. She signaled her vanguard forward then, as she bit her forepaw and let blood slowly drip from the wound.

Each member of the vanguard either carried or ushered in a small cub or fawn of every sort of creature that resided in the region. On the foreheads of the babes, she placed her bloody paw, thus condemning them to death.

The Den Mother's mind-voice—controlled by Ichneumon, the Possessor of Souls—reached out to her Pack: "A hundred souls, a hundred cycles of darkness…" One at a time, the babes were tossed into the fire that awaited them. "Now to seal the spell," she told herself, as she felt the contractions in her abdomen.

The Den Mother howled her pain as her body gave birth to a single female pup, which she marked with her bloody paw as she severed the umbilical cord with her teeth. She then kicked the infant into the mouth of the volcano like yesterday's dung.

The spirit that was once Den Mother watched from behind her own eyes as her pup fell from her toward the fiery inferno. She fought desperately to regain control of her body, but the dark creature filled her head with demonic laughter as it lightly brushed aside her efforts.

"Watch, Queenie!" Ichneumon's mind-voice teased. *"We are going to teach all of Katlyn the true meaning of terror, the way you and your kind never could before the first War of the Woods—the last time your kind reigned."*

From where the puppy was consumed into the magma, billowing columns of smoke began to climb toward the clear night sky. As the black cloud grew over the volcano, twinkling stars disappeared one after another. It continued its march toward the horizons, and though pale-blue sunlight breached the top of the Mangy Mountains for a moment, it was quickly snuffed out, and the day was reduced to gray shadows.

"You," Den Mother said, as she turned back to her vanguard. "Send out runners to Black Nation, the Winter Bears, and to all the Pack Mothers of our Green Nation. Tell them to gather at the Whirl's Eye. We no longer need to fear the light of day!"

Hatred for all that was good burned in the heart of the Den Mother as she led the remainder of the pack toward the Fubal Plains, one single word skipping through her mind as she bolted down the volcano's steep slopes: *Revenge!*

* * *

Klawed carefully watched the large male Greenwolf from the corner of his eye as it slowly stalked toward him. He searched all the avenues of his past leading up to this moment. The Kittoehee had sent him to find the Northern Beesives Hive—or at least some evidence that they still existed. Why he had been sent to the ancient passages of the Animond for this purpose remained unclear to him. He did not recall any Beesives dwelling underground.

He did not have to ponder why the Kittoehee had chosen him specifically for the quest. From his birth, Klawed had been different from the other Panthers. He was a single cub, where most litters were commonly of two or three. Most of the Panthers believed that this was the main reason he was bigger than most, weighing nearly fifty pounds more than the average Katlyn Panther.

He also stood out from the others due to his vigorous disposition and adventurous nature, which had led himself and Nep to the very borders of the world known to Panther kind, and sometimes beyond.

Klawed had dealt with the Green Nation in the past, but before now, he had only skirted the edge of their domain where their numbers were small. The pack before him had to be at least three score. At sixty-to-one, the odds drained his courage, but Klawed knew he would not turn his back on Nep, or Tailey, their newly found friend.

Thinking of the small gray cat brought more questions to mind. Why had the Cat's Eye Stone brought him here? What role did he have to play in these events that were unfolding? The little cat seemed far too focused on returning to the world of the yellow sun to be of any use to this world. And the hue-man, Megan, what was her place in this scenario? The questions seemed endless and the answers few. For now, he knew he had to clear his mind of questions and focus on survival.

The lone male Greenwolf would soon be within striking distance and showed no fear and little caution as it approached the Panther. This was a big mistake, which the Greenwolf would pay for with his life. As the lifeless body fell to the cold water of the stream, Klawed glanced toward the Mangy Mountains where Regulus, the pale-blue sun, would soon rise, but daybreak seemed a long time coming.

Klawed felt a stirring on his back and turned to see that Nep had dismounted with his bushnuts and was scurrying back into the wash. There was no time for pointless questions as he realized that the Nep had freed him of any obligations. Klawed knew he still had time to run away, but he would not—could not—desert them. Instead, he threw himself onto his back, sideways across the opening.

His thick black tail sought out the hilt of the tail-rapier and slammed itself into the opening, the muscles at the tip knotting as it filled the space, locking the rapier in place as Klawed snatched it out of its sheath and slashed the blade toward the leading attacker.

The first wave of the Greenwolf attackers tried desperately to stop before running into the wall of teeth, claws, and steel as the weight of those that followed pushed them into certain death. The stream ran red with blood before the Greenwolves fell back to regroup.

The next time, the pack advanced slowly and from every possible direction. Klawed knew he would not fare as well this time and soon they were on him.

The Greenwolves darted in and out, drawing his attention one way and striking from the other. Their fangs ripped his flesh, and sometimes, they were able to retreat before the Panther struck back, but others were caught by the throat in Klawed's powerful jaws as his hind claws shredded their soft underbellies, disemboweling them. Heedless of their losses, the Greenwolves would not turn away this deep in the battle frenzy; the flowing blood only helped feed their inner fire. Klawed knew their time was diminishing quickly.

Suddenly, Klawed heard a commotion behind him in the wash. He dared not turn to look with the Greenwolves hovering about, waiting for just such an opportunity. The thought suddenly hit him that the Greenwolves may have found a way to enter the wash from behind, but still, he could not look.

A lump of terror froze in his throat when Klawed sensed a Greenwolf coming out of the wash behind him. His body refused to respond, his heartbeat racing as he tried to force himself into action. But he could only stand frozen … waiting for the jaws of death to take his life.

* * *

Luna recognized the scents on the breeze, drawn into their passage by the pull of an avalanche of earth and stone … and a small gray cat. The breeze smelled of magic, both good and evil, mixed with the blood of death. A quiet fear of the unknown invaded the core of her being, but the presence of her people above them dominated the essence of the moment.

The flames of magic renewed the strength of her weakened body as it flowed through it. Luna sent feelers of the magical power up through the opening as she followed it quickly over the stone rubble toward the surface. Her power bypassed the Neptunian, who stood guard in front of the bush-nuts, and reached out through the opening of the wash to another being, apparently in a brief respite from a frenzied battle with her people.

The magic, which Luna sensed acted on its own behalf as much as it did to her command, froze the Panther in his tracks. Luna bolted up the wash, under the Panther, and stopped between its front legs, seeing many of her brothers lying dead.

"Stop!" Luna's mind-voice commanded the remainder of the assaulting pack.

"Who are you to give orders to the Pack of the Waterway?" asked the mind-voice of the Pack Mother, as she boldly strutted up to stand before the Panther and the small pup.

Luna knew this was a formal challenge of authority, but she could feel the coming of the sun as it climbed the back of the Mangy Mountains. There would be little time to answer the challenge—a fight-to-the-death battle for control over the pack—which she knew she would not stand a chance of winning.

Instead, Luna launched her magic into the Pack Mother, which held her immobile as it did battle with the dark magic lingering with her and her followers. The dark and white magic met in the depths of the Pack Mother's soul, the clash sending shudders through the body of the Pack Mother as the magical powers sought control over the other.

Luna felt her powers slipping. She was so small and so new with the ways of magic. She knew she would not be able to hold the Pack Mother for much longer.

Without warning, the Pack Mother broke free of the magical restraints, her fangs aimed at Luna's throat, when suddenly, a new power came into play. It was not black or white … not good or evil. No. It was an ancient force, which seemed to come from the air, the land, the water … from the inner core of Katlyn itself. The power was as red as the blood that ran through the veins of Luna's body. She felt the red magic and her white magic collect in her soul, and together, join forces to converge on the dark magic of the Pack

Mother and drive it from her soul. Tendrils of these combined forces reached out to all the pack members and rid them of the dark power that had shaped their very nature for countless cycles.

The powers faded then, leaving Luna and the Pack Mother lying in the grass, panting, their energies depleted. The pack stood about them, confusion riddling their minds.

Luna lifted her head in time to see the first rays of light from the pale-blue sun, Regulus, fall upon them. It was the first sunrise that she had ever seen. It was truly the most beautiful thing she had ever beheld, with colors beyond the shades of black and gray: purple clouds traced in red, violet, and gold set against a clear blue sky. She waited for the madness to come and destroy them all.

"Goodbye, Yahmond Yah, my friend!" Luna said, sadness filling her mind-voice.

* * *

Weenep felt her fur ruffle in the cool breeze that blew in from the north. She had spent the night in the red oak tree that overlooked the Fubal Plains, resting comfortably on a thick limb. Her densely piled fur, a mixture of reddish brown and yellow covered by her green tunic, served to keep her warm throughout the Katlyn's Spring/Fall Band night.

Her black eyes fluttered open to greet the first rays of the dawn's light. Her mind was filled with visions of the dreams that had just visited her. The winged cat had spoken gently to her of things that had passed and things that could happen in the future. Of the many things the cat spoke of, one stood out most clearly in her mind as she stretched her small limbs to rid them of the stiffness of sleep on the hard bark:

"Awake and find your destiny, *Deliverer*," the winged cat had said.

The winged cat had referred to her as the deliverer many times. *Deliverer from what? Or to what?* The questions remained a riddle in her mind as she climbed down the tree, her long curved nails making light work of the chore.

On the ground, Weenep put all questions aside and turned toward the rising sun … and a new life.

Chapter 13

ESCORTS

The smell of fresh grass invaded Tailey's dreamscape. He was resting in the hot summer sun, watching his Megan play in the small flower garden.

Her mind-voice delicately reached to him. "Look, Tailey! Look at the pretty butterfly!" The butterfly was indeed pretty with its orange and black wings, but its beauty paled when compared to the little girl, in her sky-blue and yellow polka-dot summer dress, whose finger the butterfly rode upon.

Megan plopped down in the grass beside Tailey and softly petted his fur as she examined the butterfly, which had no fear of her. Finally, the insect grew tired of the little girl's gaze and fluttered off into the breeze.

"Tailey," Megan asked, as she watched the bug fly away. "Are you going to leave me too?"

"No . . . I'll never leave you," Tailey answered with some hesitation.

Tailey felt the sting of shame. He'd never intended on being spirited off to another world. He'd never intended to say things that were not true. He had to find another Cat's Eye Stone—or maybe some other device—that could return him to his Megan. Even in a faraway world, he could feel the evil presence of the Nightman.

Wait a minute! How can this be? How can I feel the presence of a being worlds away?

This could be the key. Maybe this time he would wake up back in that tree stump, and all this Katlyn business would prove to have been a product of his subconscious: a dream, or perhaps many complex dreams folded into each other.

The possibilities seemed endless, and his mind swam back to the numbing void between dreamland and reality. In this abyss of darkness, a voice reached for him and slowly dragged him back toward the conscious world. Tailey fought the voice, wishing only to return to his visions of Megan. As clarity washed over his mind, Tailey realized that he had been painfully near death.

Once more, Tailey woke to find himself in strange company. Beside him sat a small puppy-like animal, with red and green fur. Curled in a circle around them was Klawed, with Nep and his bushnuts once again secured on his back. Next to them sat a large hairy creature with powerful arms and booted feet, wearing a brown loincloth, and a full-grown female Greenwolf with what was left of her pack. The sun shone hotly overhead.

Pain shot up the back of his neck as Tailey turned to view the motley crew around him, and he had to rest his head in the grass to ease the sharp stabbing pain that invaded his head.

"He won't survive many more blows to the head, Klawed," Luna's mind-voice informed the Panther. "I was lucky to pull him back this time."

"Thank you, Luna." Klawed paused briefly in thought. "Tailey is not of our world. He is here because of luck, misfortune, or some other unknown agent. Nep and I have made it our business to aid him and will see him to the Kittoehee, and hopefully, an answer to his dilemma."

The Pack Mother stepped forward. "Luna, it's time to settle our own dispute."

Luna quickly spoke. "I will not fight you for leadership." She stood and went over to her senior.

"We have matters to discuss, Luna," the Pack Mother said. "Walk with me."

The Pack Mother turned then to the others. "Animal, take Slim and two others and get food." She then addressed the biggest of her pack. "Spruce, take your sorry carcass and the rest of the pack and setup a parameter around our newly discovered . . . friends."

Tailey caught the look of contempt that the Pack Mother shot at Klawed with that final word.

Klawed, on the other hand, paid little to no attention to the Pack Mother. He had successfully defended their position to the dawn and killed at least a third of their numbers. There would be no love lost between them.

Tailey observed that the Greenwolves closely resembled the timber wolves he and Megan had seen on a program on the television back on Earth. The exceptions being that were dark green, or green blended with red—*Depending on their gender, perhaps?*—rather than gray and brown, and were almost twice the size. Tailey could see the wiry muscles flexing beneath their fur.

"I thought the Greenwolves feared the sunlight," Tailey said.

"Not only fear it but are driven to a maddening death by it!" Klawed replied. "But not these … or not now. From what I have seen, they are as puzzled about the matter as the rest of us."

The large hairy creature spoke to Klawed. Tailey could not understand the words he formed with his lips and shot a curious look to the Panther.

"This is Yahmond Yah, an Animond from the City of Genus," Klawed said. "He is also unsure of why the Greenwolves can now tolerate the sunlight, but he suggests that it might have something to do with the magic the puppy possesses, mixed with the magic that flowed from his ruby sword."

Tailey surveyed the wolf pack as they went about their assigned chores and noted that, while the wolves were indeed dark green, they differed widely in size and shape from bulky Spruce to the lightning-fast Slim.

The pain had subsided in Tailey's head to the point where he could likely move about the camp without adding more discomfort to himself, but he chose to remain lying on the grass next to Klawed. The size and strength of the Panther offered Tailey a measure of security as they rested, waiting for the Greenwolves to return. Tailey had many questions to ask Klawed, but he could not bring them forth past the memories of Megan and the guilt that came with them. So, he closed his eyes and dozed as Klawed and the Animond called Yahmond Yah conversed.

His sleep was not deep or all that sound, but dreams chose not to bother him this time, which allowed his rest to relieve most of his aches and pains. He awoke after sensing Klawed stir and climbed to his feet.

The Greenwolves had returned with four good-sized wild goats, two of which they placed before the Panther and Tailey.

"Go, hunt," the one called Animal then said to the sentries nearby. "The area is safe . . . for now."

Without questioning it, Klawed tore back the hide on one of the wild goats for Tailey, then turned to the other to feed himself. Yahmond Yah removed some dried fruit from his pack and offered a large slice to Nep, who happily accepted it and eagerly began consuming the morsel.

Tailey moved back to let the Panther finish eating the remainder of his wild goat, having licked the bones clean of the first. The huge Panther needed fuel and a lot of it!

The four Greenwolves made a quick meal of the other two kills and finished shortly before the Pack Mother and Luna returned. The two females quietly waited in the center of what would become a circle when the others arrived. Their wait would be short.

"I am Cleary, Pack Mother and leader of the Waterway Pack," she said, once all were in their places in the circle. "Luna has the magic, or at least part of the magic, of the Den Mother ... ruler over all the nations of the Fubal Plains."

The Pack Mother paused to let her words sink in before continuing.

"Luna has chosen not to do battle for control of the pack. She has much wisdom for one her size."

This is true, Tailey thought. The Pack Mother was in the prime of her life. Tailey had noticed the steel-corded muscles flexing under her reddish-green fur as she walked. Surely the pup, being barely an eighth of her size, would not stand much of a chance in battle.

"Still," Cleary continued, "there are other problems that must be addressed. We have seen the sunrise, and yes," she paused, "it was the most beautiful, wonderful sight we have ever seen, or *any* Greenwolf has seen since the final day of the War of the Woods... We have changed." She again waited for the words to strike home.

"I feel it. *We* feel it." Cleary's eyes scanned her people. "It is gone. The curse of Katannon, the darkness that has cursed our souls has been driven away ... or perhaps destroyed."

Tailey noticed a new tone to the Pack Mother's mind-voice. The bitter hatred had been replaced with child-like curiosity, yet she managed to hold on to the authority of her station.

"Pack, I ask you all: Where are we to go from here? Surely the rest of the Pack Mothers will see our change, and Luna tells me that her mother, the Den Mother of the Green Nation, still lives." Cleary seemed confused by this but went on. "Luna warns that the Den Mother was possessed by a creature from the darkness. Her powers will unveil us, even if the other Pack Mothers do not."

Tailey took advantage of the Pack Mother's pause. "I am seeking guidance from the Kittoehee," he said. "Klawed has told me that he has the use of magic and great wisdom. Maybe he could help your pack also."

"Oh, no!" The words echoed Klawed's mind-voice to Tailey's.

"Kittoehee! Kittoehee!?" The Pack Mother's mind-voice flowed once more with venom. "His kind are the ones who damned us to darkness in the first place!"

Recollection of what Klawed had told him before slammed Tailey back a few steps. The pain in his head was resurrected all at once.

Like black lightning, Klawed was between Tailey and the pack, his thick tail poised over the hilt of his rapier. "He is not of our world; he knows little of our history."

Luna stepped between the growing tensions, Yahmond Yah poised over her with the long ruby sword in hand.

"The curse came from Katannon, not the Kittoehee of today," Luna said. "Things change, and so do we all. To turn our heads from help is a fool's game." Luna paused, as the Pack Mother had earlier, to let her words sink in. "As you have said, we don't have many choices!"

"Well done, young-one. Indeed." The Pack Mother recognized her own tactics. "But how can we be sure that the Panther wouldn't lead us into a trap?"

"You can't be sure," Klawed interrupted, "but I give my word as a hunter-warrior that I would not lead you into any trap, and I will do all that I can to ensure your safety."

The Pack Mother studied Klawed for some time. Tailey guessed that Cleary was weighing her options. With what he knew of the two races' histories, it would be next to impossible for her to accept the Panther's pledge. Countless centuries of hatred stood between them. The Greenwolves had once slaughtered many of the Neptunians, Scantians, and Panthers. On the other hand, the Kittoehee Katannon had condemned the Green Nation to eternal darkness.

Tailey failed to see where either side could claim total righteousness. He saw the hard truth: There was no right or wrong in war . . . only suffering and death.

"Well, there seems to be no further reason for debating our dilemma," the Pack Mother said, with most of her anger in check. "Animal, Slim, and Drake, scout ahead." She turned to the others. "Escort-position two."

"Where to, Cleary?" Animal asked.

"We go to Shadow . . . to visit our old friend the Kittoehee!" she said with a hint of sarcasm.

Tailey felt the icy sarcasm of the Pack Mother's mind-voice and dreaded the thought of traveling with these would-be enemies. Klawed showed little interest in the matter though, so Tailey tried to act the same.

The three scouts bolted ahead as the rest of the party moved out, heading toward the southeast. Luna and Cleary led, followed closely by Yahmond Yah, Klawed, and himself.

There were four rows of the male vanguard, two on either side of the main party. They traveled one line a little ahead of the other, so that the view of the main body would be limited, disguising their actual numbers.

Tailey had to trot to keep up, his short legs unable to cover the ground like the others, but it wasn't hard. Tailey did not feel dragged down by gravity as he did when traveling back on the earth. Looking ahead, Luna was not doing much better than he was, hurrying to keep pace with the others.

Further ahead, the herd beasts hurried far away from the path of the approaching party. Tailey thought it must be shocking to see the Greenwolves in broad daylight. Even the xantelopes gave the party a wide berth, and from what Klawed had told him, it was highly unusual for xantelopes to back down from anything.

The Fubal Plains were a portrait of nature in balance—a balance that had been created at the end of the War of the Woods when the recoil of the Kittoehee's magic had trapped the seasons into different areas. A disturbing thought entered Tailey's mind: *How will the change in the Greenwolves affect the creatures that live now on the open plains?* Tailey knew that only time could tell how the change would affect the future of the Fubal Plains.

The rest of the day passed without event, and with the setting of the sun, the tree line of the Nep Forest came into view, and shortly thereafter, they came upon another creek bed.

"We'll rest here tonight," the Pack Mother said. "Spruce, take half our numbers and stand watch, while the rest of you hunt."

"Panther," she said, with a hint of sarcasm, "you may do as you please."

Tailey watched Yahmond Yah walk off into the growing darkness, returning shortly with an arm full of dry droppings from the herd beasts, which he stacked in a pile. Then he disappeared once more into the night and was gone for much longer. It was completely dark when Yahmond Yah returned, carrying three round turnip-like plants, each as big as his head.

Next, he sat before the dry dung pile and removed his pack. From it, he took out a rectangular-shaped stone. Tailey was surprised when the stone opened and could not restrain himself from moving closer to see what was inside.

The lid that flipped up had a flattened leather pouch affixed to it. Yahmond Yah removed a small measure of dry wood shavings from it, placing them in the recessed part of the pile. He then took a rounded stick of metal from the pouch and began raking it across the stone, sending sparks into the shavings, which took fire after several strokes. Next, the Animond placed the burning shavings near the dung and fed the flames with dry grass and small bits of dung. Soon, he had a respectable fire. Yahmond Yah then pulled his sword from its sheath, and neatly impaled the plants through their centers. He held the plants over the fire and slowly turned them in the flames.

"Klawed," Tailey turned back to the Panther. "What is he doing?"

The Animond started making low grunting sounds, which escalated to loud haw-haws; his head tilted back then, and he roared into the heavens, his free hand resting against his heaving stomach. He laughed for a long time, and Tailey was reminded of Boss Lennie back home, who was always full of boisterous laughter.

It was true that the Animond was very much like the humans in terms of shape and body structure, though the Animond were obviously much larger and hairier. Megan's father was tall and kept his face clean shaven. Of course, the hand structure between the two races was different, because the Animond had two opposing thumbs on each hand, on either side of three powerful fingers, while humans only had one thumb with four fingers.

Slowly, the Animond's mirth subsided, and as he wiped the tears from his eyes, he began to talk in that same language that Tailey couldn't understand, reaching over to the small cat and gently stroking his fur with his large digits. Tailey could not refuse his body's need to purr; his back arched and bowed to the Animond's touch.

"Yahmond Yah says that it has been far too long since he had a good reason to laugh," Klawed said, translating. "He says the box is called a *tinder box*, which the Animond use to start fires."

The Animond returned to his cooking. Tailey had noticed that he'd seemed preoccupied, with a distant look that haunted his dark brown eyes, but the laughter seemed to have eased some of his pain, if only a little.

"Tailey," Klawed said as he stood up, "it's time to hunt. Stay near Yahmond Yah. He won't let any harm come to you." Then the Panther moved silently out into the night, with the Neptunian and his bushnuts secured in place.

Tailey curled into a ball next to the fire and Yahmond Yah. His body welcomed the warmth against the cool of the night air.

Off in the distance, howls from the pack's hunt echoed across the plains. The sky was clear past the thin, low fog bank, which gave the red moon hazy fingers that waved about the stars like a giant sea of spider webs.

The firelight reflected off the exposed areas of the ruby sword Yahmond Yah held over the fire, moving about in a hypnotic dance as the Animond rotated it to cook his meal evenly.

Soon, Tailey was lost in slumber.

* * *

Seeker had climbed through the secret tunnel to the private balcony designated for the Kittoehee. The balcony overlooked the western shore of the Big Drink Lake and a large portion of the Forest of Nep. Quiet. Peaceful. It was a place for thought, offering a vantage point from which one could view the bulk of the beauty the Fall/Spring Band had to share.

The cool wind out of the north was refreshing after a long day of studying the magic that flowed through the veins of Katlyn, deep in the catacombs below the City of Shadow. It was a lonely job, but he knew that, as Kittoehee, it was his and his alone, as it had been since the age of Katanna, who had found the six Cat's Eye Stones so many cycles ago. Seeker often ended his day here on the balcony. He needed the clarity that only the wide-open space could provide. He knew that, without this stability, he would not be able to protect himself from the dreams that assaulted him in his sleep each night.

Dreams were the vessels of magic—the power that flowed through the veins of the ground. It rode upon the waves of air currents, hid in every plant and animal, and bathed with the fish in the waters. This special magic had been here since the creation of the pale-blue sun, Regulus—perhaps longer. It was gray magic, and it helped to fuse the matter that formed the universe. The gray magic saw the ever-changing future and mapped countless scenarios of what could be and what would be.

The gray magic had a name. The first of the Kittoehee had called it "Mythos." Seeker searched for the magic's true name, as all the others of the Kittoehee had done, as that name was thought to be the key to endless knowledge.

Throughout their centuries of searching for the true name, the Kittoehee had been sown only minor hints of the true future. But visions of the past, and what *could* be, had no limitations when it came to invading the mind. Those like the Kittoehee, who were sensitive to the gray magic, found many restless nights.

The single Red Cat's Eye Stone seemed like a heavy anchor set in the amulet he wore on a golden chain around his neck. It had been a gift from the Animond and was many cycles old. Seeker's once-black pelt now had so many white hairs mixed in that he appeared a gray Panther. Someday soon, he would pass his magic on to an apprentice.

Seeker focused his senses out beyond Big Drink Lake to the Fubal Plains. Dark magic was at work this night. Back in the time of the War of the Woods, Katannon had held the power of six stones to wield in combat with evil. Seeker, sadly, did not. He wondered if he had enough strength to face what was coming ... or if evil would rule Katlyn at last.

Chapter 14

DARKENING SHADOWS

Tailey's eyes fluttered open. The eerie red moonlight flooded his retinas as it neared the end of its nightly travel across the sky of Katlyn's Spring/Fall Band. Daybreak was not far off. Around the now dying fire, Tailey saw that most of the party slept. All but one.

The Pack Mother, Cleary, sat close to Luna and appeared to be watching the setting moon, buried in her own thoughts. Tailey approached her with caution, still unsure of her attitude toward him.

"The Panther," Cleary said, still watching the horizon, "decided that you needed to sleep rather than eat, so he didn't disturb you when he returned earlier."

"You do hate Klawed?" Tailey said, really more of a statement than a question.

"Hate…" The Pack Mother mulled over the word. "'Hate.' The word holds much power, but no… I don't hate him."

"Even after all the death he inflicted on your pack?" Her answer had surprised Tailey.

"You're truly not from this world, Tailey." She apparently had not been sure of this fact until now. "The Greenwolves are warriors as well as hunters. My Pack Brothers died in battle. We would not have it any other way. Warring and hunting define who we are as a people. You must understand; this is our way of life."

"The Panther," Cleary said, turning to meet Tailey's eyes, "Klawed. . . He is as mighty a hunter as he is a skilled warrior. I don't hate him. I do respect him and his skills."

Other questions began to form in Tailey's mind.

"Wait," the Pack Mother said, cutting off his inquisitive mind before the questions could start. "Yes, we are enemies, but to fail to recognize your enemy's potential could lead to a short lifespan."

"Pack Mother—"

"Call me Cleary, please," she said, interrupting.

"All right, Cleary," Tailey corrected himself. "Where will your pack go after Shadow?"

"You should eat." Cleary indicated a piece of meat with a nod of her head, while she pondered his question. "I believe the Panther caught a mirror deer."

Tailey stepped over to the meat and sniffed it carefully. This meat was indeed different from what he had eaten so far on Katlyn. The flesh was coarse but had a mildly sweet taste.

Cleary sighed then. "Since I witnessed the glory of the sunrise, I've felt a white magic growing inside me. It is filling the void in my soul that was created when Katannon's black magic was driven from us. Luna and I have discussed this event at length, and we have concluded that we are once again the Greenwolves that lived upon the plains long before the War of the Woods … resurrected!" She looked back to the moon, which was now half out of sight.

Tailey finished his meal and started to groom himself. He resisted the urge to ask more questions.

Cleary filled the silence. "Luna seeks a way to free her mother, and the rest of the Green Nation, from the power of the evil creature she saw, whom we now believe to be Ichneumon, the Possessor of Souls. We shall do all we can to aid her in the struggle against evil."

Suddenly, Luna sprang to her feet and faced north.

"Do you feel it, Cleary?" Luna asked, her mind-voice filled with dismay.

"Yes," the Pack Mother answered. "I've felt it for some time now. Evil is at work in the Low Jaw Mountains."

Tailey's eyes followed Luna's gaze. He was not sure what he was looking for, but he noted that a storm was building as the stars disappeared behind a rolling cloud bank that seemed to be heading southward. Soon, Tailey realized that the storm was not just moving in one direction but actually spreading out across the sky.

"Luna," Cleary said, tremors of fear flowing through her mind-voice, "Den Mother is summoning the powers of the Shadow Demons of Fire Nose. Never has she wielded the strength to control so dark an evil."

Tailey tracked the edge of the clouds as the pale-blue sun spread its rays of light over the rim of the Mangy Mountains. The lines of darkness and the rays of light fought for dominance of the sky. Quietly, the pale-blue sun was lost, and gray shadows began to haunt the world of Katlyn.

Tailey turned to find the entire party awake and watching the turmoil overhead. The sentries had drawn in close to the main body. Yahmond Yah stood with his powerful hands anchored at his hips, his manner reflecting the mood of the group as he searched his mind. There was something he had heard in the past about this moment . . . something his father had said. . .

The pages of his history refused to open for him. Something was barring those pages, and he wondered if any other thoughts were being held from him that he could not recall.

"We·must get to Shadow," Klawed said with a hint of urgency in his mind-voice. "Now."

* * *

Megan sat at the dinner table, picking at her food with her fork. Eating just wasn't the same without Tailey sitting next to her. She looked at his bowl, which had been kept full at her request, waiting for him. His private door failed to move to admit her friend. Her bright blue eyes once more became a pool of tears.

Her mother gently turned her daughter's head to face her so she could read her lips. "We will keep looking for Tailey again soon, but you must eat."

Clara and Lennie Simms felt terrible for their daughter. They understood how special the cat was to her—though they could never guess that the cat had more to do with her education than they did. They only knew for sure that their deaf child depended on the cat, her best friend, if for only moral support.

Lennie was saddened by his daughter's depleted state. Since Tailey had come into their lives over a year and a half earlier, he'd never seen her so distant . . . so helpless. Lennie promised himself that he would broaden his search. He had to find Megan's friend, but six months had already passed since Tailey had disappeared.

Lennie Simms had no idea how far he would have had to go to find him.

* * *

The Den Mother stared into the depths of Whirl's Eye; she could feel the formidable power that dwelt deep in the heart of the churning waters. The magic was neither dark nor light. Instead, it had a quality of its own, its source derived from the gray areas of life and death—from the parts that most beings watched but few cared to consider; the lines between night and day; the moments between the womb, a baby's first breath, and when the light in the eyes of the dying faded into darkness. "Mythos." The Gray Magic deemed to be the very fiber that held the universe together. Powerful magic. The Den Mother dared not dabble too much in its use, lest she destroy herself in the process. Calling forth the Shadow Demons was stretching her magical limits already. She would be careful not to draw too heavily on the power that dwelt within Whirl's Eye.

Three rivers came together here at Whirl's Eye, creating a vortex: the West Branch Drink River, the North Branch Drink River, and the East Branch Drink River. All these water sources flowed in from the Low Jaw Mountains. The exit of the whirlpool formed the Southern Cross Drink River.

Around these rivers, the Nation of the Greenwolves, the Black Nation, and the Winter Bears continued to gather, waiting for the Den Mother to lead them all to a slaughter of all that dwell in or near the Nep Forest on the last night of the Blood Moon.

"Fools for tools," the monster inside of the Den Mother thought to itself. *"We shall drink from the souls of many. Soon! Oh yes, we will."*

The Den Mother looked deeply into the vortex. "Show us that which the creator sends against us. We command it!"

From the heart of the vortex, the true-blue eyes of a little girl stared back at her from far away.

The creature controlling the Den Mother was enraged. *"Somehow, yes, we must destroy that child, but our plans have been delayed … at least for now! Stupid humans of earth, always in the way! Beware, little girl, you will never reach Katlyn where your power would be absolute! No! Never!"*

* * *

Weenep parted the grass and was surprised at the sight before her. She could hardly believe her eyes: A Panther, a Nep, and an Animond were traveling south and west amongst a pack of Greenwolves. IN THE MIDDLE OF THE DAY! There were flashes of gray in the grass behind the Panther. She was sure it was another cat, but she could not tell what breed it could be, or from what origin. They could be captives, she considered for a moment, but even through the shadows, she could tell that the party was not being kept together by force.

A compelling feeling urged Weenep to announce herself, but just the sight of the Greenwolves would not allow it, at least not yet. Instead, she paralleled the company at a safe distance and would wait for the right moment.

Time seemed to fly by for Weenep, and soon, Big Drink Lake came into view. The company headed for the strip of open plains that ran along the west side of the lake and the east side of the Nep Forest toward the short foothills of the Fubal Mountains. The grass here was cropped to a lower carpet. Weenep began to work her way over to the tree line and better cover.

A multitude of heard beasts flowed over the plains like waves on water. The animals gave the predators a lot of breathing space as they lived their lives upon the vast plain.

It was then that Weenep felt hot breath through iron jaws, which locked on to her. With no time to call up her magic, she knew she was a goner.

Chapter 15

BIG DRINK LAKE

The party came to a halt near the mouth of the Southern Cross Drink River where it emptied into Big Drink Lake. The pale-blue sun would have been shining brightly overhead if not for the dense blanket of clouds that held back the rays of light. The party would rest before finishing their journey to Shadow. As before, half of the pack left to hunt, while the others stood watch over the main body and took turns going to the lake for water. Klawed wondered why the Greenwolves felt it necessary for the tight security, especially on their home plain. He decided to let the matter go, assuming it was largely out of habit.

Tailey and Klawed also went to the lake. Klawed took his time; he knew that the pace the pack had set was hard on Tailey's short legs, though he seemed to get along well.

Traveling behind them were two Greenwolves. The large one they called Spruce and another they referred to as Slow. Slow was indeed a strange creature, who seemed to be the center of much ridicule and the butt of many practical jokes. Throughout the morning travels, the entire pack had taken turns nipping at his tail or distracting the oaf while he walked into a pile of fresh animal dung or tripped in a pothole.

"Hey, look! P.B. found another pile of fresh xantelope manure!" Animal would say. He seemed to enjoy dishing out the torment the most.

"Do you like that? Are you happy now?" This was Slow's standard rebuttal, always after the fact.

There was a high-pitched whining to Slow's mind-voice that tempted Klawed to take a shot at him as well, but he restrained himself. Still, he could not help but laugh at the antics the others inflicted on him.

When Slow was not in the heat of abuse, he could be found crying his complaints to the Pack Mother. "Slow, why don't you just grow a backbone and fight back?" Cleary would ask. "Are you going to be a victim all your life?" Klawed could feel the frustration in her mind-voice.

"Hey, Animal," Klawed had to ask. "What does P.B. stand for?"

Animal's gruff mind-voice answered, dripping with humor. "It means Partially Baldheaded!"

Klawed noted that the Greenwolf called Slow was indeed balding between his ears. *Must be some sort of mange,* he thought to himself.

Another thought crossed Klawed's mind: *The bushnuts Nep harvested need to be planted soon, if they're going to have any chance of growing.* Klawed was sure the same thoughts were going through Nep's mind. He would have to talk the matter over with Cleary and Luna when they returned.

Klawed paused before he drank. He watched Tailey and still he could not suppress his amazement over the size of the little cat; new Panther cubs were not much smaller than Tailey. The smallest cats that he knew of on Katlyn were the Lynx of Pussywillow Down, who were at least twice Tailey's height, if not more.

Despite the size of the gray cat, Klawed knew there was a lot more to him. Tailey was brave; his bout with the Nightwolf had proved that, and there was also the matter concerning the hue-man he called Megan, and his need to return to protect her. There was honor in his warrior's spirit. There had to be a way to send Tailey home, and he would do everything he could, within reason, to help the gray cat find that way.

The clear water was cold and helped to wash away the dust from their travel. Klawed's ears rotated while he drank, and his eyes scanned the distant shore. This was a built-in defensive instinct found in all cats, and most other animals for that matter. The watering place was an ideal area to hunt, but who was the hunter and who the hunted generally depended on who struck first.

Klawed saw the midnight-black shadows traveling between the trees on the far side of the lake and heard the snapping of twigs and low growls. *Nightwolves!*

* * *

The tight ring consisted of Luna, Cleary, Klawed and Nep, Yahmond Yah, and the Greenwolf called Animal. Tailey reasoned that Animal must be second in command of the Waterway Pack. All the Greenwolves jumped when he barked. Tailey felt out of place in this ring of beings and not just because of his size. This was their world. He knew nothing of magic, and he knew even less of the plots that were unfolding before them.

So, what if the Nightwolves were heading for the Fubal Plains? So, what if some of the Waterway Pack were no longer cursed against seeing the sun? So, what if a cloud-demon or demon-cloud, or whatever it was, was blocking out the sun? Why was it him who had been brought to this world? He had no magic, and he could not stand long in battle against creatures of this size and strength.

The cats and canines of Katlyn could surely fend for themselves. Megan, on the other hand, needed him to protect her from the Nightman. And deep in his heart, Tailey knew that he needed her also. She had become an important part of his life. He loved her, but it was not the love between master and pet. No, it was the love shared between big brothers and little sisters. Megan was his family, and he would gladly give his life to save her.

"We have heard reports that the Nightwolves were massing at our borders. We had hoped for an answer from the Den Mother, but..." Cleary let her voice trail off. The dilemma with the Den Mother was well known to all those present.

"Nep and I have another problem as well." Klawed sounded unusually tactful as he chose his words. "Surely, our company has been seen, and advance warning is traveling to the Panther King. It's our intention, Nep and I, to carefully go to Neptown, plant the bushnuts, and head to Shadow with great speed to announce your coming and offer them reasons why they should allow your pack to enter Shadow and consult with the Kittoehee."

Nep and I? The words kept repeating through Tailey's mind. "Hey, wait a minute. What about me? What about Tailey?"

"Well, Tailey," Animal said, pouncing on the opening. "You get to stay with us, so that we can kill you if the Panther happens to double-cross us!"

Tailey was stunned.

After a long tense moment, every word and sound that could describe laughter erupted around Tailey. The entire company had been caught off guard by Animal's humorous statement. Even Nep, who had been mute for days, would have fallen from his saddle if it not for the securing straps.

Soon, even Tailey had to relax and unleash his purring machine, followed by a series of meows and purrs.

"Tailey," Cleary said after regaining her composure, "what Klawed hasn't said is that he and Nep will make better time alone, but I would prefer that Animal joins them and speaks on our behalf."

Out of the corner of Tailey's eyes, he saw a lone Greenwolf running under a full head of steam toward the company from the direction of the forest.

"Slim!" the Pack Mother said. "What's the problem?"

Slim was slight of frame, and somewhat shorter than the others of the pack, but what he lacked in size was made up for in his speed and strength. His agile body flowed over the remaining distance between them like a leaf on a strong breeze, then came abruptly to a halt just short of the company and spit the small body of a creature into the grass before them.

At first, Tailey had thought that Slim was hacking up a large fur-ball, covered with saliva and foam. To Tailey's surprise though, the wet ball uncurled, stood up, and began wiping the slime from its fur and from what appeared to be a green sleeveless tunic with a brown cloth belt tied around the waist. It had reddish-brown and yellow fur, jet black eyes, and no tail. Tailey was sure it was another Neptunian, but it was much smaller the Klawed's Nep companion.

"Found this one spying on us from over by the woods," Slim said, as he spit some leftover hair from his mouth.

"This one is no threat," Klawed said. It was obvious that he was suppressing the urge to laugh.

"If that's so, runt," Cleary said, addressing the smaller of the two Neptunians, "then why were you following us?"

The word *runt* obviously struck home, Tailey noted, because the small Neptunian purposely ignored the Pack Mother and finished cleaning herself off. Her clothes were soggy. Only when the small Neptunian finished did she face the Pack Mother, her hands defiantly on her hips.

"I am Weenep, Leader Doggie!" The Neptunian's insolent tone did not go unnoticed by the Pack Mother either. Cleary's lips rolled back to reveal her long pointed fangs, but she held her anger in check.

Tailey could not refuse his own curiosity and walked past Klawed to get a closer look, and perhaps, a sniff of the small creature. The Weenep turned to Tailey, as he got close to her. She seemed as curious about him as he was about her. There was something about the creature that Tailey found appealing . . . or maybe familiar.

Klawed's Nep called down to Weenep in a vocal chatter that held no meaning to Tailey. Weenep's response was to climb up Klawed's harness and sit across from the Neptunian with the bushnuts between them. There, they resumed their conversation without a second glance at the others.

Tailey's questioning eyes sought out Klawed.

"Weenep," Klawed answered without question, "is a female of their kind and is exceedingly small for an adult. All that I know of her is that she refused to become a life companion with a Panther for reasons that only she knows." After a brief pause, he went on. "She also refused marriage and the honor of being named, so the Nep Elders in the confusion just called her Wee Nep, which soon became her unofficial name: Weenep the Adventurer."

Cleary was still suspicious. "I have little doubt that the Panthers are readying their tail-rapiers as a welcoming party."

"What you say is likely to be true," Klawed agreed. "So, I suggest that Nep, Animal, and I get on our way."

"Agreed," Cleary said. "Klawed, we shall wait here until we hear from you." She turned then to Weenep and asked, "And what of you, wee runt?"

Weenep dismounted and went over to Tailey. "I will stay with Tailey, your Immense Doggedness."

Ouch! That must have hurt! Tailey thought to himself, but the Pack Mother seemed untouched by the verbal dig.

A short time later, Klawed, Nep, and Animal galloped toward the forest and out of sight. Once again, Tailey felt very much alone.

Chapter 16

PLAINS OF CHE

Hurtling across the Plains of Che at speeds exceeding sixty miles per hour, the worker Beesive B'loris, with a full load of nectar, navigated herself over the tall grasses and flowers toward the hive of the Queendom of the East. In the distance, the trees that bordered the Long Drink River came into view. The monstrous willows, hundreds of feet tall, stood arm-in-arm, whips mingled together to form a giant wall of greens, browns, and yellows.

As she approached the dense thicket, her multi-faceted eyes scanned for a possible route into the trees, unable to fly over the top with a fully loaded storage stomach. The Beesive hovered along the edge a short distance until she found a small opening in which to enter. After a brief inspection of the opening, the Beesive flew out away from it in a large circle to gain momentum, then folding her wings to her abdomen, she plummeted threw the foliage to the dark interior.

Her wings snapped back to action as she entered the dark space, which brought her to a standing hover. Automatically, her vision switched to her night vision eyes, located just below her antennae and above her mandibles. These would allow her to navigate through the darkened grove wall to the other side.

Before she could go on, B'loris had to land to rest. The long morning flight and the gathering of nectar, paired with the exertion of entering the trees, had made her weary. Landing on a low branch, the Beesive fanned her wings to cool down her body temperature. Feeling in need of nourishment, she relaxed the muscled valve between her special storage stomach and main stomach. This would allow the smallest of measures of the sweet syrup to transfer for digestion. She had to be careful. The nectar was pure magic.

From her vantage, the Beesive surveyed the gloomy interior. On a huge tree trunk across from her station were two lines of inch-long ant-like insects going up and down the tree. The line moving downwards carried tiny pieces of leaves, which they were industriously harvesting from the upper limbs. Along the forest floor, the leafcutters carried their burdens to their nest, which appeared to be somewhere downstream.

Rested enough to move on now, the worker Beesive held her position hovering above the limb. Rotating in mid-air, she sent out a sonic hum from a special inner vocal cord attached to her wing muscles. This humming echoed off objects around her and was received by her antennae. This sonar gave the Beesive a clear image of things not readily visible to the naked eye, such as certain spider webs.

Upon confirmation that all was clear, the Beesive set out, searching the interior for a possible route to the upper plains.

Flying over the river was not a big deal unless you didn't fly high enough. The deep waters held many different types of fish. Most of which could, and would, jump several feet out of their environment to catch a passing meal.

The silver needle nose was by far the most feared fish in the inland waters. Like its cousins, the spear fish and dagger head, the silver needle nose could impale its victims with its long-pointed snout and feed on their corpses.

Locating a way out of the willows proved easier than finding a way in; it was just a matter of finding the largest ray of light and following it to its source. Fortunately for the Worker Beesive, the opening she found was large enough to fly through with fully extended wings.

Beyond lay the upper Plains of Che. In the late-afternoon light, most of the flowers were beginning to close for the coming night. Still, her multi-faceted eyes were able to take in the rush of colors from the plants that remained open for business—millions of giant-plumed flowers, whose shapes stood out boldly in the fading light of the sun. Less than an hour remained before the western sky would be ablaze with its setting. Soon, this world would be darker than the one she had just departed. The realization that she would be unable to reach the Eastern Queendom before dark signaled the Beesive to find shelter for the night. Although, she could travel at night, it would be very risky to do so. The rich load of nectar she carried would be used to nurse a new batch of queen larvae, after being turned to royal jelly and royal bread. To risk losing this precious load to a passing night predator would be foolish.

Setting her course for the hive, which was located north and east of her present position, the worker Beesive searched for a haven. Zooming over patches of purple and yellow iris, the Beesive soon came upon a vast area covered with tulips.

A brief inspection of several flowers revealed a bright yellow-petalled tulip, the center of which was full of pollen and nectar. Being larger than most of the surrounding cups, this flower would be perfect for what the Beesive had in mind.

In a short time, the Worker Beesive collected all the flower's pollen on her body hair. Then, with the hair-lined notches on her front legs, she cleaned her antennae, then brushed the pollen from the rest of her head. With her center legs, she cleaned the thorax portion of her body and transferring the pollen from her front legs to her center legs. Following this series, the hind legs cleaned off her abdomen, and transferred the pollen to the rear from the center legs. At this point, she rolled the pollen into a pellet and stored it in the built-in baskets on her hind legs, this time, shaping it shaped it into a cup, which she filled with nectar she had extracted with her proboscis. Finally, she removed large amounts of wax from a gland in her abdomen, with hooks located on her center legs, using it to seal the nectar into the cup of pollen to preserve it for her breakfast. Settling herself and her burden in the center of the flower, the Beesive awaited the night and a much-needed rest.

In time with the setting sun, the petals of her tulip started to lift, eventually closing her inside of it, forming a natural tent that would protect her against the elements of the night.

* * *

Only by viewing the Plains of Che as a passing cloud could one deeply appreciate the vastness of this multicolored land: from the sandy shores of the Mighty Drink Sea in the west; the towering heights of the Fubal Mountain in the north; and the Mangy Mountains some two thousand miles east. The northern border was a dense pine forest called the Green Divide, encompassing the foothills to the Fubal Mountain Range. From there, the plains ran southward thousands of miles to lands still unknown to the northern residents.

Near the eastern end of the Green Divide, one would find Crescent Drink Lake, the main tributary of the Long Drink River, which flowed southwest across the middle of the Plains of Che to Calm Drink Bay. The entire surface of the plains was riddled with springs and creeks that also fed the main branch. It was said among the Cheetahs that one cannot run fifty miles without coming upon drinkable water of some sort.

It was perpetual summer here. Across the plains, there was a continuous display of blooming flowers; asters, bell flowers, tulips, heliconia (also known as lobster claw), and pansies were just a short list from the massive catalog of flowers on display, scattered across a huge backdrop of grasses, clover patches, and alfalfa.

The visual effect of this landscape was enhanced by the pale-blue of the sun. Colors were deeper, bolder, because of the tinted light. Reds seemed to bleed from the plants. Blues stood out from darker shades of green. Yellows, lavenders, pinks, purples, whites, and every other pigment reached out and took hold of the optic nerves of any who called the planet of Katlyn home.

Katlyn, the football-shaped world, orbited Regulus on a stationary axis. Staying about the same distance from the sun throughout its calendar cycle now—though that hadn't always been the case—the planet's seasons were constant and unchanging. The Summer Bands were perpetually warm. Spring/Fall Bands were cool but comfortable during the day, and the late afternoon brought mostly rain. As evening settled, the rain turned to sleet and eventually to snow (or just cold on the nights free of precipitation). Then there were the Winter Bands. These smallest zones were the thresholds of the polar icecaps. To date, little was known of those frozen wastelands.

The Plains of Che were home to many creatures, big and small. One of the most outstanding of its residents were the Cheetahs. These high-speed, nomadic people could be found in small groups across the plains. Against a backdrop of yellow daisies and sunflowers, two Cheetahs stood completely still at the edge of the flowers. A short distance away stood a small herd of xantelopes, feeding on clover blossoms.

"Caser, which xantelope are you going for?" Chaser questioned.

"Look right … at the edge of the herd. There's a xantelope with a bum hind leg," Caser answered.

"I see it. Good choice."

"I guess this is it," Caser said, bordering on timidity.

"Yes," said his older brother, in a slightly agitated mind-voice.

"Do you think I have a chance?"

The reply he got was familiar to him. His older brother, Chaser, gave him that stare that plainly said, *Quit stalling, or I'll bite your tail off*

Deciding it would be best not to provoke Chaser into voicing those thoughts, or acting upon them, the young Cheetah started stalking his intended prey.

At his back, Chaser watched his brother's first attempt at hunting a xantelope. His chest swelled with pride for it was a great honor to teach the older cubs to hunt and fight. Caser, the youngest of their clan, was showing all the signs of becoming a great hunter.

Crouched low in the clover, the Cheetah moved soundlessly, with only the top of his wedge-shaped head above the clover. His cone-shaped ears stood tall, rotating toward any sound they heard. His long whiskers were held forward to help guide him through the clover until he could get a visual on the xantelope he intended to take down.

Ahead of him, the grazing herd was unaware of the pending threat stalking toward them. Around the edge of the herd stood several males, their three-horned crowned heads held high so that their large black eyes could scan the surrounding area. The bucks were fearless guards over their harem. Two of a xantelope's three-horns grew straight out from the sides of the head, just above and forward of the ears. The third grew out of the skullcap just forward and between the other two horns, arching out over the nose in a saber-like curve. They could be dangerous prey. All their horns were rounded with sharp points, and their long-muscular legs, designed for great speeds, had razor sharp hooves that could shred the flesh of any enemy.

Closing in on his prey, Caser got a close-up view of the sentry buck nearest him. As he watched, another buck came to take the sentry's place, having finished grazing himself. The replacement appeared to be older and larger, with wisps of gray throughout the blue-tick pelt, which was their most common coloring.

Just a little closer, Caser thought, as he slowly approached the buck with the bad leg.

Caser knew he had been detected when the new sentry bugled the alarm, putting the herd on alert. Soon, all the bucks were facing him in a defensive half-moon formation, with all the females behind them preparing to flee.

"Timing is everything. You must wait until they run before you can attack. Then go for a young buck in the rear, or one that is lame. Never go for a female alone. The bucks will rip you to shreds if you try." This had been the warning he had heard from Chaser so many times as they trained. And this ran through his mind as he bunched his legs under him, preparing to chase after the herd.

A signal from the bucks sent the does running away, and seconds later, the bucks turned to follow. Moments later, the whole herd was racing away at speeds of fifty miles an hour.

Behind them, a yellow, white, and black-dotted predator sprang from the clover. After only a few long strides, the Cheetah was beyond the xantelope's top speed and closing the gap on his prey. No four-legged beast on the planet could match the Cheetah's ability to maintain high speeds for such long periods of time. These lightning-styled runs required an enormous amount of energy, but fortunately for the cats, the plains were rich with game.

Caser was built for rapid pursuit, with his long legs and streamlined, powerful body. He had a flexible spine that allowed him to bring his rear feet all the way up to the front for greater strides. His non-retractable claws gave him incredible traction for his four-foot-long body at any speed.

Coming at the lame xantelope at a slight angle, the Cheetah made his move. With a mighty leap, he tackled the animal, grabbing its throat in his jaws as they fell together to the ground, cutting off the xantelope's airway. It soon lay dead.

Looking up to examine his kill, Caser saw that one of the bucks had turned around and was only seconds from running him through with its saber-like front horn. With no time to escape the charging beast, Caser braced himself for impact and the pain that would surely signal the end of his life.

* * *

The Fubal Mountains could be seen easily through the breaks in the upper foliage, even without the aid of the pale-blue sun. Following close behind Klawed, the Greenwolf called Animal kept pace with the large Panther. Animal did not seem nervous or shaken by the fact that no Greenwolf had set foot in the Nep Forest since the War of the Woods some many thousands of cycles ago.

In fact, Klawed was finding that he enjoyed his company. Animal had a strange outlook on life, but he was quick to laugh when something humorous was about, and he was a skilled hunter. Klawed did not relish the thought of doing battle against him and counted his blessings that he had done as well as he had in the skirmish back out on the plains.

All had gone well back at Neptown, where they had stopped to have the bushnuts planted. The Neptunians had been standoffish, if not shocked, to find a Greenwolf among them, but they'd accepted Klawed's explanation and had allowed Animal to enter.

Of course, the Neptunians were not overly friendly towards him and did not hide the fact that they resented his presence. Animal paid little if any attention to them.

It had taken most of the morning to summon the Scantians, whose help would be needed with the planting. Their village lay west of Neptown in the forest along the vast foothills leading into the Fubal Heights and near one of the tributaries of the Clear Drink River.

The single bushnut tree grew in the center of a large meadow that also served as the center of the town. There were no buildings or other structures. The Neptunians dwelt in the giant trees of the forest. These were not carved out holes or rotted, hollow trunks. No. Rather, it seemed as though the living trees had opened themselves to allow the Neptunians to reside within.

Two beds were prepared for the nuts on the north side of the bushnut tree. Apparently, the trees would need the night wind's help in pollination.

This day belonged to Nep, and he received a hero's welcome, for the nuts were fresh, and sprouts began to inch up from the soil with help from the Neptunians' light magic and the Scantian's soil magic.

That night, the residents of both communities celebrated. Kegs of honimilk had been imported with the combined effort of the Lynx and Animond of Pussywillow Down and were opened to toast their good fortune. The trio lapped down a quick bowl to honor their hosts, but as they had dire business to attend to in Shadow, they'd quietly melted into the forest while the crowd was distracted with the night's entertainment.

The distance to Shadow would not have been short if not for the path that had been made through the Nep Forest to the edge of the forest near the City of Shadow. The path weaved around massive old tree trunks and exposed roots. Along the way, Animal raved over the taste of the honimilk, which had been a new experience for him. The Greenwolves never had the luxuries of fine beverages on the open plains. Combining goat's milk with honey, and fermenting it, produced a lovely mild taste, but drink enough and one would find themself going to sleep early.

"We will be in view of the guards soon," Klawed said. "Are you ready for another warm welcome, Animal?"

"I can hardly contain myself," Animal answered. He could not hide his sarcasm. "Do you suppose that they'll want to have a party before I am impaled with their tail-rapiers?" There was no hint of fear in his mind-voice.

There was little undergrowth or fallen waste from the trees here. Ferns grew in patches where the light of the sun crept through the upper foliage, and mushrooms that could still the heart of a gourmet chef grew in abundance in the shadows. Giant oaks, beech, and several variations of walnut trees dominated the forest, but towering white ash, elm birch, and hemlock trees could also be found in some places. There were also many trees that were not identifiable to the trio.

The Nep Forest was a picture of health and vitality, mainly thanks to the contributed efforts of the Neptunians and Scantians, whose combined magic had washed away the scars of a war long gone.

In the wee hours of morning, all was still along the path from Neptown to Shadow. Then suddenly, the three were surrounded by Panthers, tail-rapiers poised to strike, their Neps riding low on their saddles.

Klawed had his tail-rapier half out of its sheath when he noticed that Animal had plopped down onto his belly and started cleaning his front paws, not showing any concern whatsoever.

A roar of laughter erupted around them.

* * *

Throughout the night, Worker Beesive B'loris rested in the comforts of her yellow tulip. As the morning light warmed the petal walls of her shelter, the Beesive carefully opened the package of nectar she had stored the evening before and consumed the rich liquid, sucking it up through her tubular proboscis.

In a short span of time, the worker's well-rested body was filled with new energy. Climbing to the rim of the partly opened tulip, the Beesive beheld a new day. All around her, the world was coated with a heavy dew, and with the pale-blue of the sun, the landscape appeared a ghostly white. The Beesive also took time to consume the nectar that the flower had regenerated overnight.

I must hurry if I am to reach the Hive this day, she thought to herself, as she lifted off the flower.

Heading north and east, the Beesive flew only inches above the flower tops, slowly at first to work out her knotted muscles and avoid cramps that could cause her to crash, jeopardizing the valuable load she carried. Nothing could be allowed to stop her from delivering it. Nothing!

Tonight, she would be the honored guest of the celebration. The queen would stand before the whole queendom and announce to all that she, Worker B'loris, had braved the crossing of the Long Drink River to retrieve the nectar of the Strelitzia flower. This was her daydream, as she skimmed along the multi-colored landscape.

A couple of hours into her travel, the rising sun had burned off the remainder of the dew. Another lovely summer day, as usual. Below her, the countryside was covered with a variety of daffodils, from yellow petals with yellow coronas to white petals with red coronas. Red, purple, orange, and blue pansies with brown and black central blotches littered the spaces between the daffodils.

Fluttering about the flowers were several full-sized monarch butterflies in search of mates or nectar. With their twelve-inch wingspans, boldly colored in orange on black, they were the largest of species of butterfly on Katlyn. Their colors and size give them a true look of royalty.

Ahead in the distance, the Beesive approached an area of yellow flowers, which were speckled with deep brown centers. As she approached, the worker noticed a herd of xantelopes, grazing in a clover patch beside the flowers, suddenly bolting away.

Seconds behind them, a Cheetah exploded from the clover in pursuit of the herd. Slowing her speed to a hover, the Beesive watched with admiration the graceful bounds of the attacking cat.

Picking up speed to parallel the hunting Cheetah, the Beesive was amazed at the skill of the savage beast in taking down its prey. B'loris noticed a rare event then: One of the herd bucks had stopped and was turning around to help its fallen comrade. Realizing the cat would not see the other buck in time to save itself, and without thought for her own safety or for the royal package she carried, the Beesive moved to intercept the charging beast.

Landing on its neck, B'loris grasped the charging buck, aimed her stinger for its spinal cord, and drove the two-inch spike home. The paralyzed beast folded in mid-stride. Then it fell to the ground in a twitching bundle of fur, bones, and guts, pinning one of her wings beneath it. With her jagged stinger deeply embedded, B'loris was unable to free herself without tearing out her stinger, which would kill her. So, she held on tight to the neck of the xantelope, hoping it would die before it could cause her further damage.

* * *

Believing that he had not reacted fast enough, Chaser charged toward Caser in hopes of stopping the second xantelope from killing his brother. His eyes widened with terror as he realized that he was too late to save him. Ahead, Caser crouched and bared his teeth as a last act of defiance as he awaited his impending doom.

Not willing to give up, Chaser bunched his muscles for one final lunge, hoping to put himself between his brother and the beast. Then, to his amazement, it toppled over dead. Putting on the skids, Chaser managed to stop just short of the still-spasming xantelope.

Cats of Katlyn

The brothers' eyes locked together in disbelief at this turn of events, unsure of who or what had been responsible for saving Caser's life. Slowly, they circled the beast, careful to keep their distance, fearing it might have been sick somehow, or worse, enchanted. Behind it, they found the trapped Beesive, its wing caught beneath the animal's neck and its stinger buried to the hilt.

"Now would be a good time to get me out of this thing!" the mind-voice of B'loris shouted at them.

Unsure what to do, Caser stood back as Chaser ripped into the beast's already cooling flesh with an upper fang, all around the stinger, careful not to damage the Beesive. After freeing it, he called his brother to aid him, and the two dragged the antelope from the trapped wing.

"I am Chaser, and this Cheetah you saved is my brother, Caser."

B'loris carefully fluttered her wings. The one that had been trapped under the antelope was crumpled to the extent that she would not be able to fly for at least a day, perhaps two. B'loris knew that she might as well be dead. The fate that awaited her—as a Beesive who had risked royal nectar—would not be kind. Still, if she could get the nectar home, she might be able to salvage something of her life. She had no time to waste.

"I am B'loris, a worker Beesive of the Eastern Queendom," she said. "Could one of you please give me a lift?"

Chapter 17

SHADOW

Tailey was sitting in the grass next to Weenep when the ten Panthers came out of the forest and headed directly toward them. They did not seem to be in any hurry, nor did they try to hide themselves. Instead, they moved openly toward the company, and only when they were close did all but one of the Panthers stop.

"The Elite Guard," the Pack Mother said to the approaching cat, "or at least part of it. To what or whom do we owe this honor?" Tailey noticed the return of Cleary's sarcasm in her mind-voice.

"We are here by order of King Gustar, son of Geard." The Panther seemed to be ignoring the Pack Mother's attitude. "I am Paxie Jax, First Paw of the Elite Guard. You will come with us." There was no question in the mind-voice of the First Paw.

"What if we choose not to follow you?" Cleary countered.

"Do as you will," said the First Paw. "But you will release your prisoners to the king."

Tailey was surprised when the Pack Mother seemed to relax. Apparently, she had suspected that the Panthers were there for different reasons. Perhaps she'd thought that Klawed had betrayed them after all.

"Yahmond Yah," Cleary said to the Animond, "would you be so kind as to show the First Paw your sword?"

Yahmond Yah slid the ruby sword from its sheath and displayed the handsome weapon to the Panthers.

"As you will note, First Paw," the Pack Mother said coolly, "prisoners do not carry weapons. Yahmond Yah is now an honorary member of the Waterway Pack. He saved one of us from the devils that dwell below, and he will always have a place among us." She then turned to Weenep and Tailey. "These two are also under our protection."

The Pack Mother seemed to be avoiding the subject of Klawed, Nep, and Animal. In fact, Cleary was quick to cutoff any further need for questioning by agreeing to follow the Panthers to the king, pointing out that such had been their intention in the first place.

So, the Panthers fanned out, and the mixed company followed them south along the shore of Big Drink Lake.

The pace was slow. Tailey had time to drink in the beauty of the world around him. Even in the gloom caused by the dark clouds, Katlyn's highlights managed to show through. The lake was home to a large variety of waterfowl. Birds with long necks and legs waded through the lily pads and reeds in the shallow coves and bays; the lake at this time was almost literally covered with every color of bird imaginable.

A small herd of white-tailed deer grazed in the short grass along the edge of the forest. There were several bucks in the group, but only one of them stood out to be the leader. Tailey counted at least sixteen long antler points reaching for the sky. The rack was set wide on his crown, with hints of gray about the tan portions of his coat. When the Panthers finally came too close for the deer, they bolted into the forest; the white bottoms below their tail signaling danger as they disappeared.

Other creatures scattered before the Panthers; some Tailey could name or thought he recognized, but there were quite a few critters that he had no clue as to what they were.

Weenep stayed at his side as they traveled. She was not at all like the Neptunian that Klawed called his life-companion. Tailey found her annoying at first, with her almost constantly chattering mind-voice, but after a while, he began to appreciate the vast knowledge she held of the world around them.

Another interesting quality she possessed was her ability to take an answer to a simple question and expand it to the point of distraction. But one thing was for sure, Weenep had a thirst for knowledge and was not bashful in her methods of gaining it.

The lake was not nearly as wide as it was long, but it was indeed a "Big Drink!" They had traveled all day, and only now as the shadows deepened did the heights of where the Mangy Mountain met the Fubal Mountains become clear. The mouth of the Fe'line Valley, which cut between the two mountain ranges, came into full view. The Mangy Mountains seemed worn and ragged, pale in comparison to the towering snow-covered beauty of the Fubal Mountains at their side.

Paxie Jax called for a short rest. No one left to hunt, but that did not matter as food was the last thing on Tailey's mind. He wondered what was happening to Klawed and Nep, and even more so, whether Megan was all right or if the Nightman had managed to get to her.

The rest was brief, and soon they were back on the trail. Through the darkness, Tailey saw the large Greenwolf called Spruce make his way over to him. "Tell me of your world under the yellow sun, Tailey." Spruce's mind-voice was high pitched yet slowed by a mental drawl. He seemed friendly enough though, as far as canines went.

Tailey found it challenging at first but was pleased to find that the story-telling helped to distract him from his present problems. Weenep remained unusually quiet, hanging on his every word as though he were revealing the truth of some great mystery. Tailey supposed that his very presence here on Katlyn could be considered a mystery of sorts, but he knew the greatest mystery was how he would return home.

Time passed quickly, and before long; the Fubal Mountains' base was in view. They turned more southwesterly then, keeping the edge of the Nep Forest to their right. Tailey saw dark shadows in the trees and along the mountains. Others said nothing about it though, so he remained quiet also.

They came upon a high wall of stone that continued a long way into the woods. Tailey was surprised when they rounded the end of the wall. He had expected to find more woods, but instead, he found himself looking at a large meadow. One tree stood in the clearing near to the base of the mountain with a large stone dais off to one side of it. The area was illuminated by large, glowing white mushrooms and red bushes. The light was not bold, but it was enough to show the travelers that the clearing was surrounded by Panthers and their Neps.

"And the jaws close," Spruce said to no one in particular.

Gradus—a fellow Greenwolf—was standing poised behind Slow. Gradus was slender in build, like Slim, but taller ... and maybe meaner. His eyes seemed too close together somehow as they tracked Slow's waving tail while Spruce was voicing his revelation, and it was in just that moment when the temptation became too great. Lightning-fast, Gradus nipped the tip of Slow's tail, which launched the whiner into the center of the clearing. Then came the sound of hardened steel whistling through the air.

* * *

Caser could enter the giant Hive but no further than the opening to the main inner chamber. The entire structure was lined with hexagonal cells, which Caser could easily see by the light from the single round orb suspended from the center of the dome. Caser had noted in his approach to the Hive that there were five domes centered around a lone tower-like structure.

Thousands of Beesives labored about the chamber, all with a particular chore or purpose to complete, and they worked tirelessly at it. At their work, the Beesives emitted a steady hum or buzz that was annoying to his ears.

Caser had left Chaser and the rest of the clan shortly after the top of the day. He had taken it upon himself to see B'loris back to the Eastern Queendom to repay her for saving his life, and after several bursts of speed to hunt and feed, they had come within sight of the Eastern Hive. B'loris had asked Caser to slow his approach then, so that she would be recognized. This would ensure that their intentions would not be misconstrued, with the bonus of not being stung to death.

It had come as no surprise to Caser, or B'loris, when they had been met at the front approach to the hive. B'loris had gladly transferred her precious load of nectar to her fellow workers, who'd rushed it off to the royal chambers for processing. Then they'd been escorted into the hive by several guardian Beesives. B'loris had said earlier that there were many different classes of Beesives, but to Caser's eye, they all looked the same.

"Queen B'liner," B'loris said to Caser, introducing her to him as the dome fell silent.

The queen had entered the room surrounded by Guardian Beesives. She looked the same as the regular Beesives, with large compound eyes, long antennae, an abdomen covered with yellow and black hair, golden brown hair over her thorax, and a smooth black head. But the queen was twice the size of all the others, and her movements were much slower than her subordinates.

"Welcome, Cheetah," B'liner said to Caser with her mind-voice as though B'loris were not there standing beside him. "You are the first non-Beesive to enter the Eastern Hive since, well. . ." The queen searched her memory. "It would have been the Brew-Master of the Lynx, many cycles ago!"

"I am honored," Caser said, remembering his manners.

"You should be." Her words were tinged with acid. "My question . . . is why." She looked to B'loris, as if noticing her for the first time. "Be brief."

"I saved him from an untimely death," B'loris said rapidly, "and he in turn saved me and helped to return the nectar to the queendom."

"Let me correct you, foolish one." There was nothing kind in her mind-voice. "You saved him *and* put the food for the queen larvae at risk!"

"But I—" B'loris started to appeal, but the queen cut her short with a wave of her front leg.

"But I *nothing!*" Queen B'liner fumed. "You know that the punishment is death for intentionally risking the nectar of the strelitzia."

Caser was stunned by the queen's words. Only now could he appreciate just how much B'loris had sacrificed to save him. She was a hero to him, not a traitor. She should not lose her life for saving his. What could he do? There were tens of thousands of those two-inch stingers in this dome a lone, at least. And who knew how many others were elsewhere nearby. The queen placed little to no value on his life, so he was sure his words would mean even less.

"Today," the queen resumed flatly, "is indeed your lucky day, B'loris, because today, I need a *volunteer* to go north on a quest. I am sure you will be that volunteer."

"Of course," B'loris said quickly, shifting uneasily before the queen.

"Collectors near the Green Divide reported that dark clouds are massing over the Fubal Plain and deep over the Mangy Mountains. These appear not to be mere storm clouds but something more sinister. The queendom would like to know what threats lie on the horizon. Now be gone with you, before I change my mind."

B'loris left in haste, yet there was something about her manner that reminded Caser of the condemned walking toward oblivion. Caser knew that, with her damaged wing, B'loris would not make it far, but the queen's tone had made it clear that her decision was final.

The queen turned to Caser once more. "Don't be quick to judge me, Cheetah. You don't understand our ways. I am old, and my time is short." The queen's mind-voice lost its harsh acidity then. "Without the magic found in the nectar of the Strelitzia flower, my workers cannot make the royal jelly and bread that transforms certain larva into queens. Without new queens, there will be no eggs to repopulate the colony. Thus, the end of the hive."

Caser caught the queen's meaning, but death still seemed like a harsh punishment for someone who was trying to help another. The world of Katlyn was not easy on the weak or the unfortunate. Indeed, Katlyn was a wild and untamed world where only the strong would survive—*could* survive.

"We thank you, Cheetah," Queen B'liner continued, "for all that you have done. You may spend the night inside the hive under our protection."

"The Cheetah are a people of wide-open spaces and are troubled in close quarters," Caser said tactfully. "Your offer honors me. Still, I would decline, with hopes that your hive would not be insulted."

"Beauty be the flight of the Cheetah," B'liner said formally. "Go in peace."

* * *

It disturbed Klawed that Animal had detected the surrounding presence of the Elite Guard when he had not, but Klawed was a creature who enjoyed a good laugh, and it was easy to find humor in this situation, with the Greenwolf choosing to ignore such a looming so brazenly, deadly threat in lieu of personal grooming. In doing so, of course, Animal had proven his mettle once again. He would be a formidable foe to reckon with in combat.

Paxie Jax, an old friend from cubhood, now walked beside him. "So, you're the First Paw?" Klawed asked, mildly surprised. "What happened to old Raker? He's been the king's number one since we were cubs."

"Weird story behind this one, Biggy." Paxie tried to hide the stress in his mind-voice by using his cubhood nickname for Klawed. "Raker went to the Fubals shortly after you left on your quest. He was going to hunt mountain goats and get some much-needed rest. When the searchers found him, he and his Nep lay dead, deep in the mountains. Their bodies had been torn to ribbons. Whoever or whatever killed them was long gone."

"Raker only reached old age," Klawed mused, "because he was the best warrior in the Kingdom. He would not fall easily."

"We found no tracks or any scent that might reveal the murderer's identity. In fact," Paxie continued, "Raker's tail-rapier had not been drawn, and no other signs of resistance were visible."

Klawed let the subject drop as they entered the clearing at the base of Shadow. Before them, the company of the Greenwolves were resting in the short grass. Tailey and Weenep rested as well, near the stone wall with Yahmond Yah, Cleary, and Luna. The group seemed safe and in good health, except for Slow. Slow faced the blank stone with his back to the group. The dark cloud of his sulking hung over him like a thunderstorm over troubled water, still unhappy at being caught unaware by Gradus and almost skewered by half a dozen tail-rapiers as he'd leapt abruptly forward, startled at having his tail suddenly nipped.

Klawed could not resist smiling inwardly at the events that had led to the Greenwolf's present state of mind. The timing had just been too perfect. The Panther was certain that Slow would always be a target, a victim of the hidden anxieties that plagued the very core of his life's pattern. Slow's only alternative would be to become the aggressor, channeling that anxiety into aggression toward someone else. Klawed thought that unlikely. In any case, Slow actually seemed to thrive on the attention, regardless of the pain he would have to endure to gain it. He was no spring cub after all, and Klawed was sure that he had been through this chain of events many times in the past. Klawed had to wonder how he had survived as long as he had.

Putting Slow from his mind, Klawed made his way over to Tailey, while Paxie Jax, the First Paw, left to find the king to announce their presence. The king would come to them there. The Greenwolves were still considered the enemy regardless of this pack's present status and would not be allowed into the heart of the city. Entering the city would make little difference to the coming conference. The meadow, which housed the gate-tree to the city, had been laid out with the intention of entertaining visitors that were not apt climbers.

Not all Neptunians who resided in Shadow were strapped to the backs of Panthers. No, there were many others who dwelt among the great cats, both Neptunian and Scantians. Their purpose for being there was simple: There were things that the big cats were not able to do efficiently for themselves, such as certain types of grooming and cooking—not all Panther meals were raw, right off the bone. The others also performed general tending of the city. In return, the Panthers provided safety to their world. This was not a land of masters over servants. No, the Neptunians and Scantians came and went as they pleased as honored, equal, and respected members of the Panther Kingdom. The different races were bound in friendship.

"Only the pale-blue of the sun can explain the beauty of Shadow, Tailey, my friend," Klawed offered. "Welcome to you." With a sweep of his paw, he called out, "Welcome to you all. Be at peace here. No harm would dare fall on the guest of the Panthers." Klawed pointed toward the base of the cliff where the Neptunians were preparing the evening meal. "By the smell, I believe our good Neptunian chefs are preparing bison, and those who have never eaten a cooked meal are in for a rare treat."

Luna and Cleary joined the pack to hear the details of Animal's trip. Klawed's Nep dismounted, removing his saddle and harness, and putting them aside, then motioning to Weenep to join him. Together, they disappeared into the forest. Tailey and Yahmond Yah watched the Panther roll around in the soft grass, free of his burden of what must have been many long days.

Little noises could be heard: the sizzling of fatty meat cooking on the iron racks; bird calls overhead; and leaves rustling in a west wind that had traced the happenings of thousands of cycles that had silently passed into dust. Klawed laid quietly on his back, drinking in the peace that came from being home after having been gone for a long time.

A lone Animond came off the gate-tree and strolled toward Yahmond Yah. The Animond wore a loose-fitting forest-green tunic with a wide leather belt around his middle. The long brown hair on his head had been braided into a long tail that hung down the middle of his back. The hairy towers met each other halfway between the stone wall and the gate-tree. They did not embrace as lovers do, or as old-time friends. Instead, they bowed toward each other with their hands entwined before them in a solemn gesture. They spoke briefly and then approached Klawed and Tailey.

"This is Onlooker Jib, Ambassador to the Panther Kingdom," Yahmond Yah said, formally introducing his new companion to Tailey and the Panther, who was already familiar with the ambassador. "I noticed earlier that your battle harness is in need of repair, and I would like your permission to take it to where the task can be completed." In the halls of Shadow City, the Animond had built a small satellite community, with sleeping quarters, meeting centers used for eating and worshipping, and work stalls for crafting with plant fibers, leather, and crysteel, an almost magically strong mixture of onyx crystal and steel.

"Of course," said the mind-voice of Klawed as he courteously nodded to the Animond. "Onlooker Jib, my old friend, we must talk when time permits. I have a tale that should be told."

"I've been waiting for your return for just that reason!" The Animond's bass voice rumbled with excitement. "I'll bring the honimilk and lots of it."

The Animond retrieved the saddle harness and returned to the gate-tree, but Yahmond Yah stood and took a long hard look at the bewildered Tailey before taking his leave.

"What was that all about?" Tailey asked.

"They want to make some repairs to my gear," Klawed replied.

"No, no. The look," Tailey said. "What was with the look?" Klawed shrugged his front shoulders. He had not noticed anything unusual.

* * *

The chamber of Seeker, the Kittoehee, had been constructed deep below the main passages of Shadow. Very few of the residents had the slightest idea of where it lay, or where these passages might lead. His talents required silence, for the voices that spoke to the Kittoehee were not audible to the ear of a normal cat. Through the magic of the Red Cat's Eye Stone, paired with his own, he was able to hear the voices of the past, bits of the present, and small hints of the future—the quiet voices of the patterns of Katlyn.

Seeker recalled the stories of old, when the Great Cats of Katlyn first struck out on their own after the magical war of the Indigo Mountains which lay south of the Mangy Mountain Range deep in the Summer Zone, when the Gray Circle had first battled Ichneumon in the catacombs. The Cougars, Panthers, and Lynx, accompanied by the Neptunian, Scantians, and new-found friends, the Animond, had traveled north and eventually settled in the regions where they still resided to this day.

Refocusing, the Kittoehee recalled the voices of his magic telling him of the coming of Klawed and the rest of the party. He had warned King Gustar of their approach and directed a welcoming/security party to lead the king's guest to the meadow before Shadow City. He'd also seen the struggles of the various groups of Katlyn to maintain their current positions in its ever-changing patterns.

His old bones felt the vibrations of the king's private messenger coming to summon him to join in the welcoming committee. Dragging himself to his feet, Seeker chose to meet the messenger halfway and so made his way back to the upper passages. Along the way, Seeker gazed at his world of studies with loving eyes. He would miss Shadow and his homeland. Mythos, the gray magic, had showed him the way, and his journey was soon to begin—a journey from which he saw no return.

Chapter 18

KING GUSTAR

King Gustar paced his bedchamber unable to rest. He'd known of the storm brewing on the borders of his kingdom even before hearing the warnings of the Kittoehee. He was the direct descendant of King Panthera and Queen Moona, the first sovereigns of the Panther Kingdom. Like all those who'd come before him, Gustar had keen instincts, reactive to the attitudes of the birds, deer, trees, and the very air about him.

Gustar was not long into his reign over the kingdom. It had been only seven cycles since the passing of King Geard, his father. Gustar stopped before the mirror-deer pelt, hanging near the entrance to the royal chambers, and gazed at his reflection in the pale-blue light that passed through the opening that served as a window in the far wall. His forehead bore the star-shaped patch of white hair that was the marking of his royal heritage. His limbs and chest bulged with the muscles of a Panther in his prime. The harness that he wore had fine jewels embedded along the black straps and on the saddle. At the center point of his chest, where the straps crossed, the family's crest hung proudly. The crest was a tooled golden shield, bearing the likeness of Panthera. A rich, red cloth with golden tassels lay under the black saddle, and anchored along one side, hung his tail-rapier. The sheath and hilt were also made of gold with multicolored jewels and precious stones set along its length. All these fineries were gifts fashioned for him by the Animond. The get-up was heavy and only for ceremonies and celebrations. Only his father's blade would accompany him into battle.

"He has arrived," a Neptunian's mind-voice announced from the outer chamber.

"Please enter," Gustar called back, "my old friend."

Seeker entered through the maroon curtains that served as a door. His head and tail hung close to the floor; the whites of his eyes streaked with red. This startled Gustar. He hadn't seen the old cat look this bad since his mother, Queen Randra, wife of King Geard, had died giving birth to his sister some thirty-five cycles ago.

Gustar's mind soared back in time, remembering being near his father when the Kittoehee had come from the birthing room, where he'd aided the Neptunians who labored in medicine. They had struggled to stop the queen's internal bleeding but failed. "Queen Randra now stands with the maker, My King."

King Geard had been crushed, and Gustar could remember only the sensation of being lost. It had taken quite a bit of time for his father to regain his mind. Gustar had spent that time with his new sister, and the Kittoehee had watched over the kingdom. In her dying moments, his mother had named her daughter, calling her Liliana, after the flower she most loved.

Gustar had centered his young life around raising Liliana. King Geard, although stable-minded, stayed apart from his daughter. Gustar guessed that his father somehow blamed her for his wife's death. The king was never harsh or bitter toward her, but it was as if his eyes refused to see her.

"You seem tired, old friend," Gustar said, although the truth of that was plain to see. "You should make time to rest."

"I will have time to rest in the grave, my King," countered the Kittoehee.

"As always, right to the point." Gustar knew not to press the matter further. "We shouldn't keep our guest waiting. Let us be off."

They made their way out of the royal chambers and up through the passages that led to the upper floors of the city. The Animond had carved the city in the granite face of the cliff. Their skills were displayed on every wall. Gustar noted each carving as they passed and still could not suppress the awe he felt in the realism of each piece of work. Scenes from near and far lay etched on the timeless walls of the Panther's keep, with only the lack of detailed color keeping the scenes from being reality. *Where would we be without the help of the Animond?* Gustar thought.

Somewhere, lost in the folds of time, the Animond had taken on a special love for Panthers. Their numbers varied from time to time, but some were always about. They mostly tended to the repairs and upkeep of Shadow, but each would also add to the sculpted beauty of Shadow's inner self. The Animond were quiet folk who tend to their own affairs, noble yet never snobbish or unpleasant to be around.

The king's Nep slid into his saddle. The Neptunian wore a fine hooded riding cloak over his loincloth made of fine white animal fur. The cloak was decorated with fancy feathers and jewels lined to the edges.

Makeup for the show! Gustar joked to himself.

A quick look back showed that two of the Elite Guard had once again taken up their position without notice. The late First Paw Raker's finest warriors were always ready, always waiting in the shadows to protect their king. As they drew closer to the gate-tree, others of the guard took up their places to the front and rear of the king, his Nep, and the Kittoehee. Gustar's father had once told him that a king was never truly alone. Gustar had always had trouble understanding the meaning of those words until he'd had to step forward and fill his father's office.

Few of his people were to be seen. Most would be in the main hall for the evening meal, where he would usually be at this hour. Tonight, he would have business to attend to before dining—dire business he would prefer to avoid if he could, but for a king, there was no hiding from reality.

The shelf above the meadow of the gate-tree was all but deserted save for the Elite Guard. Some of the upper limbs of the giant oak tree had grown into the stone of the shelf, forming a bridge across to the trunk and out across to the meadow. The gate-tree had been a gift from the Scantians for helping them in the War of the Woods. The Scantians were wise in the lore of wood, and their magic centered around the growth of trees as well as other larger sacred bushes and plants.

Gustar remembered the old tales of how the Scantians had been able to convince a great oak to grow in such a manner as to form a natural bridge from the meadow and to the Shadow City shelf. The tree, honored to be at the center of such attention, had submitted to their will.

Amazing, Gustar thought, as he always did when considering this feat.

The tree had bent itself to the mountain, anchoring its thick limbs into the shelf and was thus able to form a bridge to the meadow. For thousands of cycles, the tree had stood strong, allowing the Panthers passage back and forth.

Nightfall was coming early under the cloud cover, and a stiff chill came from the north wind as the sun set somewhere in the west. The king and his vanguard made their way down the wide gate-tree.

First Paw Paxie Jax was, as usual, one step ahead, and had prepared the guests to receive the king's presence.

"Welcome," King Gustar said, as he climbed upon the stone dais near the gate-tree. "Klawed, you seem to be traveling with strange company in these troubled times. I will ask for your full report soon, but first I will show courtesy to our time-honored enemies." Gustar turned to Cleary and Luna, who stood next to Klawed and Tailey, with the pack closely behind them. "The floor is yours."

"Thank you, Gustar, King of the Panthers," Cleary said as she took a step forward. "I am Cleary, Pack Mother of the Waterway Pack. My pack and I have seen the sun, and all the wonderful colors of the daylight." Cleary paused to let the full impact of her statement sink into her audience. "As you can imagine, King of the Panthers, we have no one of our kind we can turn to. We are as lost as pups . . . and in need."

Gustar considered this for a moment. "The fact of your coming here tells me of your sincerity to find answers in a peaceful manner." His father had often spoken of the time of peace he hoped would come between the Green Nation and the Panther Kingdom. Could this be the beginning of that new era? Gustar knew he must be careful not to insult them, yet he was not ready to drop his guard either. "Pack Mother, you and your people are welcome to stay and pursue the information you seek. The lines that have been drawn between our kind are old, yet strong. I ask you to be patient as we seek to open new doors."

"Your hospitality honors us. Thank you," the Pack Mother said as she took her place back among her people.

Gustar then turned to Tailey. "Who and what are you?"

* * *

B'loris felt the rush of wind brushing her wings and fur as they passed over the plains. Although her wings were finally capable of flight once again, she preferred to hold fast to the back of the Cheetah. This was a dream come true. To be carried along by the swift cat was more exciting than she had ever imagined it could be.

It was true that a Beesive could reach the same high speeds as the Cheetahs, but they could only maintain that speed for a brief period. And it was different to be a rider. She observed the world as it rushed rapidly by and enjoyed the independence from navigation. It was like free-falling across the horizon.

Caser was indeed a missile, and B'loris could not help but admire his cunning endurance. She could feel his massive, elastic muscles expanding and contracting under her six legs, which held fast to Caser's low-piled pelt. Caser's long tail flowed after the cat like the tail of a kite on a windy afternoon. Speed consumed fuel, and Caser would have to hunt soon or chance running himself to an early grave.

Ahead, the Fubal Mountains towered over the giant pine trees that made up the Green Divide, the sharply defined border between the Summer Band and Spring/Fall Bands. Overhead, the black clouds churned to an ominous rhythm all their own. Unnatural. Spoiled. These were the very object of her quest and getting closer with the Cheetah's every bound.

B'loris could feel Caser's momentum decreasing.

"I must hunt," Caser said, "and be free to maneuver. Wait here."

B'loris raised her wings and released her grip on the Cheetah's back. The wind on her clear wings lifted her off Caser's back and up into the sky, as Caser continued into the distance in search of game.

Food was also on her mind, and she scanned the area for flowers that would be plump with the rich nectar that was the main staple for the Beesives. B'loris did not have to search long to find her meal in a land of constant summer, where life was renewed with each new day.

B'loris took the necessary time to fill her storage stomach. She had never traveled beyond the Plains of Che and had no idea when she could find more plants to feed from, so she would take whatever measures she could to be prepared for whatever might lay beyond the towering pines and mountains.

B'loris thought back to the night when she'd walked out of the Eastern Hive and the lost feeling that had followed her. It was weird that she'd felt so helpless and alone, when in fact, all Beesives hunt for nectar independently on a regular basis. It must have been the nature of her journey that had troubled her so much. She remembered how, after retreating from the hive, she had been cursing herself for ever risking the nectar for the queen larvae to save the life of a cat when Caser had walked up to her out of the darkness and insisted on helping her on her quest. *What a noble creature.*

Now though, B'loris felt the rush of a new freedom, and she enjoyed the excitement of not knowing what might lie over the next rise. She was sure that Queen B' liner had meant for this quest to be her death sentence, but B'loris now saw herself at the start of a new life.

Will I return to the hive? B'loris asked herself. Of course, she knew that she would. She needed to deliver the answer to this mystery, as she owed the Beesives that much. But when she'd finished giving the queen her report, she decided that she would leave and continue exploring her newfound independence. Secretly, she hoped to stay with Caser and the free-roaming Cheetahs.

B'loris took to the air and headed in the direction that Caser had gone in hopes of catching up with him in time to watch the Cheetah finish his hunt. Her flight was much slower now with her storage stomach full of nectar, yet the excitement of watching the graceful Caser in action fueled the beating of her wings, carrying her over the surface of the Plains of Che.

Time passed quickly, but still Caser was nowhere to be found. The multifaceted eyes of the Beesive scanned the areas she passed by, and though she saw plenty of game the Cheetah could feed upon, there was no sign of him.

A wave of urgency swept over B'loris. She needed speed, and there was only one way to get it; she dumped all her nectar stores in midflight. A wave of guilt washed through her at the thought of wasting good nectar, but she felt she was out of options. With her load lightened, B'loris climbed higher into the sky, increasing her speed with the hopes of broadening her field of vision. *Where could he be?* This question kept running through her mind.

Ahead, the banks of the Long Drink River came into view, as well as the bridge that crossed it and the southern shores of Crescent Drink Lake. B'loris remembered once traveling this far north of the hive. It had been on her first flight, fresh from the hatching cells. She and a hundred of her comb-mates had followed the veteran Worker Beesive B'nine on a weeklong tour of the Eastern Queendom. There were no borders drawn in the grass, but B'nine had pointed out highlights of the terrain to serve as markers to help orientate the newcomers—her own would-be replacements.

Ahead was one of those markers: a stone bridge built across the river by the Animond for the Lynx of Pussywillow Down, who used the bridge to travel to the Eastern Queendom to gather the honey they used in brewing honimilk, a beverage enjoyed by Beesives and cats alike.

B'loris continued over the bridge toward the pines of the Green Divide. The air about the Green Divide held a light electric charge from the constant clash of the atmospheres of Summer and Spring/Fall Bands. Rainstorms formed and dissipated in a matter of minutes. Whirlwinds spanked the tops of the trees, which stood unyielding in the test of time. All this drama was painted on the titanic canvas of the Fubal Mountains, whose jagged peaks met the black clouds she'd come to investigate like massive columns holding up a broad, darkened ceiling.

Soon, B'loris was overwhelmed by the strong aroma of pine as she entered the silence of the Green Divide. The needle-covered floor absorbed whatever noise might intrude upon the eerie solitude that filled the dark void between the ancient tree trunks. Whatever life existed among the pines stayed hidden as the Beesive navigated in the direction of the Fubal Mountains.

The night-vision eyes of the Beesive guided her safely through the gloom. There seemed to be no end to the pine forest as time dragged slowly by. Caser had vanished into thin air, but B'loris trusted her instincts, which were guiding her into the unknown, and hopefully, to her new friend.

The terrain under the canopy was hilly—a hidden highlands leading into the mountains. B'loris flew near the surface. Just over a rise, she beheld the apron of the Fubals and the edge of the forest. The pale-blue light of Regulus rained down from the heavens along the base of the mountains. The curtain of light slanted into the pine forest but didn't penetrate far. Still, there was enough light to allow B'loris to switch back to her multi-faceted eyes.

The Fubal Mountains rose sharply from the edge of the pine forest. No shrubs grew to hide the rocky face of the mountains that reached into the ominous clouds overhead. B'loris turned right and followed the slim gap till she came upon a place where the sliver of a ravine climbed between the towering peaks.

Small fingers of gravity pulled at B'loris as she propelled herself into the darkness surrounding this strange landscape. She felt unnaturally tired, the power slowly draining from her body, but the rush of her urgency to find her friend compelled her onward into what she was suddenly certain was a well-laid trap.

The top of the ravine came suddenly, where the narrow ravine passed between the peaks to the range beyond. That's where she found her friend Caser, standing frozen before a creature she had never encountered or heard of before. It was as large as the cave mouth from which it seemed to be emerging. Only its head, neck, and front shoulders could be seen. The wedge-shaped head and long neck were covered with diamond-shaped scales. The scales were dark red and ended at in orangish fur at the base of its neck and ears. The ears were long-lobed, with black tufts raising from their tips. Its jaws opened to display its long fangs and pointed teeth. A long-forked tongue darted out of its mouth. B'loris expected some sort of howl, bugle, or shriek to follow the stifling air that rushed from its maw towards her and Caser, but instead, the air carried a low sound like gentle rain falling among the flowers yet tainted by an eerie undertone that pulled at the fibers of her being.

B'loris willed her wings to leave the hover she held over Caser and began circling the Cheetah, who once more began walking toward the monster. Caser seemed not to see or hear her desperate attempts to reach him with her mind-voice.

B'loris finally landed on his back, staring up at the monster. She would face the same fate as her friend. She would not—could not— abandon him.

Two white plates stood wide open in the places where the creature's eyes should have been on either side of its wet black muzzle, which sniffed constantly at the air. Drool dripped from its gaping jaws and ran down its long neck as the beast waited patiently for its meal to walk forward to its doom.

Desperate times sometimes require desperate measures, and B'loris knew her options had narrowed to one. Exercising extreme care not to bury the barb of her stinger, B'loris drove it home just above Caser's tail. . .

* * *

Megan sat quietly looking out through the glass of her bedroom window at the mounds of snow that had drifted about the Simms' home. The full moon overhead cast eerie shadows across the winter wonderland. Santa Claus would be coming this night, and she prayed that Tailey, her cat—her best friend—would be with him.

The little girl reached out with senses that surpassed any child who had not lived with deafness. Megan closed her eyes and saw her friend. Tailey was in a dark place. She could feel that he had other friends nearby, but she did not see Santa Claus anywhere.

Megan realized that Tailey would not be home this night. Tears ran down her cheeks as she nestled into her soft blankets.

Goodnight, Tailey. I love you!

Chapter 19

MYTHOS

The festivities around the great fire were a true celebration of life. The Neptunians, wearing brightly colored costumes, danced about the blaze, doing leaps and somersaults and other amazing feats of physical endurance. One Neptunian summoned three balls of light and juggled them high in the air, while other Neptunians did stunts through and all around them.

On the dais near the gate-tree, a small group of Scantians played musical instruments. They wore matching outfits, so Tailey was under the impression that they performed together regularly. There were a couple of wind instruments and a few stringed instruments being played, varying in shape, size, and string count, as well as many drums of several shapes and sizes. The music was light and lively. Even the Neptunians tapped their toes and snapped their fingers. Several Scantian and Neptunian couples bounced in front of the band. The ladies wore colorful tunics with bright cloth belts while their dance partners wore the common dark-brown loincloths. Most of the Neptunians were half the size of the Scantians, except Weenep, who was no larger than one of Megan's dolls. She was with a small group of her people, who Tailey assumed were her friends or maybe family. Weenep wiggled and swayed to the music with her hands above her head, her fingers snapping to the sound that carried across the meadow.

Tailey noted that, although the dancing Scantians were taller than the Neptunians, they were shorter even than Megan. They wore bright yellow tunics with wide brown cloth belts at their waist, although most of the Scantians lingering around the meadow wore brown or red tunics. The male Scantians had long flowing blond hair, which they tied behind them, while the females wore braids done in many different fashions.

Off to the side of the merriment, the Greenwolves that made up the Pack of the Waterway lay around with full stomachs. Cleary and Animal were on one end of the row, watching the merriment happening about the meadow with intent eyes. Slow seemed entranced by the music and stood, pointing at the dais, with his tail an obvious target for his brothers to ... well you know. Funnily enough, the Waterway Pack saw that Slow was interested in something other than crying and whining and decided to leave him to enjoy the show.

Maybe people can change, Tailey thought as he got up from where he sat with Luna and Yahmond Yah, making his way over to the area where the meat had been cooked. There was a small piece of meat on the ground, left over from the feast earlier. Hardly a mouthful for the massive Panthers, it was exactly right for a midnight snack for Tailey. He was lying in the low grass, gnawing on the morsel, when Seeker came up to him. "Tailey, please follow me."

Without waiting for an answer, the Kittoehee led Tailey back into the shadows. They walked along the stone face where the gate-tree leaned over toward the city. Tailey scanned the faces of those gathered in the meadow. The merriment was still going strong, yet no one seemed to notice the old Panther and the gray tomcat as they moved about the area.

Suddenly, the Kittoehee walked into the stone face and disappeared into a hidden fissure in the stone face that Tailey had failed to notice earlier. He took another look around, and sure enough, no one was aware of what he was about to do. Then he entered the narrow opening.

Inside the wall, Tailey found himself in complete darkness. He could hear the Panther ahead of him, so he followed its soft steps. Soon his night vision got hints of light from the golden moss that started to appear more regularly. Then they came to a three-way intersection, and the Kittoehee led Tailey down the descending passage, which snaked through the stone. As they traveled, the glowing golden moss multiplied to make the shaft easy to track.

Through the many intersections, the pair made their way steadily down into the maze.

Finally, they walked into an almost black passage. Again, Tailey had to use his other senses to navigate his way. Then suddenly, a red glow lit the area before Tailey. The Kittoehee mumbled something, and all around the arena-sized chamber, plumes of fire lit randomly. The light was brilliant at first, then died down to a softer radiance.

Tailey found himself and Seeker on a large balcony with a low stone wall that lined the curve from bulkhead to bulkhead. A small channel at the top of the wall was filled with fluid that lit up along with the rest of the torches, and there were stone benches and rest areas with a few soft-looking pallets along its curve. A small trickle of water was flowing out of a small crack and collected in a natural bowl in the stone floor. The water channeled to a small notch where it overflowed out and down into the cracks in the floor.

Seeker motioned Tailey to join him on one of the benches. Tailey jumped up onto it, and as he landed, all the flames went out. "No need to fear, Tailey. Let your eyes readjust to the darkness, and as you do, look out over the area leading up to our balcony. It will take a moment, but then tell me what you see."

Tailey blinked his eyes many times and then closed them for a couple of moments. Ever so slowly, Tailey opened his dark blue eyes and looked around, becoming aware of the very faint glow coming from small gray veins, like spider webbing, all around him on the walls and floor of the arena!

"The gray veins are a small part of Mythos, the gray magic. The power between life and death. The power of luck or chance if you will. The very pattern of creation! With much time and training, you can clearly hear the past and some of the present. The future comes in tidbits, mainly in my sleep, but it is never a sure deal. No. The future is unstable, constantly moving," Seeker said softly in his mind-voice.

"I know what Klawed told you along the trail here. He is practically right, but there is so much more for you to know. For example, most Panthers believe that Katanna was the first Kittoehee of the Panthers, but no, that is not true. That is just a story told around fires to keep the evil spirits of the night at bay." Seeker said this with a hint of sadness in his mind-voice.

"How do you know all this?" Tailey asked, finding his mind-voice. "Why do you tell me this now?"

"You are not from this world, but from Earth. Right?" Seeker stated boldly.

"How do you know of my ... my Earth?" Tailey's mind-voice stumbled.

"Close your eyes and listen to the truth." Seeker's mind-voice grew softer. "Tinconder was there at the making of the world.

"As I said, the past is clear to me," he continued. "The maker told the Panther Tinconder that he had made our planet in the aftermath of the building of your world, the Earth. The maker told Tinconder that our world's pattern had been fashioned after yours, except the maker left this planet under feline control. Our world is call Katlyn, which means 'pure.' Our world was meant to be a place of serenity. The maker felt that, without humanoids, it would be free of evil. Instead, wickedness found a way to corrupt the maker's pattern. The blame clearly rides on the back of the Wizard Lars and the members of the Gray Circle, who invoked the magic of the Gray Cat's Eye Stone to bring the monster insect to our world."

No! Tailey screamed to himself. *Not the great Lars!* Tailey tried to reject the mere thought of his world being responsible for delivering evil to this paradise, but he knew the truth. It had come from his own father's mind-voice that night under the apple tree in the middle of the hay field, so long ago: *"We, the Cats of Earth, had no idea where the Gray Circle had disappeared to."*

"Do you now see any similarity between our worlds?" Kittoehee asked calmly.

Tailey was floored. The Kittoehee was right. There were a lot of similarities. The cats were much larger than at home, but they still were cats. He remembered when he and his companions had first exited the Low Jaw Mountains to a vantage point overlooking the Fubal Heights and the area where it stepped down to the Fubal Plains with the mountain ranges in the far background. In reflection, he remembered one winter night when he and Megan were watching a program on the television about a faraway land called the Serengeti National Park in the land called Tanzania. The Serengeti housed a grand display of herd beasts of every size and shape, flowing like rivers across the open plain. The views of the multiple herds had a lot in common with the Fubal Plains. There were also many similar trees, he realized now that he was thinking about it.

The most compelling argument for comparable world patterns was the one thing that all cats shared: the mind-voice! *Wow!*

Seeker's argument started to make sense to Tailey. Yet he felt lost being so small in such a huge world. So many options flowed through his mind. Tailey folded his legs under his body and lay down facing the veins of magic, his eyes seeking anything that would stop his life from spinning out of control. Soon his eyes felt heavy. *Too much honimilk!* Tailey thought as his eyes closed and slumber overwhelmed him.

Chapter 20

DILL TUCK

Dill Tuck sat quietly, looking over the plateau that had served as a base for the Tuck family farm for many generations. Rows of grains, fruits, and vegetables were laid out in neat, well-cared-for rows. In the sandy soil along the south edge of the plateau, the Tuck family had planted several long rows of grapes. Dill's eldest son, Chawn, and his younger son, Qustin, worked with sharp knives to prune away the old growth to make room for the upcoming season. Dill noted that the boys would be done soon. Despite their youth, the young Scantian were diligent workers and quick with their hands.

The land beyond the boys stepped gradually down toward the edge of the Nep Forest. On a bright day, Dill could see Scanterville, the home of the Scantians and a place he visited many times since his own youth, which seemed ages ago.

Dill picked up the book from behind him on the woven bench. The cover and inner pages were clear coated to give the book life far beyond its normal span, but the coating had been applied long after the writers had given it life, so the pages were sometimes hard to read.

The book was a collection of journals from the generations of Tucks who lived on a world far from Katlyn. They called the world Scanton, due to its small size compared to the four giant-sized planets that shared the same sun, Denebola, as a part of the Leo system.

Dill read:

1336 AM (After Maker)

My daughter, Gasmone, will be wed today to the Freeman boy, Gosh. He comes from a good upbringing and will be a welcomed member to the Tuck family.

Today also marks the end of another bountiful harvest. Reports from around the planet indicate that it is our best! We thank our maker for this world, with its limitless farmland.

Four vessels have landed near our Capital City of Plenty. Each vessel was filled with ambassadors from the four giant worlds, Neptune, Triviania, Watartar, and Firmatia. They claim to have come in peace.

- Abor A. Tuck

The beginning of the end, Dill thought to himself as he set the book aside and fished a leather pouch from his jacket pocket.

From the pouch, Dill removed a broad brown leaf, which was dry but still moist enough to manipulate. He rolled it between his fingers until the entire leaf was tubular in shape. Then he licked the tail edge, his saliva helping it to hold its shape.

From another pocket, he removed a flat, round piece of glass, which he held up to the afternoon sun. The glass lens condensed the rays of light onto Dill's leaf, and in moments, the tip of the leaf began to smoke. Dill gently sucked on the unlit end and began to enjoy the mild flavor of the tobacco. Wisps of smoke rolled off Dill's large mustache and then floated out into the distance on the soft southern breeze. Dill admired the glass piece as he relaxed. It had been a gift from his old friend Onlooker Jib. The Animond was long overdue for a visit to the Tuck Farm. Dill had put away a large pouch of tobacco for him. They had shared many evenings on the knoll, conversing and enjoying each other's company over fine tobacco.

Dill thumbed deep into his book and read:

1399 AM (After Maker)

Father died last month, and I am just now taking up his writings as he had done for his father and his father's father... Abor Tuck was a fine Scantian and a great father, and I, Revor, hope to continue their works, so that the future generations will learn from our successes and failures.

The Scanton Government has grown to be an absolute power among the five planets. 'He who controls the food, rules!' Father once said. It also appears that the power is corrupting people who were once giving and caring.

Even on our remote farm, we hear rumors of trade embargoes, forced starvation, and pending war. We pray to the maker for salvation, and to send our latest president guidance to stop the turmoil growing between the worlds

- Revor A. Tuck

Dill again put aside his book and brushed his long blond hair back from his sky-blue eyes. Fair hair and skin were a Scantian trademark. The Scantians were twice the height of a Neptunian, with slender builds and long flowing hair reserved for their heads. The males sported long mustaches, the length of which were a matter of station, and the females' hair would often have to be braided to keep it from dragging on the ground.

The Scantians had little body-hair. They covered themselves with cloth woven from fibrous plants. Generally, they wore long tunics with tight pants, and wore leather boots when such were available, but most often they wore heavy socks in wooden shoes of various shapes. The Scantians were not hunters of animals, so it was rare to see leather in their wardrobes. The materials they wore most commonly were dyed to match each individual family's chosen colors. The Tuck family sported a dark green, with black borders.

Dill's jacket was made of fine tooled leather, which had been another gift from Onlooker Jib. The jacket was a work of art; the two front pockets had rearing Panthers embroidered on them. The inside of the jacket was lined with chainmail, the loops of which were jet-black and so small that the finest point could not penetrate it. Onlooker had told him that these loops were not metal or stone but rather a mixture of crystal and steel, named crysteel, which would never fail to protect him.

Dill shifted himself back toward the north side of the farm where a titan-sized blue spruce grew at the base of the Fubal Heights. Below the tree, the roots formed a home for the Tucks, who took great care of the tree in return. The Tucks were not like the rest of the Scantians, who devoted their lives to the trees that made up the Nep Forest. No. The Tucks remembered the old ways of life, mainly because of the book, and loved the smell of rich, freshly turned soil and a large variety of foods and drink. Unlike the other Scantians of Katlyn, the Tucks enjoyed being apart from the main body of their people, free to make their own choices—free to live their own lives.

The farm had always done well. After each harvest, Dealy—Dill's wife—would load the kids and grandkids, as well as any excess goods, onto the carts and go to visit her parents in Scanterville. The trip was good for them. The kids would get exposure to the church, see their relatives, and get to know other Scantians outside the family, maybe even future mates.

Dill opened the book to the last entry, and read:

1436 AM (After Maker)

Revor (my father) and my uncles left the farm to join the army today. There are reports that Firmatia has sent a massive force of war machines to destroy our world. Father told me in secret that he did not believe what President Devastator was telling our people, but he would go, as the draft in times of war was a law of our people.

A fifteen-year-old boy should not be burdened with so much, Dalven, my son. You are the oldest of your siblings, and this weight falls on your shoulders. Take this book of your past and this sword, which has been a symbol of our family's freedom since the coming of the maker. Take them. Follow your heart, but never forget your past.

Mother said we all should attend church this night. Somehow, my heart tells me she is right.

- Dalven W. Tuck

Dill nearly jumped out of his skin when he looked up to find Dealy sitting next to him.

"Drink?" Dealy asked. Her grin was filled with mischievous intentions.

Dill accepted the tall cup and took a long pull of the contents. "Beer! You've been into the special drums again." Dill tried to sound aggravated but failed miserably. Dealy knew his weaknesses all too well, and a cool cup of beer was one of them.

"Well," Dealy said, "me and the other girls were thinking . . ."

Here comes the pitch, Dill thought to himself, studying his wife of forty cycles as he shut out the noise flowing steadily from her delicate lips. Time had been good to her. Her face was smooth and round, bordered by her long blonde hair, which still had wisps of red highlights, though now the red was joined with silver-gray.

". . . all of the wagons and carts are loaded. . ."

Four children later, Dealy still had a petite build and smooth features. She usually wore long flowing dresses with a knitted sweater, depending on the time of day. She was getting just a little broad across the rear-end, though of course, that observation, Dill reasoned, would be best kept to himself. She had always been a good companion and a loving mother.

". . . so, you can see, it will take a couple of extra days to—Dill, are you listening?"

"Uh, oh yeah, couple extra days, sure. Take what time you need. The planting can wait until your return."

"We'll be leaving soon," Dealy said, as she got up to walk back down the knoll. "Come see us off."

All that, just to get a good beer, Dill thought to himself.

* * *

Four dark beings stood at the edge of Whirl's Eye, looking into the deep water the vortex.

"Yes! Very well done. The Winter Bears have destroyed most of the Cougars of the Fubal Highlands. Those left are being routed to the Nep Forest near Scanterville, where our combined forces of Black Nation and Winter Bears will finish them off, along with the Scantians and the Neptunians. The might of the Green Nation will deal with the loathsome Panther Kingdom!" Den Mother gloated. "It is time for us to strike again!'

"We agree," said the Ichneumon the Possessor of Souls, in its primordial wasp-like form. "The time is ripe."

As its counterparts charged off into the darkness, Ichneumon took wing. "But first, we have a score to settle with a certain gray cat and his friendly Kittoehee."

* * *

Weenep's snoring made it impossible to sleep. Tailey paced the floor of the small room that had been assigned to him. Weenep had insisted on bunking with him. She had proclaimed in front of the entire Panther court that Tailey would be her life-companion, no matter how much he argued against it.

"Please, Weenep, be reasonable," he'd said. "I am leaving this world as soon as possible. The world under the yellow sun is nothing like Katlyn. The humans believe that cats are ignorant, a species many notches below what a human would consider an equal in the eyes of the maker. They think of us as voiceless pets, contributing little or nothing to their society. On my world, you would more than likely be killed as vermin or caged as an exotic pet for their entertainment."

"And you're in a hurry to return?" Weenep had countered. She was having trouble understanding Tailey's point. "This hue-man, Megan, must be very special."

Tailey understood Weenep's point all too well. Humans were not the most appealing creatures to reside near, but Megan was different. She knew the true meaning of friendship. If it were not for her, Tailey knew that he could make Katlyn his home. In the brief time that he had been on Katlyn, Tailey had discovered that this land was a cat's dream. The air, food, and water were all pure and fresh. There were no automobile tires to avoid, nor humans to please or elude.

To make matters worse, the two Animond, Yahmond Yah and Onlooker Jib, had come forward with a harness just his size, with a small saddle and bags attached to it, along with a saddle blanket, which had chainmail sewn to the outside. They said the armor was made of crysteel, of which they'd had a couple of small pieces left over from an earlier project.

And to top it all off, the Animond had formed the final piece to cover Tailey's head. He would have argued its use, but Weenep had hushed him, reminding him of what Luna had said, that the next blow to his head could be his last. She took the liberty of securing the helmet in place.

Tailey viewed himself in the mirror-deer hide that hung on the wall. The get up was lighter than it appeared. In fact, even with Weenep on board, he did not feel any restrictions or discomforts. The helmet thing, or whatever Weenep had called it, was extremely comfortable. There were large openings for his ears. The liner was soft, but its shape conformed to his head in a way that was neither loose nor sloppy. The back edge hung loose about his front shoulder like a short cape. The black over his gray fur looked appealing. If it were not for the two-inch silver spike that was mounted just forward and between his ears, he would have given the get-up his complete approval. But the spike made him look like a miniature gray rhino—an animal he and Megan had once seen on the television.

Finally, Tailey grew tired enough to sleep through the worst of Weenep's snoring. That night, he was visited in his dreams by faces he was almost sure were from his past. Words of encouragement accompanied the faces, but without clear knowledge of who had spoken to them, they would leave little impression on him the next day. The hits to his head were beginning to take their toll. Tailey's past was slowly slipping away into darkness.

Chapter 21

DIFFERENT WAYS

Klawed pounded the ground hard as he sped along the edge of the Fubal Mountains toward the coast of the Mighty Drink Sea. He had never been this angry in his life. There had been times in the past when he had not totally agreed with King Gustar's decision, but this time the king was completely wrong.

Klawed remembered his argument with Gustar: "Who cares what fate may have come to the Cougars of the Fubal Highlands?"

"Klawed," Gustar had interjected, "the fate of the Cougars may be the fate of our Kingdom if we ignore their plight."

"Is the curse of Katannon still at work?" Venom had filled Klawed's mind-voice. "The Cougars all but laughed in our faces when Shadow asked them to send aid in the War of the Woods! Let us recall, Your Highness, what the Cougar Ambassador said then: 'Cougars are above these minor skirmishes.' Your father would never have forgotten the lack of action those cowardly Cougars displayed!"

Silence had engulfed the throne room then with the Elite Guard poised with their tails above the hilts of their rapiers, Gustar's ears low on his head. Klawed had struck a nerve.

"Like my father," the king said, his mind-voice clearly greatly restrained, "I will not forget the loss of two-thirds of our people. But the fact remains that the plight of one does not outweigh the needs of an entire kingdom."

The king's words, Klawed had to admit, were true. "Well, at least send Paxie Jax in my place. He has the skills to protect Tailey from a world that is completely foreign to him," Klawed suggested, with a hint of remorse for the cheap verbal shot he had taken at the king.

"No Panther will continue with Tailey."

"What!?" Klawed's anger leapt back to the surface.

"Silence! Before you say something you can't take back, Klawed!" The king's mind-voice was hard as crysteel, and the silence that fell over the room was as thick as good stew. "Your mission is clear. Go! Now!"

Pain shot through Klawed's limbs and deep into his body. He looked in all directions and then down at his paws. All four sets of claws were buried deep into the black soil. How long had he been standing in one place? Klawed had no idea, but his muscles were cramped and sore from the tension.

Suddenly, a noise from behind him sent Klawed's body into action, doing an about-face in mid-air and landing in a crouch, claws extended, ears laid flat on his head, lips curled back to expose his fangs, and his tail-rapier waving menacingly overhead.

"All that just for me! Klawed really you shouldn't have." Onlooker Jib found out in the next moments how hard it was to catch one's breath and do a deep, belly rumbling laugh at the same time. The effort had Onlooker Jib doubled over, leaning hard on a nearby tree. Between the gasps for air and the haw-haws, Onlooker Jib managed to say, "Gustar should light a fire under your tail more often. You've traveled an entire day's distance in half the time. I didn't think I'd ever catch up to you guys!"

Apparently, Nep had loosened his securing straps when Klawed had stopped, because he landed then on the ground next to Klawed, curled up in a ball of humor.

Klawed was helpless. From his crouched position, he dropped to his belly, his tail and rapier lifeless in the grass behind him, claws retracted, lips pursed over his teeth, and his ears back on duty scanning the area around them for the sound of any nearby threat. He could not join in their laughter, but he did wait patiently for theirs to subside.

Onlooker Jib removed his backpack and used it to cradle his head as he plopped down beside Klawed and Nep on the grass. The last of his rumbles subsided as he rolled toward the big cat and threw his thick, hairy arm around Klawed's neck. "Don't worry yourself, my friend. I spoke to Yahmond Yah before I left, and he said that his search to find a way to free his Yana lay along the same line as Tailey's. And as you already know, Weenep has befriended him. So, you see, he is in two capable sets of hands, and maybe even more by now."

"So, what brings you sniffing my trail, Jib?" Klawed asked, as the Animond rolled back on his back.

"I am off to visit another old friend," Onlooker Jib said, as he reached above his head and started fishing through his pack. "He and his family live near your destination and north of Scanterville a bit."

"I see." Klawed rested his head on his front paws. The exertion of his self-enforced speed, and the challenging route he had taken, was taking its toll. "Well, if the scouting reports are accurate, then you'll be better off with us."

Onlooker Jib was not a warrior, and from what he gathered, the Cougars had been attacked by what were described as large, white beasts that numbered into the hundreds. Anything that could route the Cougar Pride, which numbered well into the thousands, had to be extremely dangerous.

Klawed searched his memory for clues to the invaders' identity. There had been a time when they had been exploring the north above the Low Jaw Mountains, where they crossed over to the Winter Band, looking for traces of the Sabretooth Cats, also known as the Gray Circle. The cats of the Gray Circle had been described as bulky with long hair, the logic of which seemed probable, as they would be creatures who were more at home in colder climates.

There on the frozen wastelands, they'd came face to face with a white beast that was at least twice the size of Klawed. The creature, which they would later call a Winter Bear, charged them from over a bank of snow. Klawed had only had time to draw his tail-rapier and brace for combat. In the closing bounds, the ground beneath the Winter Bear had given way, and to the surprise of Klawed and Nep, had plunged into the icy water they'd had no idea was even below them.

They had been quick to make the most of the lucky break and had bolted back towards the south. The encounter had been brief, but Klawed had been left with the impression of a creature with incredible dexterity and strength.

Klawed had decided then that they would not travel the frozen Winter Band again unless they went with a lot of friends. The entire Elite Guard would do nicely.

Now, thinking of the "white beasts" that had routed the Cougars, he fervently hoped that scores of the enormous and fearsome Winter Bears had come down from the frozen realms to join forces with their enemies against them.

"Here. Drink this," Onlooker Jib said, as he set an empty stone bowl in front of Klawed Katz, who had been totally occupied with his own thoughts, filling it with liquid from his canteen. He then held out the canteen to Nep, who refused the offer after watching its contents being poured.

"Onlooker Jib," Klawed said, trying to sound matter-of-factly as he examined the contents of the bowl. "It appears to me that somebody . . ."— Klawed hesitated to voice his observation—" that somebody has taken a leak in your canteen."

"I suppose it does," Onlooker Jib said, as he poorly mimicked Klawed's indirect approach to the subject. "Ah, but the taste," he said, as he took a long drink from the canteen. The fluid quickly formed a golden arch as it spewed from the lips of the Animond. Foam ran from the corners of his mouth and down the hair of his chest. "Is much better cold."

The restraint that held Klawed's anxious nature at bay collapsed instantly, and the big cat lost himself in a cloud of body rumbling laughter, tears running from his golden eyes.

Onlooker Jib looked upon his much younger friends and was reminded of something his late mother had once said: *Time is the curse of our soul, and laughter shields our soul from the burden of time.*

* * *

"The visions gained through the power of the gray magic makes my decision clear to me. Our fates are similar, Tailey and I," Seeker said to King Gustar, pleading his case. The king was having trouble accepting the Kittoehee's decision to join Tailey on his quest to find the magical means to return to his world of the yellow sun.

"You can't leave us without your magical protection now, with the threat of war looming heavily in the air!" Gustar was getting a good taste of the frustration that Klawed must have felt only hours earlier. Seeker was a Panther of his kingdom, but the magic that made him the Kittoehee put him beyond Gustar's authority.

"Gustar, you are a good and wise king, regardless of the short amount of time you've spent in office. Your father, I am sure, is proud of you ... as we all are, Gustar." Seeker used care in exposing his intentions. "When Katannon battled Ichneumon, the Possessor of Souls, he had the power of six of the Cat's Eye Stones, plus his own considerable powers."

Seeker gently probed the amulet that hung from the gold chain around his neck with the tip of one claw. He was ashamed of the words that had to be said, but he would say them. His station required that it be so. "Throughout Panther history, the Kittoehee have searched through the gray magic of Mythos in hopes of finding the one power that would destroy Ichneumon. Our search, as you well know, has been fruitless."

"Is there any chance of locating the five Cat's Eye Stones that were lost to us?"

"I wish it were that simple, but the magic of the stones serves those of their own choosing. They may be with us for a moment or for centuries. We have no control over them. Take, for example, the Golden-Brown Cat's Eye Stone that brought Tailey to our world. It too is gone from us." Seeker hung his head in frustration. "Even if we had the six stones, it would be only a repetition of the past. The six are not enough to destroy the Ichneumon! We can only hope to find the seventh stone, the Gray Cat's Eye Stone—the mother of the six. Just maybe, with it and the powers we now possess, we can finally put an end to the Possessor."

The Kittoehee was ashamed of himself for holding back knowledge from his king—his friend. There was another detail that the gray magic had yielded to him: There was another source of magic out there, and though it was not on Katlyn, it would play the greatest role in the evil being's final destruction.

King Gustar knew all too well that what the Kittoehee had said was true, but his mind's eye refused to see the finality of the situation. Gustar could not accept defeat on these terms, not to the Green Nation, not to the Black Nation, and especially not to Ichneumon, the Possessor of Souls.

"What advice will you leave us with, Seeker?" Gustar asked, finally accepting that the Kittoehee was compelled to fulfil his own role.

* * *

Paxie Jax had agreed with Klawed about the plight of the small cat, Tailey, who desperately needed to return to the world of the yellow sun. But orders were orders, and he would follow the king's word even to his death.

There were three other generals besides himself meeting in the king's private situational chamber, which had been set aside for planning and plotting the location of troops and the enemy. The center of the room was filled with a raised dais, its surface another Animond work of art, which had a carved map of the known world of the Panthers.

Bulldory, First General of the regular army, was the first to offer his report. "Scouts from the northern borders of the Forest of Nep just reported that the entire Green Nation was on the move from Whirl's Eye, heading directly toward Neptown." He indicated their route of travel with the aid of his Nep, who drew their attention to the appropriate places on the map. "The scouts lost track of their numbers at ten thousand!"

"And what of the Nightwolves, Rammino?" Paxie Jax asked the general of the east wing.

"It seems that the Mangy Mountains housed far more of the Nightwolves than was ever expected. We have no tally of their numbers, as most of our scouts were caught in an ambush . . ." General Rammino fell silent for a moment. "The bulk of the main body heads directly toward Scanterville. They make no attempt to hide their course or objective. We estimate their number around five thousand strong," General Rammino finished. "They take no provisions. No sign of a siege encampment." Rammino hesitated then before continuing. "No, my friends . . . Their aim is a route. A massacre if you will. No prisoners. No quarter."

"And none will be offered," said King Gustar.

"What of General Hiker of the west wing?" Paxie Jax asked. "What awaits us in the Fubal Mountains?" Paxie Jax dreaded to ask, fearing what might be coming from that direction.

General Hiker had also grown up with him and Klawed. Hiker was the smallest of the three, but what he lacked in size he made up for with lightning reflexes and skill with a tail-rapier that very few could match in battle. His size and skills made him a natural for mountain patrol, and in a short span of time, he'd climbed the ranks to general of the west wing.

"The mountains are clear for now. I have a battalion of Panthers, one thousand strong, camped near Scanterville and awaiting orders. I also still have four platoons searching the Fubal Mountain for the murderer of old Raker." Hiker's whiskers on the left side of his muzzle began the familiar twitch that always signaled that there was something bothering him.

"Hiker, we've been friends a long time," Paxie Jax said, irritated that Hiker always had to be coaxed into offering the information that bothered him the most. "There is more, right?"

"This morning ... a runner brought word that a Beesive and a Cheetah were found nearly dead. They seemed to be heading toward Shadow City up through the Fe'line Valley. They appeared to be traveling together. The squad that found them were able to stabilize their conditions and are bringing them to Shadow City as we speak."

"What would a Cheetah and a Beesive be doing this far from the Plains of Che? Let alone traveling together." Paxie Jax mused over the information. "Were they able to say what happened to them?"

"The Beesive uttered one word before she blacked out," Hiker said, and after another hesitation, told them what it was: "'Monster!'"

Paxie Jax did not like the way things were beginning to stack up. He sat next to Gustar and watched the Neptunians place the figurines representing their enemies in the reported positions on the map. Unsure of what the creatures were that had attacked the Cougars of the Fubal Highlands, the Neptunians used small white stones to show their locations.

Paxie carefully focused his mind-voice so that only the king would hear. "If the white beasts swing into the Fubal Mountains, we would be cut-off from any escape in that direction, Your Majesty."

"Escape!" Gustar said in return, maintaining the offered privacy, the word souring the tone of his mind-voice. "There will be no escape. Ichneumon will haunt us wherever we go."

Gustar searched the eyes of those around him and spoke to his subjects. "We will stand and fight on our own ground, at times of our own choosing."

"But, Majesty," Bulldory interjected, "we are outnumbered at least two to one by the Green Nation alone. Not to mention the Nightwolves, and the white beasts from the north, whom I suspect are what Klawed once described to us as 'Winter Bears.'" Bulldory was not a coward by any definition, but these odds spoke for themselves. The others, except for Paxie Jax, nodded in agreement with Bulldory.

"We are hunter-warriors," King Gustar stated flatly. "If we do not stop the Possessor of Souls, its evil will possess our entire world, and even what lays beyond it, sooner rather than later."

The room remained silent for some time. Paxie Jax thought back to the days when Geard had ruled the Kingdom of the Panthers. Gustar's Father, Paxie Jax was sure, would have reacted the same way.

"Hiker, take your battalion to Scanterville, and do what you can for them." Gustar turned to Rammino. "Take your battalion and secure Neptown against the Greenwolves. Bulldory, hold your station until we hear from Klawed" Then he said to all of them, "Generals, in the end, bring all our friends and allies here to the city. Shadow will be our final stand against Ichneumon, the Possessor of Souls."

Chapter 22

PRETTINESS AND THE BEAST

The Fe'line Valley cradled the Between Drink River and passed from the bottom of Big Drink Lake to where it merged with the Our Blood River and then flowed into the top of the Crescent Drink Lake. The water descended a slow natural slope to the river basin. The river itself was wide but shallow, its swift current boiling over the rocks and larger stones that lined the riverbed. Stands of pine trees lined the fringe of the Fe'line Valley where the valley climbed into the western Fubal Mountains and the Mangy Mountains that bordered the east side of the valley. Open grassland paralleled both sides of the river. Herds of large-antlered animals grazed on the plush grasses and ran off towards the mountains at the sight of the mixed group as they made their way toward the edge of the river.

"Look!" Luna exclaimed to no one in particular. "Sunlight!"

Tailey had seen it too but could not get himself as excited as the young Greenwolf. Tailey tried to put himself in her place for a moment but failed. He could not imagine living in a world without sunlight, although the dark cloud—a product of the Shadow Demons of Fire Nose—was beginning to dampen his hopes of finding a way home to his Megan.

Fe'line offered a grand view of the southern horizon. The black clouds ended near what Weenep called the Green Divide. A veil of pale-blue sunbeams shone down from the heavens and traced the lines of mountains and towering pines.

Beyond the edge of light, clouds raked the treetops. These clouds hung far lower than the black-rolling clouds that hovered unnaturally over the north like a foul mood. The lower clouds churned continuously, rising, and falling on ever-changing drafts of air. Funnel clouds appeared and dissipated in moments. Heat lightning spider-webbed across the horizon in sporadic streaks.

Weenep's mind-voice interrupted Tailey's thoughts: "Long ago, the seasons changed throughout a cycle of time. Some stayed longer than others, but there seemed to be a natural order to their passage. Rarely did the one season meet another, but when it happened, the seasons would struggle for control. Most of the encounters were brief, and eventually, the leader would give way to the follower. Then came the War of the Woods, and the Curse of Katannon, which banished the Green Nation from the light of day. The curse was far more powerful than anyone could have imagined. It is said that the backlash of the curse confused the seasons to the point where they no longer knew their natural order. Summer and winter met and fell in love. Summer admired winter's soft white face, and in turn, winter worshipped summer's warm gentle touch. But summer and winter knew they could never be together and grew apart. In their wake, spring and fall met and disagreed with each other's principles. To this day, spring the conveyer of life and fall the harvester of death do battle above the Green Divide, keeping apart a love that could never be."

The small party stopped next to the water to rest. Yahmond Yah, the towering Animond, and Seeker the Kittoehee had been leading the way. Luna, the young Greenwolf, followed closely behind them. Weenep rode on Tailey's back. Next to them Cleary, the Pack Mother of the Waterway Pack, appointed the swift, sleek Slim to act as Luna's guardian. He traveled at will around the group, serving as a lookout.

Bringing up the rear were two patrons of the Elite Guard. They were sisters of two separate litters, Falsity, the eldest, and her younger sister, Truth. King Gustar had insisted that, if the Kittoehee felt that he needed to leave Shadow on Tailey's quest to find the means to return to the world of the yellow sun, then there would be some sort of guard accompanying him. Paxie Jax had chosen the sisters because they had served General Hiker 's left-wing mountain patrols before being transferred to the Elite Guard. Being females of their species, they were lighter and more easily adaptive to the changing terrain. The sisters were also fearless hunter-warriors, which they had proven of themselves many times in the past.

Tailey was beginning to see a pattern between the Panthers and their Nep riders. The Nep that rode with Klawed, for example, had the same personality traits as the huge Panther. They both found humor in the most unexpected sources, yet they were brave and honorable.

Falsity and her Nep both wore a band of braided leather dyed pinkish across their brows, with matching tail feathers from some bird affixed to the band on the right side of their heads. Their appearances were neat and prim, with the Nep's tufted ear hairs even seeming to be waxed into fine matching points. The Nep's sleeveless tunic was pinkish red with a wide, white cloth belt around her waist. As they sat in the grass during their rest, Tailey sat in wonder over how they reflected each other's appearance, as they fussed with their accessories and fur.

Tailey then turned his attention to Truth, who was watching her sister's makeup ritual. She turned toward Tailey, disdain written plainly on her face as she rolled her eyes, exhaling loudly as she lowered herself into the grass.

"You got that right, girlfriend!" Weenep said, agreeing with Truth's assessment.

Truth was just the opposite of Falsity. She was not sloppy or messy, as the truth of reality can often be. No, Truth and her Nep were plain, not feeling the need for ornaments, glitter, or objects that would stand out and mask her natural self. Truth was half the size of Klawed, and like her sister, had a sleek, powerful frame that was always ready for the hunt or combat. Similarly, Truth's Nep wore a plain brown sleeveless tunic with a black cloth belt around her waist.

Weenep released her securing straps and went to the river to drink. Tailey decided that this would be a good opportunity to converse with Seeker about where they would search for the lost magic that might help in the upcoming conflict and provide a means to return him home.

The Kittoehee, Luna, and Yahmond lay in the grass closer to the rushing stream. Seeker rested on his stomach with his forepaws spread out before him, and Yahmond Yah on his side with one arm supporting his head while the other gently brushed the hair along Luna's back. Luna, the proud daughter of the Den Mother of the Green Nation and would-be inheritor of the throne and its power, lay flat on her belly with her limbs sprawled in all directions. Her small-bushy tail spanked the top of the grass as it wagged to the rhythm of her pleasure. There was no doubt in Tailey's mind that Luna was completely bonded in friendship to the Animond. Tailey knew of the situation surrounding Yahmond Yah's abducted bride and guessed that the companionship they were sharing was helping to heal Yahmond Yah's torn heart.

Slim bolted past Tailey, and in a few bounds, was across the river and heading toward the tree line that skirted the Mangy Mountains. Slim had been on the run most of the morning and showed no signs of growing weary. As he passed out of sight, Tailey could not help but admire the Greenwolf's speed and agility.

Tailey had been startled by the run-by dogging though and was quick to find a place to sit with the other three.

"We are heading for the Animond City of Genus," Seeker said to Tailey as he settled among them. Tailey was surprised that the Kittoehee knew his question before he could form it on the tongue of his mind-voice. "Tailey, would you please tell me once again of your trip to this world?"

Tailey's minds-eye traveled back to the world of the yellow sun. The picture of Megan's face was clear in his mind, but the circumstances surrounding his need to return was becoming slightly clouded. The night of his encounter with the Golden-Brown Cat's Eye Stone remained vivid, so that was where he chose to start his narration, ending it with the night of the clash with the Nightwolves.

Yahmond Yah was absorbed in the tale. Tailey realized that, since he and Luna had started traveling with them, the Animond had not heard the complete version. Tailey noted the Yahmond Yah seemed extremely interested in the part when Klawed's Nep had returned to the cave tunnel to search for the Cat's Eye Stone that had spirited him to this world. The Animond spoke then, but as usual, Tailey couldn't understand him.

"He says that he has something in his pack that you might find interesting," Weenep translated. She had come up from behind Tailey to stand next to him, her tiny hands anchored firmly at her sides. A cool breeze ruffled any reddish-yellow fur that was not covered by her dark red halter-style top and matching loin cloth, as well as the black tufted hairs on the tips of her ears. Weenep's black, white-less eyes sparkled even without the aid of sunlight.

The Animond dug deeply into his backpack, and what he removed startled the whole group. Fitting easily in Yahmond Yah's palm was a slender, tubular object. One end of the black tube was tapered to a point, and a silverish ring was set into the blunt end. Another ring was similarly set about three quarters of the way toward the other point. The tube itself was about four inches long and smooth and free of any symbols or runes. The only decoration was a golden-brown stone set into the silver near the open end of the tube, which Weenep realized was a scabbard. "Wow! A mini tail-rapier!" she exclaimed.

"The Golden-Brown Cat's Eye Stone," Seeker breathed. The Kittoehee was obviously and happily shocked.

* * *

Cleary, the Pack Mother of the Waterway Pack, traveled back to the region they called home along the banks of the Clear Drink River. Her pack traveled behind her in silence as they crossed the Fubal Plain.

For the first time in her life, Cleary found herself unable to make an adequate choice to meet the circumstances of the problems presented to her. She could not in good faith order her pack into war against the Panthers or their allies, realizing that their ancestral enemies were no longer the light-stealing monsters they had seemed in the past. And yet, to join with them was utter treason against the Green Nation, and that was completely out of the question.

The combined powers of Luna's white-magic and the ruby-red magic of Yahmond Yah's sword had changed her own magic forever. Cleary needed time to reflect on the power that was continuing to grow inside her, and she refused to commit her pack to any side until she could sort the matters out completely.

There seemed to be many mysteries to sort out, and it would take time to find those answers, but Cleary was happy about her decision to send Slim to act as guardian and protector on the behalf of Luna. There was something special about the young Greenwolf, and Slim was second in her ranks only to Animal—who was most senior—his mind working as fast as his body.

Luna had insisted on helping the gray tomcat, Tailey, find his way home. There the hue-man girl, Megan, was in trouble from an evil figure he called the Nightman and needed his help. Yahmond Yah had joined the quest while noting that he felt a certain kinship with Luna. Cleary knew they had been through quite a lot in their last adventure, with Yahmond Yah saving Luna in the deep catacombs after she'd escaped the dark creature that had possessed the Den Mother of the Green Nation. In a way, she had saved him in return after the loss of his bride when they'd joined minds, healing his body, and setting his mind at ease.

Cleary could only hope that they could continue to protect each other in the days to come.

* * *

The scout Winter Bear rounded the base of the titanic oak that grew along the edges of the Forest of Nep and and the Clear Drink River. The trio of Onlooker Jib, Klawed, and Nep had little time to brace themselves against the attack. Klawed launched himself in front of the Animond, knowing that his friend was not a warrior.

Klawed's tail-rapier leapt from its sheath, the thin blade swaying like a cobra above his head, ready to strike. The Winter Bear rose on its hind legs, making even the seven-foot Animond look small in comparison. Klawed felt the heat on the back of his neck from Nep's light magic as it condensed between his small, lifted hands.

Klawed ducked under the first swing of the Winter Bear's attack, its scimitar-shaped claws raking the air above Klawed's head and barely missing Nep's face. Klawed was not new to this world of combat though and countered-jabbed his tail-rapier at the Winter Bear's throat. The Winter Bear slapped it away with ease with the return stroke of its huge paw. Klawed used the momentum of the slap to launch his tail-rapier into a series of slashes, marking the Winter Bear's chest with a bloody "X."

Nep was having trouble summoning the light through the heavy cloud cover, and the balls that he did manage to send at the Winter Bear were meager at best. Nep concentrated them on the Winter Bear's beady black eyes and head, hoping to blind it at least temporarily and give Klawed the opportunity to destroy the beast. But if the light-magic had any effect on the Winter Bear, it did not show.

The combatants circled each other, striking at every opportunity. Blood flew in all directions as the maneuvering became more intense. Even Nep had superficial gashes across his chest and down one leg.

Klawed caught sight of Onlooker Jib out of the corner of his eye. The Animond stood close to the giant oak. Klawed could easily see the inner turmoil that washed through his eyes as he found himself torn between his Oath of Peace and his desire to help his friends.

"Jib!" Klawed's mind-voice shouted. "Warn Gustar!"

The slight distraction was all the Winter Bear needed. The Winter Bear rose to stand on its hind legs once again, but this time, it added an unexpected twist and swung at the two in full force as it rose. The hit missed Klawed entirely, but Nep caught the bulk of it, ripped from his securing traps and flung against a nearby tree, where his lifeless body slid down and settled motionless on the ground.

Klawed turned and charged to his friend's side. His nostrils could smell death as he approached his fallen, life-long companion. "Come on, Nep. Wake up. We have so much more to do, you and I." Tears stung his golden eyes as he turned back on the Winter Bear, stomping toward them, still up on its hind legs.

Rage enveloped Klawed's soul—a rage that reached deep into the very fabric of his being. Klawed drove his tail-rapier into the ground, releasing it and abandoning it there. Klawed was no longer himself. The spirit of the feline rose through his crouched body. His long black tail stretched flat behind his body with its tip snapping back and forth to the cadence of his rage. His ears laid back flat on his head, and his lips pulled back to display his fangs and teeth. A primordial roar escaped his throat as he launched himself at the Winter Bear. It was not the battle cry of a soldier but the sort of roar that defined the most primal parts of feline nature. Ferocious. Ruthless. Wild.

At the same time, the Winter Bear slammed both front paws down towards the Panther, intent on crushing him. The two met then in mortal combat. Klawed's jaws locked onto the Winter Bear's throat, his claws shredding the chest and abdomen of his adversary.

The full weight of the Winter Bear fell on Klawed, who could taste his enemy's blood in his mouth, even as he heard his own bones cracking as he was slammed to the ground. Consciousness left him.

Chapter 23

WHISPERS IN THE WIND

Caser opened his eyes as he raised his head off the cushion and looked about the small room. The walls were pale-yellow stone, and across the room, a white curtain blocked off what Caser assumed to be a passageway. The wall opposite the entrance had a square opening, which allowed pale-blue rays of light to brighten the room. The four walls were not smooth; each of them had images of cats etched into the stone, caught mid-action in various poses. The room had several beds lining two of the walls—one of which he was currently occupying—with cloth mattresses stuffed with grasses set on stone blocks.

On the bed closest to the white curtain lounged a small creature with grayish-brown fur covering its back and limbs of his body, and black hairs that tufted its pointed ears. The Neptunian wore a white tunic with a white cloth belt around its waist. Caser had heard stories of the Neptunians who rode on the backs of the Panthers but had not actually seen one until now.

B'loris rested on the bed next to his. She appeared whole and intact, apart from the white bandage wrapped around the base of her stinger, yet she appeared slimmer, weaker, and very frail. Caser tried to rouse her with his mind-voice but failed to penetrate the depths of her slumber.

"She was on the edge of death, like yourself, when they brought you both in from the mountains," the Neptunian said. "She just about tore her stinger out when she removed it from your backside.

Caser examined himself and found the bandage near his tail.

"Starvation is the biggest threat to her health. We pumped her full of honimilk, which is the closest thing we have to nectar. Now, it is only a matter of time." He looked at her for a moment. "If she is strong, she will have a chance, but . . ." The Neptunian let his voice trail off, his small hands open and his arms spread wide on either side of his body.

Caser understood the gesture all too well. "Where are we?"

"You're in one of the secondary infirmaries in Shadow City, the Kingdom of the Panthers," the Neptunian replied. "I am called Mendion. I work as a healer."

The Neptunian hurried from the room, and Caser dropped his head back down onto the cushion, feeling drained of strength. He knew he needed to hunt but could not imagine accomplishing even the simple feat of standing.

Back through the curtain, the Neptunian returned with two bowls and placed them near Caser's head. Caser lifted his head to examine the contents. The larger of the two contained a white milky fluid, and the other had small chunks of meat that did not look or smell quite right.

"I suspect plains people aren't familiar with cooked food or honimilk. I think you'll find both will agree with your stomach," Mendion said, as he turned back toward the curtain to leave. "But eat slowly as you haven't had solid food for at least a couple of days."

Caser fished out a couple of chunks of meat with his tongue and slowly chewed as his mind wondered. *A couple of days?* Everything seemed kind of fuzzy, and he found that he couldn't quite remember how he had come to be in this place.

Caser finished his meal and lapped up the white-milky fluid Mendion had called honimilk. The drink tasted far better than water. It had a smooth, creamy texture, which a flavor much like the nectar B'loris had coaxed him into trying back on the plains. Caser felt strength slowly seeping back into his body, but he knew that he would not be back to his old self for a while longer.

The curtain parted abruptly, and a Panther with a white star on his forehead passed through it into the room.

"Welcome to my kingdom," the Panther said. "You'll forgive us for not receiving you in a more formal environment, but war is upon the kingdom and time has been limited for ceremonies."

"Okay, sure," Caser said, at a loss for words.

"Let me introduce myself," the Panther said. "I am Gustar, King of the Panthers."

Caser tried to raise his body.

"Please, there is no need for formalities," Gustar said, stopping him. "You need rest, Cheetah. I am glad that you have survived—"

"Excuse me, Your Highness," Caser interrupted. "I am Caser, son of Sprint and Sway, of the Windswept Clan. My friend here," Caser indicated with a nod in the Beesives direction, "is B'loris, worker Beesive of the hive of the Eastern Queendom."

"Thank you, Caser," B'loris said, as she climbed to her feet. "But I can speak for myself."

Caser, without thought, was up and at her side with a flood of questions about her health and what he might be able to do to improve her condition. The king's presence was all but forgotten in his wave of emotion.

"Ah, Caser … the king," B'loris said, directing Casers' attention back toward Gustar, who stood patiently watching their reunion.

"What brings you good people of the Plains of Che this far north?" Gustar asked.

Caser started the narration—his memory returning as the story enfolded—and brought the king up to the point where the siren call had lured him into the mountains. B'loris picked up the story from that point, as that was where Caser's memory failed him. Caser and Gustar sat in awe over the description of their fight for freedom from the monster that had accosted them.

"I have no knowledge of this monster," Gustar said, after giving the matter some thought. "But I will encourage you both to rest and regain your strength here in our home. There are tasks that must be accomplished. Tasks upon which our survival relies, feline and Beesive alike."

* * *

Yana, the new queen of the TIG, returned to the fiery passages below the Triplets with her TIG-Horde and TIG-Workers in tow. The ebony sword she held before her guided her every step toward what she was determined would be the end of those pitiful Animond.

Above Yana's head, the city that had once been the home she loved so well—the home of her family and the memories of a people saved from the clutches of evil many worlds away—slumbered in the dark of night. Beneath the sleeping gentle giants, a branch of the evil that had threatened their existence so many cycles before sought once again to destroy them.

The cavern where Yana the TIG-Queen stood was enormous. The walls and ceiling were jagged, with no certain pattern or shape. A crater of boiling magma filled the center of the cavern, and around it, the TIG-Workers were stationed at even intervals. The black onyx crystals at the tops of their staffs glistened with the red glow of molten stone and the igniting flames from the gases that escaped into the air. Standing behind the TIG-Workers, the TIG-Horde stood like muted derelicts without direction.

Yana studied the ebony blade. It told her of the war being waged, and of Ichneumon, the puny creature she would soon get to crush. The Possessor of Souls was truly evil, but she would not share her black throne with anything or anyone.

"Look about you, Yana," the ebony sword whispered into her mind. *"The TIG are no longer what they once were. Only you can make that claim to the power. With every cycle, the TIG grow weaker. Look, Yana, at the helpless sheep that once were powerful enough to stand beside you as your servants. The old queen forgot her own direction; she forgot her goal of ruling the whole of Katlyn and beyond. Instead, the old queen settled on ruling the underworld ... until you came and cast her aside.*

"Command me, My Queen! Would you have the pitiful TIG-Horde punished for failing you? Would you have the Animond destroyed? Would you rebuild the TIG to its former glory? Command me, My Queen, and it shall be done!

The bride of Yahmond Yah sought to regain control of herself. Yana saw the horrors the ebony sword was compelling her to do. She could not destroy her home, family, and friends, or reject the Oath of Peace she had been preparing to swear to on the day of her marriage to Yahmond Yah. Together, they would have shared their lives and love with the world and all that dwelled therein.

Yana could feel the presence of Yahmond Yah not far away. Her mind reached for him, needing his strength to rid herself of the compulsion of the evil sword, and for a moment, their hearts and mind joined. A fiery red magic flowed into her, combining with her soul. With all her might, Yana tried to cast the dark blade into the magma pit, but it would not be undone so easily and laughed at her efforts.

The darkness once again drove Yana's spirit deep into the recesses of her body, but as she fell into herself, she sent a message of love through the remaining strands of crimson magic to Yahmond Yah: "Let me go … or the darkness will destroy you!"

Slowly, Yahmond Yah's magic faded back into the void of the distance between them, and the dark side of Yana's new persona—the side made up of greed, lust, hatred, and fear—took control of her body once more as she held the ebony blade lovingly to her chest. The evil magic that made-up the sword's being reached into Yana, compelling her to use its powers.

Blackness radiated out to the TIG-Horde. The TIG-Horde had failed her in the capture of Yahmond Yah and the young Greenwolf pup in the ancient Animond city. This TIG-Horde would never fail her again.

The TIG-Workers began their demonic chanting around the magma pit, holding their staffs out towards it. The power within their staffs' black onyx crystals burst forth, collecting in a glowing sphere that hovered above the center of the bubbling liquid stone. The sphere of evil acted as a magnet and beckoned the TIG-Horde toward the magma pit. Blindly, the TIG-Horde walked to the edge and beyond, dropping to their deaths without question or reason.

Yana worked the sword through the air about her like a witch's wand directing the incarnations of an ugly spell, her lips forming words without making a sound. Then a blood-curdling scream burst from Yana's throat as the last of the TIG-Horde plunged into the magma. Black waves of evil followed the termination of the TIG-Horde's descent into the molten magma, causing the magma to erupt from its birthplace.

As the chamber began to fill with the blazing, flowing rock, the TIG-Queen and her workers retreated quickly back into the dark underworld. Above them, the Animond slept on, blissfully unaware of the molten lava that was slowly rising to steal from them . . . everything that they were.

* * *

The giant trees that had once formed a canopy over Scanterville burned silently under the dark clouds that blotted out the afternoon sun. A few trees remained untouched, but that would change once the north wind swept out of the Low Jaw Mountains with the coming of night. Bones of dead Scantians littered the ground. The tide of Nightwolves had stopped to feast on its victims . . . and even on any of their own who had fallen as the Scantians fought for their lives.

Scattered among the bones were a few swords, daggers, and knives, as well as other implements that had been used in place of real weapons. The Scantians were poorly equipped for battle on any scale. The attack of the Greenwolves appeared to have been swift, sudden, and merciless.

Dill Tuck made his way silently through what was left of Scanterville. His heart was laden with grief as he approached the stand of ash trees that had been home to his in-laws. Dealy's family had put up a good fight, and he found the bones of many Nightwolves as testimony to their valiant efforts, but in the end, all had been lost.

Sorting through the bones, Dill looked for evidence he dreaded to find, though he knew where to look. There among those who had chosen to fight for their lives, Dill found the silver broach that had belonged to his mother . . . which he had given to his wife.

Dill sat next to Dealy's remains. He let his fingers trace the edge of the silver maple leaf he grasped tightly in his left hand. Thunder rumbled through the fibers of his heart, and lightning flashed around the icy-blue centers of his eyes, leaving red streaks that channeled the tears flowing from the building rage deep in his soul.

Memories of the life they had shared flashed through his mind. They had been born on the same day of the same cycle, seeming destined from birth to be together. The family ties between the Tucks and the Dews reached far back to their old world where they'd had neighboring farms. Even though the Tucks had refused to abandon their old ways and become one with the forest, the families had always remained close.

Dealy was kind and loving, yet strong of mind and body. She had not deserved this end.

"How can I go on without her?" Dill asked the smoky air around him. "Revenge?"

The answer came from one of the roots of the family's ash tree, which reached up from the soil and gently laid itself across his shoulders in an embrace. Dill listened quietly to the wisdom of the ash tree, which was soon joined by that of the rest of the forest, passed along from one root to another until it could reach the lone Scantian. Silently taking it all in, Dill returned the ash tree's embrace as grief flowed from the wound in his heart. He watched quietly, as all around the place once known as Scanterville, the roots of even those trees destroyed above ground by the fires of violence, reached from the dirt and sorted through the remains of the fallen, retrieving their servants and gathering them down into the soil, leaving the bones of the Nightwolves to the elements.

In the eerie hush that followed, Dill found a way to continue with his own life, watching as part of the ash tree root began to reform itself into a longbow and then detach itself from the rest, dropping into Dill's hand. The bow was as tall as himself and flawless. Its fibrous string had also come from the root, but Dill found it smooth and flexible as he tested its draw. Dill could feel the life-force of the tree in his hands.

A nearby maple offered up from itself a wooden quiver, which he swung over his shoulder. As Dill marched out of Scanterville, the remaining trees dropped arrows with wooden feathers and broad heads from their limbs, which he gathered as he passed by. The living quiver expanded to accommodate each shaft and hold them safe.

Dill would not become a victim to vengeance or hatred. No. Dill Tuck would now be a champion of the Nep Forest, but more importantly, a champion of the maker. He would do his best to return peace to his homeland, even knowing that peace always comes with a price.

The wind out of the north spread the embers and flames through the remaining trees. Dill felt their silent screams of pain as they passed from the world of Katlyn.

Chapter 24

VISIONS

The wings of darkness took rest on a perch high in the Mangy Mountains. It would observe the gray tomcat, learn its weaknesses, and strike at just the right moment. "We must be closer, yes. We must. So, all of us can feel when to possess those who would be the object of our defeat."

* * *

Every day, the hunting grew poorer. The Nightwolves had killed or driven off the bulk of the larger beasts populating the mountains. The lack of food compiled with the countless hours of travel, which the group was pushing themselves to achieve, left Tailey tired to the bone. But when they did finally stop to sleep, rest would allude him, thus denying Tailey any quarter from his suffering.

During their rest periods, Weenep, Falsity, Truth, and the other Neps helped Tailey learn to use the tail-rapier that Yahmond Yah had fashioned. It took many days of constant exercise to build Tailey's tail muscles enough that they could expand inside the hilt and hold the blade tightly enough to remove it from its sheath. But now he could draw and use the weapon, even though he felt very clumsy and awkward with it on.

Tailey lay near the Panther sisters, Falsity and Truth, drawing in warmth from their larger bodies. Tailey had placed the small tail-rapier close to his head in such a way that he could gaze into the depths of the Cat's Eye Stone that had been set into the hilt. Just as he had done every night since the stone had come back into his possession, Tailey searched for a way to unlock its powers to send him home to the land of the yellow sun, and to his Megan.

The Kittoehee could not provide much help. Seeker could only say that the stones acted for their own secret ends. But this only brought more questions to Tailey's mind. Why would a stone, or the magic that dwelt therein, choose to bring a cat with so little to offer to a world in such desperate need of help? What could he do that would bring an end to Ichneumon or the TIG dwelling deep under the face of Katlyn? *Could this all be a dream after all? Will I wake and find myself at the foot of Megan's bed?* Many thoughts flowed through Tailey's mind.

Tailey knew in his heart that he was not in some dreamworld.

He felt slumber over taking his body. To his amazement, the Cat's Eye Stone began to pulse as it had back in the tree stump. Tailey wanted to call out to the others but found he was unable.

The powers of the stone once again controlled Tailey as he faded into darkness.

* * *

Neptunian fireballs streaked across the sky in an arch and crashed into the swarm of enemies that raced across the charred clearing that had once been Neptown. The air weighed heavy with smoke from the once proud trees of the forest now lying like fallen soldiers in the aftermath of conflict. Many other bodies lay with them, feline, canine, and bruin, torn to pieces under the paws of those who sought victory over the others. The battle was still young, Gustar knew, and to hope for a simple close to the bloodshed was futile.

General Rammino's east wing had met the bulk of the Greenwolves at the edge of the Nep Forest and had done well to slow their approach to Neptown, but in the end, the overwhelming numbers of Greenwolves had driven the east-wing forces back to the forest and eventually to Neptown, where the Panthers had combined with General Bulldory and the main body of the Panther Army.

The Greenwolves stopped their attack long enough for the Black Nation to join them from their conquest of Scanterville, and the Winter Bears from their decimation of the Cougars of the Fubal Highlands. Now the three forces charged headlong into battle with the Neps and the Panthers as the few remaining Scantians raced among the trees, giving what comfort they could to the trees they could not save. The remaining Scantians tried to extinguish the flames that were consuming the trees, many of them dying in their efforts.

Together, thousands of tail-rapiers waited for the countless horde that plunged through the flames and smoke toward the end of all that was good in a world that could have been a paradise.

Tears stung Gustar's eyes as he removed his father's rapier from its sheath. Gustar did not cry for his troops, nor for himself, but for Katlyn and the innocence of those who had been driven mad.

* * *

Liliana, Gustar's sister, led the young and the old Panthers out through the secret passages of Shadow, which opened into the Fubal Mountains.

"Shadow will fall if a single Panther remains within," Gustar had said to Liliana before he left to confront the enemy. "When our retreat brings us to the gates of Shadow, it will be our last stand."

"Our warriors are strong," Liliana argued. "What if—"

"Yes! We are strong, but our numbers cannot compare to those who oppose us." Gustar hesitated a moment. "Without the magical aid of the Kittoehee, we cannot hope to stand against the forces converging on the Nep Forest."

General Bulldory ordered one hundred of the regular army, with Major Vinicunca and Princess Liliana, to lead the way for the civilians to escape. Liliana felt the weight of her station. The white star on her brow felt unbearably heavy as they left the black passages for the mountains beyond.

For the first time in her life, she regretted being the daughter of a king. From birth, Liliana had been shielded from the duties of her station by

Gustar. He was the leader of their people, and his son would follow him. But Gustar had never wed and had no offspring to take his place.

* * *

B'loris held fast to Caser's coat as he bolted down the river valley of Fe'line toward the Green Divide and the Plains of Che, beyond the atmospheric disruption. B'loris knew they would soon part ways to give warning to their separate peoples of the menace that would soon invade from the north.

They would part company at the stone bridge that spanned the Long Drink River. There, B'loris would continue to the Western Hive and then back to her home queendom in the east, while Caser would travel to his people. There he would spread the warning of Ichneumon, the Possessor of Souls, and request any aid they could muster for the coming war. But in private, Caser and B'loris had agreed that whatever aid could be sent would almost certainly be too little and too late.

* * *

Seeker waited in the darkness. Sleep for the Kittoehee had been brief but long enough for his dreams to link with Mythos and reveal events that would take place this night. Mythos, the gray magic that dwelt between life and death, had no conscience. Mythos was simply the past, present, the future—what was and what might have been. Truth and lies rolled into a ball of light and darkness known as the universe.

The Kittoehee called quietly on his own magic, and with it, he formed a veil of sleep, which drifted down over the sisters Truth and Falsity like morning dew. *The sisters have no part in tonight's events* Seeker thought to himself. *Sleep will keep them safe and out of the way.*

The Kittoehee lay there quietly, his mood darkening as he waited for the chain of events to begin: a countdown to what might be his own demise and an end to the known world of Katlyn. It was in Seeker's heart to wake his traveling friends and flee from the forming terrors that were readying to accost Katlyn, but flee too where? Evils as great as Ichneumon and the TIG were impossible to hide from for long, and of course, his station as the Kittoehee—a companion of the light—would not allow him to turn his back on what he believed to be right or good for Katlyn.

Seeker knew in his heart that Gustar was not faring well against the combined effort of the Winter Bears, Black Nation, and Green Nation. No dreams came to him to tell of the Panther's, Neptunian's, and Scantian's folly, but the smoke from the burning forest hung like a death shroud over the land. Seeker refused to dwell on the matter. He knew that his magic would not make any significant difference in the outcome of that battle if he were there. What could make a difference would be finding the mother of the Cat's Eye Stones, if he could only do so, or perhaps even the magic of the Northern Beesives. The gray magic had given him clues that were now leading him to the Triplet Mountains and the Gray Cat's Eye Stone. But now Seeker knew that this avenue would soon be closed to him in a way still unclear at this point.

The wings of despair had flown toward his soul when another avenue was opened to him. Mythos had showed him images of a lake, the surface of which was smooth and shimmered like glass, with lights dancing over its surface. In the background of the lake stood a tree the size of a mountain, its base reaching halfway around the lake. Seeker was sure this was home of the Northern Beesives, but the only clue to its location in the vision was Tailey, standing on the lakeshore.

Suddenly, Seeker noticed the Golden-Brown Cat's Eye Stone set in the hilt of Tailey's tail-rapier begin to pulse, its magic forming a clear chamber around Tailey and lifting him into the air before spiriting him off toward the Mangy Mountains in the north. Seeker studied its path closely, knowing he would soon have to follow, but other events needed to occur before he could continue his quest.

The silence in the small camp was absolute, as though all the elements of the night were taking a holiday. Even the insects were eerily still. Seeker absorbed the quiet surroundings, savoring them like the company of old friends. This was the way of his world. Although there had been times in his life when Seeker would have enjoyed being a part of the normal world, his station as the Kittoehee required his complete concentration. Seeker had put those common desires—those cravings—behind him long ago, in his early youth. Silence was no longer a requirement. It had instead become his friend, lover, and comfortable companion.

Seeker studied the resting travelers. Falsity and Truth, always separate yet together, lay head-to-tail, forming a dark circle. Their Neps were nestled in the warm center of the sisters' bodies.

The tightly wound Slim had decided to rest but only after Seeker had reassured him that his magic would warn them of any danger. Luna, the would-be Den Mother, nestled close to him and Yahmond Yah.

A wash of sadness came over Seeker as he studied the Animond. Yahmond Yah's life was about to change again. Yahmond had been through so much, with his escape from the TIG and the loss of his bride, but he had awakened the red-magic powers that dwelt in the ruby sword, which meant two things: a great evil was alive among the Animond once more; and with blood on his hands, Yahmond would never be able to recite the Animond's Oath of Peace, which was the heart of Animond culture here on Katlyn. Yahmond Yah and his people did not deserve what fate had in store for them, but Seeker knew that, with all the magic in the world, he could do nothing to change the course of destiny. There were times when Seeker hated having brief visions of the future, and this was one of them.

The chain of events he had been waiting for began simply, with Yahmond Yah rustling in his sleep. All too soon, the rustling turned to violent thrashing as he screamed Yana's name over and over.

"You cannot help him," Seeker said to Luna and Slim. They had been awakened by the turmoil. "For now."

Yahmond Yah struggled with his dream for some time, his arms and legs flailing in the darkness as he rolled and tossed himself about the camp, Agony gripped his body as he fought unseen demons that reached for him through the black soil.

Finally, Yahmond Yah found the strength to break away from the invisible fingers that gripped his soul and lunged to his feet. In the same motion, the ruby sword appeared in the grip of Yahmond Yah's powerful hands. Crimson lightning leapt from the ruby crystal as Yahmond Yah stabbed the blade at the evil clouds hanging ominously overhead.

A scream of a thousand deaths escaped from the throat of Yahmond Yah as he inverted his grip on the sword and drove it deep into the soil between his feet, steam erupting from the heated soil and rising into the air. The entire area glowed crimson as the magic traveled toward the bowels of Katlyn. The Animond held fast to the sword hilt as he willed its magic into battle with the darkness.

Seeker watched the hopeless struggle before him. There was no aid he could offer to the Animond. Guilt mixed with helplessness attacked his tired soul.

Patience fool, Seeker thought to himself. *Your time to strike back will come all too soon.*

Time stood still for what seemed forever. Suddenly, Yahmond Yah could no longer sustain his driving force behind the red magic of the ruby sword. The magic that dwelled under the soil surged toward the surface, causing a backlash of the red magic towards its wielder. The bulk of the blast tossed both ruby sword and its bearer many feet from the others. Yahmond Yah lay motionless in the gloomy aftermath.

Luna and Slim rushed to his side.

Falsity and Truth remained asleep.

Seeker had held the same position throughout the night. The Kittoehee could sense through his magic that Yahmond Yah was physically sound. Instead, the Kittoehee focused his attention on the three mountain peaks known as the Triplets, home of Genus, the Animond city. Seeker did not have to wait long for the final links in the chain of events that would set his own path in motion.

One after the other, the tops of the Triplets exploded, and fire and brimstone flowed from every crack and fissure. Fire and ash filled the air and rained down on the land. Evil rode the fiery stallion, destroying everything in its path. Seeker could hear the laughter of evil amongst the roaring of the volcanoes.

Abruptly, Yahmond Yah surged to his feet. Complete horror was painted on his face as he bolted off into the night with the ruby sword still clenched in his fists.

Luna and Slim dashed after the Animond. Seeker bid them a silent farewell. He knew he would not be seeing them again.

* * *

Having said her goodbyes, B'loris let go of the back of Caser's neck and caught the wind under her wings. Up she went, and as she gained a little altitude, it helped to bring the whole landscape of the lower Crescent Lake area into view. Flowers lined the waterways and the stone bridge that spanned the Long Drink River.

B'loris hovered long enough to watch her friend bolt across the stone bridge, into the flowers, and out of sight. The Beesive still could not help but be awed by the cat's absolute power. The long powerful strides of the Cheetah were always a remarkable sight. Then she turned west and started her climb to reach the lower jet-streams.

As B'loris made her ascent, she passed over Pussywillow Down. She could see the herd beasts that produced the milk that would be combined with honey from the Beesive Queendoms to make the Honimilk blend.

It was dangerous to travel these rivers in the sky, with their wind shears that could drive you straight down, out of control. These winds could happen anywhere but were most common by the mountain and over open water. Beesives with a full load of nectar and wax had no reason to be this high up.

As B'loris reached the swift currents in the air, it was only a matter of reading their direction, then riding them towards the Mighty Drink Sea to the Western Queendom of the Beesives, far faster than she could travel without them. She did not even have to beat her wings to make the coastline by nightfall.

Chapter 25

MIRROR - LOOK INTO MY EYES

The full rush of the melee swarmed about Gustar. Tail-rapiers sang their death songs as they whistled through the air toward their intended victims. The first wave of attackers were canines. The endless line of Greenwolves and Nightwolves crashed head-on with the rapiers, claws, and fangs of the waiting Panther Army and its Neptunian riders.

There was no retreat. The first wave perished as the second wave renewed the assault. The second wave was at least twice the size of the first. Some of the giant Winter Bears were mixed into the swarm of Greenwolves and Nightwolves, and several of them were converging on Gustar's position. The king slashed the last Nightwolf before him, bringing him down, then braced himself to meet the Winter Bears, approaching up on their hind legs.

As the space between the bears and Gustar closed, First Paw Paxie Jax and four others from the Elite Guard filled the void. Outsized and outnumbered, the Elite Guard plunged into battle with the fierce savagery that set the king's guard apart from all others. The Winter Bears would have plenty to deal with before they could hope to kill the Panther King.

There was little time to dwell on the Winter Bears with the Greenwolves closing in from the sides. Gustar met the Greenwolves, demonstrating the true nature of his birthright to the throne. He had been trained not only in the art of leadership. Gustar was also proficient in the use of tail-rapier, tooth, and claw—quick and with deadly precision.

Gustar was a hunter-warrior, and a true king, but even the greatest soldier can fall to the unseen. Behind the king, one of the Winter Bears had slipped through the Elite Guard and was seconds away from delivering a crushing blow to Gustar's head.

The king turned in time to see the giant paw falling toward him, but to his amazement, the Winter Bear froze mid-swing and fell to the ground dead. A long wooden shaft had pierced its brain.

* * *

The ash bow was alive. It would allow Dill Tuck to fully draw an arrow with ease, and upon releasing it, the bow would propel the arrow with such force that it could go through several enemy assailants before stopping. Dill was careful when choosing his targets.

Through the burning trees and thick smoke, Dill Tuck watched the battle of Neptown unfold. He had trailed the Nightwolves and the Winter Bears through the Nep Forest.

The trees had charged him with the mission of finding and destroying the hosts of Ichneumon, the Possessor of Souls, thus putting an end to its evil influence and attempted conquest of the world of Katlyn. Its hosts were not easily found amongst the ever-shifting thousands in the melee, compelled by forces of both darkness and the light.

Dill Tuck was not an expert soldier, and his skill at eluding detection left a lot to be desired. If not for his family's sword, his jacket of crysteel chain mail, and lightning reflexes, he would have been dead long before now.

A gust of wind cleared the smoke from the center of the melee, and in that path, three characters stood out from the rest. A Winter Bear, a Nightwolf, and a female Greenwolf stood together, looking around as if examining the battle scene and strategizing amongst themselves.

These must be the hosts, Dill Tuck thought to himself, *the leaders, driving their forces to attack.*

An arrow was notched and drawn in one swift motion. Dill Tuck had hoped to get the hosts in line like this for one clean shot, but the events on the battle ground changed so rapidly that he knew he must shoot now or lose his chance altogether.

In the heat of the moment, Dill Tuck misjudged his range. The shaft flew high of the target. As the smoke closed his window of opportunity, Dill Tuck watched the arrow impale the head of a Winter Bear near the front lines.

Better than missing the enemy completely, I guess, Dill thought as he headed to a new location, hoping to gain a better angle on the hosts.

* * *

The air smelled sweet and fresh and carried a slight chill. A gentle rustling of a million leaves dominated all other sounds that might have been present. The sand under Tailey's belly was warm and comfortable.

Tailey knew he should open his eyes and meet whatever circumstances the Cat's Eye Stone had delivered him to, but he felt so good just relaxing in the bliss of ignorance. He knew from the very feel of the ground that he had not arrived back to his home under the yellow sun and didn't care to wake in any other place.

In the scheme of things, though, curiosity always soured the milk. Tailey found that he could no longer resist the building urge to open his eyes. Snapping them wide open proved to be a mistake though. The pale-blue of the sun stung Tailey's eyes, having been out of direct sunlight for so long, and he rubbed them with the backs of his paws. Then he slowly tested the light, giving himself time to adjust to its brilliance.

During this adjustment period, Tailey used his tail to explore the contents of his tail-rapier's sheath. The blade was secure in its place. He could feel the rounded surface of the Golden-Brown Cat's Eye Stone still set in the hilt. Tailey felt relieved. The stone was his one and only known avenue to return to Megan.

When he was able to finally look around, Tailey found himself alone under a mid-morning sun. The eastern sky harbored no sign of clouds, but where the late-afternoon sky began, the black demon-cloud from Fire Bane drifted ominously. Smoke from the burning forest rolled forth beneath the demon-cloud, rising into the clear blue sky in flowing wisps. Tailey found the display beautiful.

Evil, with a pretty face, he thought.

"Evil is what dwells below the surface," Weenep said, in a matter-of-fact way.

"Weenep!" Tailey snapped his head around to find Weenep flashing him a toothy grin. "You ... you're here!"

"I managed to strap myself back in the saddle before the stone could spirit you away," Weenep said, sounding pleased with her accomplishment.

"What of the others?" he asked.

Weenep had no answer for Tailey, as the Cat's Eye Stone's sleep spell had caught her as well. She could only shrug her shoulders without comment. Her lack of knowledge made Tailey nervous; she always had an answer to everything.

Tailey put his questions aside and began to survey their surroundings. They were in a deep, round, crater-like valley, its walls covered with grass and small shrubs. Jagged rocks reached through the vegetation in places like fingers clawing at the sky.

A couple of feet past the sand where Tailey stood lay a surface as smooth as glass, covering most of the valley floor. Somehow, the surface did not reflect the sunlight's glare but captured only images of the surrounding valley instead.

It was in that reflection that Weenep realized that what they had mistaken for part of the valley wall was actually a tree—a mountain-sized tree! Its exposed roots encompassed half the edge of the shiny surface. The two amazed travelers gazed up at the tree's upper limbs in awe of its grandeur.

"Don't even bother asking, Tailey," Weenep said, ahead of the tomcat's thoughts. "I've never seen or heard of this place." Weenep paused then added, "But isn't it incredible?"

"Indeed," Tailey had to agree. Then Tailey turned his attention back to the reflective surface, wondering at its seeming ability to reflect some things and not others. He approached it with caution and sniffed the area closest to the sand.

"Water!" Tailey was surprised and confused all at once.

"Water?" Weenep's eyes widened. "It can't be. . ."

Weenep released the safety straps from her harness and was quickly beside Tailey on all fours, sniffing the surface and nodding her head in agreement. "Should be water, all right."

They gazed at their own images for some time. Before long, they found themselves taking turns at striking poses and mimicking other beings that they knew, letting go the frustrations and tension that had been building over the course of their long travels and the endless search for solutions.

Tailey puffed out his chest and strutted stiff-legged before the water. "I am Super Cat! Blah!"

Weenep fell over, completely losing control of herself. Her hoots and chirps echoed across the valley. Tailey was suddenly reminded of Klawed and Nep and their love for situations like this. Tailey found himself wishing they were here with them to enjoy this moment. He could not help but wonder where they were and when—if ever—he would see them again.

Tailey's attention returned to the mirror-like water. Gently, he nudged the surface with his muzzle, then carefully drank from the shiny plate. He had expected the water to taste stale from its apparent lack of motion, but instead, he found the liquid icy cold and overwhelmingly refreshing. What bothered Tailey was that no matter how much he disturbed the lake, no waves or ripples blemished its surface.

For the remainder of the day, Tailey and Weenep foraged for food and explored the valley. There had to be a reason the Cat's Eye Stone had brought them here, but what that reason might be did not appear obvious in any form or fashion.

Up to this point, Tailey had relied on the other cats to provide food, but he would have to rely on his own wits and resources here. There was always smaller game available, overlooked by the big cats with their enormous appetites, but it could feed him easily. Tailey knew that, somewhere in his past, he had been taught the fine art of the hunt—though who those teachers had been and where he'd received his lessons were now a mental blur. He could still recall his failed hunt for the mouse in the hollow log, though, which had ended in the tree stump, marking the beginning of his journey from his world under the yellow sun to Katlyn.

Weenep scurried to a small shelf on one of the stone fingers. Snacking on some roots, she watched Tailey intently as he crept through the grass and bushes in search of game. Before long, Tailey happened onto the scent of a small rodent, which Weenep would later inform him was called a meek.

Tailey began the instinctive and mechanical feline stalk, following its scent through the grass until he got a visual of the small creature. It was sitting still in the tall grass. The meek was larger than the mouse of his previous hunt. It had long shaggy brown hair covering its entire body except for its round pink ears, which lay tight to its head, and its nose, which was flat on the end instead of rounded like that of a mouse. All these characteristics meant only one thing to Tailey: food.

As Tailey loaded his body to spring, the meek darted out of range, long before Tailey could act. The meek stopped under a bush then, his back to the cat, who once more slowly closed the gap to attempt another lunge. Tailey found it strange that the meek did not appear to have acted from fear or show any real sign that it realized danger was near. This ignited Tailey's temper, as a threat does not like to be ignored.

His hunter's mind started checking off a list as he started his attack:

Coiled to spring? . . . Check.

Target in range? . . . Check.

Launch? . . . Check.

Altitude good? . . . Check.

Airspeed good? . . . Check.

Claws extended? . . . Check.

Jaws in position? . . . Check.

Impact with target? . . . Imminent!

A thought occurred to him then: *This is when something would go wrong.*

And, of course, something did. Tailey's calculations would have been perfect were it not for the spike that rose from his helmet, which pierced the limb of the bush under which he'd attempted to launch himself. Of course, the bush was hardy and strong. Tailey found himself fighting to free his head instead of capturing the meek for dinner. He watched as his meal made a leisurely escape into its burrow at the base of the bush.

Weenep fell from her perch, hysterical from laughter. Tailey's pride, although shattered, refused to acknowledge Weenep's enjoyment of his failure. Instead, he resumed his hunt, now choosing insects as his prey. The hopping bugs that dwelt in the tall grass were easier to catch but were somewhat lacking in taste. Anything was better than nothing though, and the bugs did fill the empty void in his stomach.

Weenep had regained her composure by the time Tailey finished his bug supper and joined him for a snooze in a thick patch of soft grass near the giant tree root on the west side of the lake.

The moon was just a sliver, hanging high in the night sky. Rays of light in the eastern skyline told of the coming of morning. Though stars could still be seen, Tailey noticed a puffy cloud drifting on the upper air currents, the approaching dawn tracing its bottom in violet. It seemed odd to Tailey to see the stars after being for so long under the evil canopy of the demon-cloud from Fire Bane, the once-dormant volcano in the Low Jaw Mountains.

Weenep awoke, and together, they walked to the edge of the lake for a drink. The icy water drove off any sleep that might have lingered in their bodies.

Tailey and Weenep sat in the sand then and discussed the light show on display high above their heads.

Suddenly, their attention was drawn down to the lake. There, skimming just above the surface, were thousands of small yellow lights, flying in intricate patterns across the lake's entire surface.

"I can't be sure, Tailey," Weenep said with soft mind-voice, "but I believe those lights are the Northern Beesives."

Tailey and Weenep were completely amazed. The small lights stayed yellow at first, their pattern confined to horizontal sweeps. Time stood still for the observers as the lights began to blink in every color imaginable. The pattern was abandoned then, and the lights danced outward in every direction, then looped back toward the center of the lake.

Tailey felt compelled to draw his tail-rapier, for reasons that eluded him. Still, he held the rapier poised over his head, its tip pointed skyward. With a quick glance up, Tailey saw that the gold-brown Cat's Eye Stone was glowing brightly.

The lights seemed to recognize the stone, and each in turn came to it, circling the rapier before returning to the dance. Tailey and Weenep were awestruck when the dance suddenly changed, and the entire swarm condensed into a near fog and began circling the Golden-Brown Cat's Eye Stone as one.

"We know of you." A thousand mind-voices spoke as one. "Evil is coming. Prepare." Tailey was not sure if the lights were speaking to him, Weenep, or the stone. But the message was clear enough. "Remember," the voices continued, "only through her eyes can Katlyn be completely free of the evil of Ichneumon, Possessor of Souls. Remember!"

The first rays of pale-blue from the sun rolled over the rim of the Mangy Mountains then. The small lights reacted by pulling themselves into a spiral that flew upwards into the upper reaches of the mountain-sized tree, disappearing into the leaves.

Lost in their own confusion, Tailey and Weenep watched the sunrise.

* * *

Ichneumon, the Possessor of Souls, could feel the great evil at work beneath its feet. Its mandibles and antennae twitched in anticipation of what might happen next and curiosity at what evil dwelt below the Mangy Mountains.

"With great care, this evil could be one with us . . . oh yes, it will." Ichneumon drooled at the thought of becoming more powerful.

Ichneumon had been present when Tailey had been spirited off by the gold-brown Cat's Eye Stone, carrying with it the small thread of evil it had attached to the cat undetected, which would save it the strain of having to find it once again.

It could tell that the evil below was beyond old ... older than time itself. "We must be careful. Yes, we must!"

The dark creature took wing once more and flew toward the Triplet Mountains. The fire from below began to bellow from the mountain's heart. The search for the ancient evil would take time. "The tomcat can wait . . . for now."

Chapter 26

GATHERING THE MASSES

Megan and her father sat at the breakfast table. Lennie Simms sipped at his coffee and stared out the kitchen window, watching the spring rain spatter on the sill. Megan waited patiently for her cereal to achieve the proper sogginess; she liked it that way.

Clara Simms, Megan's Mother, was busy fussing over preparations for the roast beef supper they would have that night. The silence behind her at the table was unbearable. She turned around, "Okay, what are you two stewing over?" Clara asked her husband while her hands signed the same question to her daughter.

"With all this rain, the snow will be gone fast, and it will be time to till the garden," Lennie said over the rim of his cup.

"Fiddlesticks, Lennie Simms," Clara retorted. "Fiddlesticks!" Clara thudded the countertop with her clenched fist. "And your story, Miss Megan?" Clara's lips and hands worked as one.

Megan's voice was higher than need be, but it was hard to control her tone as she was unable to hear it. "Tailey is coming home tonight," she stated flatly. She had no idea why or how she knew that, but something was stirring in her head that told her that her friend was coming home.

Clara and Lennie looked to each other in shock. There was no hint of humor in their daughters' voice, but Tailey had been gone for so long that they knew he would not return. They both had ideas of what might have happened to their little girl's cat, though they would keep those ideas to themselves.

Megan looked at both of her parents. She could easily read the turmoil on their faces. "He is! He is! I don't care if you believe me!" Tears burst from Megan's eyes as she bolted from the kitchen, up the stairs, and into her bedroom. Megan threw herself onto her bed and buried her face into the pillow.

I know you are coming home! She refused to accept the doubt that she saw in the eyes of her parents.

* * *

Gustar stood with his back to the stone wall. Above him, Shadow—the home of his people—was dark, quiet, and abandoned as he had ordered. Liliana should have left with what was left of his kingdom's people by now, moving deep into the Fubal Mountain, and maybe farther.

In counsel, Seeker had told him that Ichneumon, the Possessor of Souls, would not bother to destroy the city if no one remained. "Ichneumon seeks our souls, not our possessions. Leave the city and save yourselves so that our ancestors can come home someday." But Gustar would not leave without trying to rid Katlyn of Ichneumon's evil, even if it meant giving his own life in return.

Somehow the hosts of the Possessor of Souls had maneuvered around the Panther Army and brought fire to the gate-tree. Now all the Panthers' escape routes were cutoff in that direction anyway. Here, before their beloved city, the king and the remainder of his army prepared to die. They had fought well, but the combined horde of the Winter Bears, Black Nation, and Green Nation seemed unaffected by their losses and now charged headlong to finish the destruction of the Panther Army.

Regardless of the fire, smoke, and countless enemies, Gustar's world was dying all around him from the simple lack of sunlight; the greenery had been fading well into brown even before the all-out offensive had begun. There was nowhere to run, and nowhere to hide. *This evil must be stopped, here and now, or the entirety of Katlyn will be lost.*

King Gustar, Son of Geard and Randra, removed his tail-rapier from its sheath and braced himself for the arrival of the enemy front lines, its canines and Winter Bear rushing relentlessly towards him.

Suddenly, from the west, Major Vinicunca, Princess Liliana, and the one hundred Panthers of the regular army charged into the mass of enemies, taking them completely off guard, and allowing the left wing a chance to cut their way to Gustar and the bulk of the remaining Panther Army.

From the direction of the Fe'line Valley, several hundred Cheetahs raced into the fray. Their fangs and claws tore into the east side of the advancing horde. On the back of one of the leading Cheetahs rode a Beesive, B'loris, grasping tightly to Caser's back as they rushed forward, having together fulfilled their promise to bring with them into battle whatever help they could muster.

This day would prove to be full of surprises. From overhead, the buzz of millions of beating wings could be heard, almost felt, by those passing beneath, as the combined forces of the Eastern and Western Queendoms plunged from the swirling heights and down into the enemy masses.

"No life will be lost in vain!" Gustar's mind-voice screamed to his expanding army. Gustar and the Elite Guard led the charge into the center of the canine/bruin masses, their tail-rapiers cutting and slashing, even as the Cheetahs tore into the melee with claws and teeth and Beesives died with every sting, taking enemies down with them.

The forces of the Winter Bears, Black Nation, and Green Nation were taken off guard by the newcomers; their attack was stalled briefly in the confusion, but soon gore flew in all directions once again, and screams of agony mixed with hatred filled the air as the dark creatures resumed their assault.

Wave after wave of Beesives converged on the Winter Bears, who slapped at the swarms, showing largely indifference to the multiple stings, while scores of Beesives died in each swipe of the White Bears' paws.

The tide of war refused to turn in the favor of those who fought for the good, but Gustar refused to fall to despair and continued fighting a losing battle.

* * *

Dill Tuck disliked everything about his present location. The angle was all wrong, smoke and flames from the burning trees blotted out his view most of the time, and he was further from the action than he would have liked, making a clean shot difficult, if not impossible, but he had little choice in the matter.

Through the transit from Neptown to the foot of Shadow, he had taken many shots at the three hosts of the Possessor of Souls. All had missed their intended targets for various reasons, the main one being his poor archery skills.

Now he was down to one arrow, one final chance for redemption for the forest. More by chance than plan, the last arrow was brother to the ash bow—gifts from the same tree.

Through the thickening smoke, only one host was in view, the Winter Bear. As the minions of evil charged toward Shadow, Dill came to the decision that the death of one host was better than none. He hoped it would at least help the Panthers and their allies in some way.

It was a long shot, but Dill notched the arrow, drew, and took aim. *Now or never!* he thought, as he released the wooden shaft. Then the smoke closed back in around his target, once again blocking his view.

* * *

Tailey and Weenep spent the day mulling over the events of the past few days—their encounter with the Northern Beesives that morning. Then there was the mystery of the titan-sized tree, and the reflection-selective lake—or what they assumed was a lake. In their discussions, they had given these mysteries names that seemed fitting: the Mountain Tree and Mirror Drink Lake.

In the afternoon, Tailey and Weenep took a timeout from pondering for the pursuit of food and drink.

Weenep, once again, lounged easily, munching on roots, and watching Tailey in his quest to capture the elusive meek. The meek did not fare as well this time around and ended its existence as a filling meal for the gray tomcat.

The pair finished the shaded afternoon exploring the root base of the Mountain Tree. The trunk of the Mountain Tree was smooth and surprisingly soft to the touch. The bark's surface seemed to be made up of many shades of grey, but upon closer observation, they could see that there were also thin, reddish-brown veins that webbed across its entire surface as high up as they could see. There was no debris beneath it, nor any other indication that the tree might be sick or in the fall of its lifespan.

When evening returned, the pair made their way back to the soft grass on the south side of the lake. Sleep followed them closely.

A blow to the back of Tailey's neck jolted him out of slumber and launched him into action. In one bound, Tailey spun around to face the dark, wasp-like creature standing over their sleeping place.

The light of the quarter moon illuminated the area clearly.

Weenep backed slowly away from the creature. Then she turned and vaulted onto the saddle on Tailey's back.

"Ichneumon, the Possessor of Souls," Tailey said.

"We meet again, tiny cat," Ichneumon's mind-voice invaded Tailey's mind. "Really, you didn't need to travel so far to be destroyed, but seeing how you did, we will gladly do away with you." Ichneumon rubbed its front legs together with anticipation. "And then . . . we will possess the girl. . . What's her name? Oh yes, Megan; yes, she will be with us!"

The truth of the situation became all too clear to Tailey. If not for the crysteel chainmail he wore, he would now be possessed as well, but even with its protection, he would have to fight to avoid destruction.

How can Ichneumon know of Megan?

Tailey had yet to fully realize that, in a way, they had already met in battle, beneath his own yellow sun, but the very thought of anyone or anything threatening his Megan brought a raging fire to Tailey's soul. As his knotted tail removed the rapier from its sheath, the Cat's Eye Stone began to glow, its amber radiance piercing the night.

On Tailey's back, Weenep's light-magic began to build as Tailey threw himself at the Ichneumon.

Ichneumon, not viewing Tailey as a threat, meant to simply brush away the advance with a sweep of its front leg. Instead, Tailey's tail-rapier sliced through the limb almost flush with the creature's body. Whitish-yellow pus boiled from the wound as the severed limb fell to the ground. The creature quickly took wing before Tailey could inflict more damage.

"Come back!" Tailey's mind-voice shouted. "Coward!"

Weenep's fireball followed the Possessor of Soul as it ascended, impacting the creature's posterior, leaving a scorch mark just above its stinger.

It was obvious to Tailey that Ichneumon had not expected any noticeable resistance from either himself or Weenep, but Tailey would show no mercy for anyone or anything that would consider hurting his Megan. He sprinted up the valley after the creature, but he was wrong to assume that having been able to strike an effective blow had been a sign of the creature's weakness. Ichneumon, the Possessor of Souls, was a product of an ancient evil and made few mistakes twice.

Evil magic, dark and forbidding, collected about the creature, and with Tailey's closing bounds, it released the black lightning of its fury. The bolt hit Tailey square on the forehead and sent him and Weenep tumbling backward down the slope.

* * *

Weenep untied her straps and vaulted clear from Tailey's back just as his weight would have crushed her. She knew she could not help him if she died on his back. Her escape sent her rolling further down the slope from where Tailey lay motionless in the grass. Weenep could not tell if he was alive or dead. Ichneumon flew over them, landed next to the shoreline, and began advancing towards them. There was no time to check Tailey's condition; she had to concentrate on calling up more of her magic.

In the darkness, Weenep's magic was slow in coming compared to the dark powers of Ichneumon, who unleashed its lightning long before she could complete her spell.

Weenep saw its power blasting through the air toward her and swiftly placed what little light she had gathered between herself and the coming impact, her quick reaction the only thing that saved her from taking the full brunt of the impact, though it still sent her hurtling backward through the air. She landed next to her friend.

I am sorry, Tailey, Weenep thought to herself as she lost consciousness.

* * *

Seeker reached the top of the valley just in time to send his powers down to help cushion Weenep's crash landing. The sensitive finger of his magic told him that both Tailey and Weenep were alive, though Weenep had fared far better than Tailey, whose life was hanging on by a very thin thread.

Back in the clearing where they had camped, Luna and Slim had disappeared in pursuit of Yahmond Yah, who had dashed into the night toward the Triplet Mountains, and had not returned by morning, when Seeker had dismissed the sisters Falsity and Truth, and their Neps, to return home to Shadow. "Inform the king of what has happened. Tell Gustar that I now travel to what I hope is the hive of the Northern Beesive and will send to him whatever help I can find."

The sisters had argued that they were his vanguard, by order of the king, but Seeker had cut their argument short, suggesting that if they did not leave of their own free will, he would simply cast a spell on them, leaving them no choice in the matter.

"Truth, Falsity, and my dear Neps, I know that your hearts are in the right place, but where I now go, no other should travel. Your destinies rest along other lines. I say this plainly, my intention neither to deceive you, nor question your orders. It is the gray magic of Mythos that has given this insight to you . . . through me."

The girls could not argue such a point and did as they were asked.

And now, Seeker found himself face-to-face with the ancient Ichneumon, Possessor of Souls, pure evil, dark, and powerful.

"You are weak, and you are old, Kittoehee!" Ichneumon said to him, his sinister mind-voice echoing through Seeker's mind. "Your powers are petty compared to the evil that we possess, and we will soon possess yours as well."

"Your babble doesn't scare me, dark fool," Seeker replied dismissively, "though your foulness surpasses any I have encountered."

"Please, Kittoehee, your compliments are overwhelming," Ichneumon's mind-voice held an unexpected gleam of humor. "Yet there was a time in the near past when we would have agreed with you completely. Now though, we have found a lovely new source of evil, stronger even perhaps than our own, which very soon will be one with us."

Seeker surmised that it was talking about the TIG-Queen and the ebony sword. There were dark powers below the surface of Katlyn, and if Ichneumon deemed those powers to be superior to even its own, then he had no choice but to believe the monster. Ichneumon had to be stopped. Now. Before it could possess that dark, ancient evil as well and become an unstoppable force, conquering not only Katlyn but perhaps other worlds beyond Katlyn's sky.

Magical lightning filled the space between the combatants. Their powers met about halfway between them, sending magical sparks ricocheting off into the dark.

Seeker launched sonic blasts, channeling them along his tail in shattering waves of power. The Red Cat's Eye Stone pulsed from where it hung on the Kittoehee's amulet, adding fuel to his inherent magic.

The Possessor deflected the blast, which exploded into the walls of the valley, but it had served the purpose of distracting Ichneumon, so that the white lightning of the Kittoehee could draw nearer to its target.

Ichneumon countered the attack, calling black snakes to rise from the dirt and coil around the Kittoehee. With his tail, Seeker brushed the snakes away with ease, but again, the power shifted.

Tricks and counter tricks. Neither the Kittoehee nor the Ichneumon would give up or give in to the other. Both were aware that there could be no quarter given. There was a large gray area between good and evil, but neither side could allow themselves to recognize it, because if they did, the very definition of existence would decay, and the universe would fade to gray. Mythos would be eternal.

Unexpectedly, the Ichneumon lurched for a moment then, its powers seeming to fail him briefly, and it took flight, evading the Kittoehee's magic. When the fight resumed, now with the Possessor now hovering above the lake, its powers appeared weaker to the Kittoehee.

Suddenly, thousands of small yellow lights approached from above the distant shore near the base of the Mountain Tree. The Northern Beesives had chosen this moment to attack. At the far shoreline, behind Ichneumon, the

Northern Beesives worked their magic, and as they crossed the lake, a wave began to form.

The wave grew larger, and as the flying swarm closed on the center of the lake, it followed close behind, building, towering, cresting high above Ichneumon, the Possessor of Souls, as the Kittoehee kept his white lightning flowing toward the creature to keep it distracted.

Not until it was engulfed by the giant wave did the creature realize it had been set up.

Seeker broke off his attack then and watched as Ichneumon struggled against the wave's magic. One by one, the Northern Beesives plunged into the wave, and with the sacrifice of each, the water grew denser, binding the creature more firmly in place. But even after the last Beesive entered the water, Ichneumon still fought towards the surface.

Seeker—Kittoehee first to King Geard and then to his son, King Gustar—knew what must be done. Using his magic to levitate across the water toward the wave and its struggling captive, Seeker thought of times that had passed, all the friends he had known, and all that he might have gotten to know better. He knew that it was time for the magic of the Kittoehee to pass on to its next wielder . . . after this one final spell.

Seeker did not hesitate to do what he knew must be done and entered the water—which had been grown more solid with each life given into its embrace—and staring into the eyes of his enemy, his defiant mind-voice offered his final words: "Your time is over, monster-spawn."

The Kittoehee then released the spell that would freeze the wave completely ... and all those who were trapped inside.

Ichneumon's last words went unheard as the hardened wave tilted back and then sank beneath the surface of Mirror Drink Lake, leaving not a single ripple to mark its passing:

"There are more of us yet."

Chapter 27

OMEGA

King Gustar could not believe that he was still alive. His body was covered with blood and gore, but most of his wounds were superficial. Still, his body was close to complete exhaustion from the exertions of battle. Sleep seemed like a distant friend—one that would be most welcome when it finally arrived.

Liliana was in bad shape. A Winter Bear had delivered four long rips from her front shoulder, down her left side, to her hind quarters. She had lost a lot of blood.

The Neptunians were busy attempting to close her wounds. Gustar wanted to be near his sister, to help her through her pain, but the duties of his station would not allow him to be pulled away from what must be done for the good of the Kingdom.

"Generals Bulldory, Rammino, and Hiker have perished," said Paxie Jax, First Paw of the Elite Guard, offering his report to Gustar. "The count is not complete, my King, but I've estimated our losses to be four-fifths of the regular army and three-quarters of the Elite Guard." Jax stopped to shift his weight from his mangled rear-left leg. "Still, we fared well compared to the Cheetahs and the Beesives."

Gustar could read the pain written on the First Paw's face and dreaded the rest of the report.

"Of the seven hundred Cheetahs that came to our defense," Jax looked down and forced himself to go on, "only five are alive. The Nightwolves were concentrated on the east side, and they soon learned that the Cheetahs weren't skilled with extended battle, nor used to organized warfare, being independent and widespread."

The king looked about him. Death was at every turn, the Beesive bodies far outnumbering the rest.

"Ichneumon's victory over the Beesive was complete," Paxie Jax said, watching his king's examination of their surroundings. Shock and dismay ruled the moment. "For every Beesive that died from claws and teeth, a thousand perished by losing their stingers."

"Complete? Did none survive?"

"One, Your Highness," Jax answered. "Only one." The First Paw nodded toward the edge of a small clearing, near the stone wall that had once reached into lush forest. In the bloodied mess, it was hard to tell the living from the dead, but then he saw them: Caser Cheetah and worker Beesive B'loris. The pair sat mutely together. Gustar could not imagine how they must be feeling at this moment. Gustar wished there were something he could say or do to ease their pain. *"I am sorry"* would not be enough. After they'd had a few days of rest, he would make it a priority to speak to them. They were heroes.

The King of the Panthers continued to examine the remains of the war. There had to be a reason the Green Nation and their allies had suddenly broken off their attack and run from what would have been a sure victory. It did not make any sense.

On the northern horizon, fire from the distant peak continued to spew high into the wee hours of morning. The ground shook, sparks flew up into the demon-cloud. Then . . . suddenly, an eerie silence washed over the world. The fire and sparks dissipated, and the shaking ground stilled. The smoke from Fire Bane no longer rose to feed the demon-cloud, which weakened and began to dissolve in the fresh eastern breeze. Regulus made a grand re-entrance over a land that had been lost in darkness.

Gustar found the three hosts of the Ichneumon shortly after sunrise. They lay like fallen dominoes all in a row, a Winter Bear, a Nightwolf, and a female Greenwolf, a single hole bored neatly through the necks of each by an arrow that was still lodged in the old female Greenwolf at the end of the row, whom Gustar assumed to be the Den Mother.

It was now evident what had happened. With one swift stroke, some unseen agent had destroyed the Ichneumon's hosts, and without leadership controlling the multitudes with their black magic, the dark forces had fallen to confusion and chaos.

The king returned to the area that was being cleared of the dead, to be used as a temporary camp, and conveyed his findings to the survivors.

The Panther civilians—among them the keepers of Shadow: the Neptunians, Scantians, and a few Animond—had not traveled far from their home city and returned shortly after daybreak to relieve the soldiers, continuing the process of dragging the dead to the fires of the lost trees, so that their souls could be released from their mortal bodies.

Across the battlefield, a small group of Greenwolves trotted toward Gustar and the others. Paxie Jax was the first to struggle to his ragged paws, his tail-rapier drawn and held ready for combat.

Gustar pushed past Paxie Jax. "Rest your blade, my friend; it's the Waterway Pack."

Cleary, Animal, and the others stopped before Gustar. "We have come to help put our fallen brothers and sisters to rest, and to offer your kingdom any aid that we can give."

Cleary and her Greenwolves were challenging the line that had been drawn between their forces.

Gustar sighed. "A step towards a new world." He knew that he had to put aside the past and look to the future. "The way will be rough . . . but come. You have a place among us. Welcome to the pale-blue light."

* * *

Onlooker Jib returned to the injured Klawed after having found no safe way to reach Shadow to warn anyone of the Winter Bear they had faced and what had transpired. He was sure the king had his hands full with enemies and was by now fully aware of what dangers they were facing. The evil nations and the Winter Bears did not travel in secret.

Onlooker Jib did what he could to aid the Panther. Several of his ribs appeared to be broken. He likely had a concussion from being slammed on the ground, and Onlooker suspected internal bleeding as well. Klawed's breathing was shallow, and there were moments when Onlooker thought Klawed had died, but the Panther refused to yield to the darkness.

Nep had not survived the impact of the Winter Bear's attack. Onlooker Jib was sure that Nep had died instantly, before slamming into the side of the tree. He took Nep's body to one of the downed trees engulfed by flames and still burning. There, the ashes of Nep would be given back to the forest that he loved.

Now all that could be done was to wait for Klawed to either wake or pass onto darkness.

"Maker," Onlooker Jib prayed. "Thank you for your love. We could use some more strength. Amen."

Much later, the shaking ground woke him from an uneasy slumber, and when stillness returned, the Animond regarded Klawed. The Panther was breathing normally.

* * *

Luna and Slim found Yahmond Yah on his knees, weeping uncontrollably before the Triplet Mountains, where molten lava flowed from the heights to the valley below and beyond.

"What are we going to do now, Den Mother?" Slim asked Luna.

Slim could feel it too: The Den Mother of old was dead, and it was Luna's time to assume her birthright.

Luna let her magic nudge its way gently into the Animond. His soul was deeply wounded. Luna could not heal him completely, but she did all that she could. Only time could heal the rest.

Finally, Yahmond climbed to his feet, completely devoid of emotion, and followed the Greenwolves back toward Shadow and the Fubal Plains.

* * *

Dill Tuck passed through the smoldering forest toward Scanterville. Dill was not sure what had happened to stop the war, but he found strength in the sight of the invaders retreating towards the plains.

At the edge of Scanterville, Dill stopped before the charred stump of the Crying Tree, where the Spring of truth had once flowed. The dark magic that surrounded the Black Nation had collapsed the deep veins of water that had fed the magical spring. The sight of the ruined tree, near a stagnant pool of water, overwhelmed the Scantian, and he dropped to his knees. The Crying Tree was more than a source of magic; it was a symbol of the freedom to which so many before him had rallied . . . and died. His grief was doubled at the thought of his own family's deaths.

Dill's arms hung by his sides as tears flowed freely from his eyes. Death would be much easier than the thought of living without Dealy and their children, but death was not an option. There were other Scantians that still lived, and only together would there be any chance for survival.

"Dealy . . . I miss you so much," he said to the empty air, his eyes closed. He needed to hear his own voice, to be sure of his own existence before he could hope to find a way to go on.

"I love you too," Dealy answered, moving forward from the shadows, and kneeling beside her husband.

* * *

In the Hives of the Eastern and Western Queendoms, the worker larvae were growing rapidly. Soon, there would be enough Worker Beesives to start the process of gathering nectar to fortify the hives all over again. Thus began a new cycle of life on the vast Plains of Che.

* * *

Weenep had pulled herself from the darkness long enough to move closer to Tailey's body and hold onto him tightly. It was over his prone body that Weenep witnessed the final act of Seeker, the Kittoehee, concluding his spell and disappearing beneath the water's surface, subsumed by the now unmoving crest of the wave.

Suddenly, Weenep felt an unyielding sleep coming over her, holding her eyes open just long enough to see the Golden-Brown Cat's Eye Stone, set in Tailey's still drawn tail-rapier, start to glow . . . and then pulse.

Then there was nothing but darkness for some time.

Weenep felt herself drifting out of slumber, unsure of how much time had passed. She felt motion but no resistance or drag. She willed her eyes to open and found herself floating over her own body, looking down at it as it held onto Tailey. They were in some sort of clear bubble. All around them, multicolored lights zoomed past.

She willed her spirit body to change its orientation in the space and saw lights of all shapes and sizes streaking toward them from every angle and then passing them by.

Weenep found it odd that she felt no fear. She was strangely comfortable, just watching the light show. Weenep recalled Tailey's description of his trip from Earth to Katlyn. *Looks like we are going to your house, Tailey,* thought Weenep, as sleep overtook her again.

* * *

Barry Newman Perkins lay still on the bed, facing the blank wall. The prison's psychiatric wing had been his home for close to a year. The pastor stood in the doorway, observing the madman through the steel bars, thinking that the facility seemed disturbingly quiet for being so early in the evening. He also noted that Perkins had not moved a muscle since he'd arrived at his door, even when he'd announced his presence.

Did he not hear me? he wondered,

Pastor Mailor had visited this ward many times during the twenty years he'd resided in Jackson, Michigan. The inmate he was visiting today, Barry Newman Perkins, was a murderer, cold and unfeeling. The air around the man always seemed to reek of evil. Imprisoned for life for the grisly murder of a young girl, Perkins had escaped over a year ago and was stalking and plotting to murder another, this one much younger, up north in Antrim County.

Pastor Mailor stepped close to the bars, bowing his head to pray for the strength needed to face the evil before him. Then he began praying for the prisoner. At first, the pastor felt that his words were falling on deaf ears, but then he heard Perkins's cry out . . . and then fall silent.

Looking at the man, the Pastor Mailor noticed a disturbingly large, weird-looking insect, like a bee or a wasp, climbing up the wall above the man's cot towards the slightly opened window. It seemed to be missing a limb, having only five where it looked like there should have been six. The pastor watched, oddly horrified, as it climbed through the bars and flew away.

Looking back down towards the cot, he noticed then that Barry Newman Perkins was no longer breathing. The pastor watched in silence for what seemed an exceptionally long time, just to be certain—he told himself—that he wasn't imagining things. Eventually, he called out for help, knowing in his heart that the monster before him, Barry Newman Perkins, was finally dead and would never again hurt an innocent child.

* * *

Weenep managed to revive Tailey long enough to remove his battle gear, which she hid under some leaves that had drifted into the hollow tree stump. She'd woken up a few moments before. Through the opening above her, she noted that the light was fading rapidly. There was a smell of rotted wood and something far worse that she couldn't identify drifting in the air.

"Come on, Tailey, wake up!" Weenep said, nudging him.

Slowly, Tailey came out of his daze.

"Oh, what is that taste? And that awful smell?" Tailey's mind-voice asked dryly.

"You tell me," she said, in a tone that he found less than encouraging. "Welcome home, I guess. Now let's get out of this place." Weenep tried several times to jump to the rim of the stump but failed. "Wow!" she said in disbelief. "This place is a drag. Really. I feel heavy . . . like there's a weight tied to me."

Eventually, with a considerable amount of effort, they made it out of the stump. In the darkness, Tailey recognized their location and headed towards the lights that were shining in the distance.

"Tailey, what's that annoying smell floating all around?"

"Humans," Tailey said, a certain sadness in his mind-voice. "It's humans."

* * *

Clara and Lennie Simms and their daughter, Megan, sat at the dinner table, preparing to enjoy a wonderful beef roast, with all the trimmings, including Megan's favorite: mashed potatoes and beef gravy.

Megan had cried out her frustrations earlier about Tailey, but with a few words of encouragement from Mom, she had managed to enjoy the rest of her day.

When the time came for the evening meal, Megan had volunteered to set the table, and her parents noted that she'd set places for four, like she'd always done when Tailey had been with them. A small plate sat next to hers, without silverware. Clara and Lennie didn't have the heart to tell Megan that her cat, her friend, was most likely dead, so they chose to remain silent.

"Megan, would you please say grace?" Clara asked, forming the words carefully with her lips while signing with her hands.

Just as the family bowed their heads to give the blessing, the small pet door in the kitchen creaked open, and through it stumbled a disoriented and confused gray tomcat. Megan's sharpened senses must have somehow felt the strange movement in the room behind her because she bolted upright in her seat.

"Tailey!" she screamed as she bolted from her chair and rushed to her friend's side. Carefully, she stroked Tailey's matted hair, checking him for injuries, and paused briefly over the old scar that was all that remained of the deep scratch he'd received from the wild rose bush all those many months ago.

Clara and Lennie Simms stared in disbelief; they would never doubt Megan's word again.

* * *

Looking through the kitchen window of the Simms' home, two dark eyes watched the little girl scooping up Tailey, the gray tomcat, and holding him to her chest. Tears of joy flowed freely down the little girl's face as she stroked his back and neck. There was no doubting the sheer joy in this homecoming.

After watching silently for some time, the small, shadowy figure withdrew from the deck and made off into the quiet forest.

THE END

Authors notes

Thank you, readers, for taking this journey with me. Now, if you please, I would like to clear up a couple of things: I didn't actually come up with the term "Kittoehee." That came from my daughter, Megan. When she was a toddler, I would call out to our cat, saying, "Here, kitty-kitty! Here, kitty-kitty!" but she must have heard "Here, kit-toe-hee! Here, kit-toe-hee!" as that is what she would always call out when she wanted to find him. Thus, the Kittoehee was born. My lovely wife and I found it endearing, and I had to use it somehow, some way, somewhere.

The original Tailey wandered into our lives many years ago. Tailey was not with us exceedingly long, but he will always hold a place in our hearts.

A special thank you to my wife, Lisa, for all her help and understanding, and to Pat, Wanda, and our clients at the barbershop for your constant sources of inspiration.

Clara and Lennie Simms characters were tailored after my late grandparents on my mother's side. I hope I managed to capture the essence of these people, whom I grew up respecting and loving for their kindness and compassion in raising thirteen children in trying times. To the memory of my late mother, Bonnie, who will be forever my songbird of the morning.

I give credit to Bill (Dill), his son Shawn (Chawn), and his son Justin (Qustin) for inspiring part of the Tuck family. Thank you to Dennis (Animal), Bruce (Spruce), Grady (Gradus), Jimmy (Slim), and Jerry (Slow)—we were a part of the maintenance crew in a canning company in Michigan many years ago—for your inspiration of the Waterway Pack.

Anyone I have known in my life has a good chance of finding their essence in any of my writings, and so I thank you all.

CPSIA information can be obtained
at www.ICGtesting.com
Printed in the USA
JSHW060747300722
28636JS00001B/9